CONSTANTINE CAPERS

CAPERS

There Comes a Midnight Hour

CONSTANTINE CAPERS

There Comes a Midnight Hour

NATALIE BRIANNE

Searose Press

MMXXIV

To my niece, Geneil.

As you well know, good books contain a fair amount of truth. Whether the author puts a piece of their soul in each of their characters or creates a world that mirrors their own, there is something real to be found in each page.

And so, I wish to give you a bit of truth as you embark on your own journey. Remember that all of us wear masks. To protect ourselves, to protect others. To give us courage or confidence when we think we have none. Or to conceal one's true intentions.

In a world of false faces, I hope that you are able to see people how they truly are. And I hope that when you wear a mask yourself, that you will let your true self shine through it.

Do you not know that there comes a midnight hour when every one has to throw off his mask? Do you believe that life will always let itself be mocked? Do you think you can slip away a little before midnight in order to avoid this? Or are you not terrified by it? I have seen men in real life who so long deceived others that at last their true nature could not reveal itself . . .

In every man there is something which to a certain degree prevents him from becoming perfectly transparent to himself; and this may be the case in so high a degree, he may be so inexplicably woven into relationships of life which extend far beyond himself that he almost cannot reveal himself. But he who cannot reveal himself cannot love, and he who cannot love is the most unhappy man of all.

Søren Kierkegaard

Miss Samira Blayse
4 Swan Walk, Chelsea, London

Correspondence

Detective Byron Constantine
22 Rue Geoffroy l'Angevin, Paris

November 17, 1888

Dearest Madam,

Here is my first letter, as promised. I've arrived in France along with the other members of the Scotland Yard team. I've settled in well enough, although it is strange to be in another country. For so many years, I kept close to Palace Court in fear of my memory, or lack thereof. Why, just a few months ago, it would have been impossible. But I suppose so many things have become possible since I met you.

I must say that your new sketch of Durant has been a monumental help in our search for him. By showing it to people at each of the ports, we were able to determine his path rather easily. He left Spenston Park and took the train directly to Dover, where he took a steamer to Calais, France. From there, he took a rather serpentine route that ended in Paris. As far as we know, he's planning on disappearing here for a while.

We have plans to meet with the Parisian police force tomorrow to discuss our actions going forward. Things are rather against us in this investigation and the boys from the Yard are already bringing up a complaint. The situation is a bit dire, I will admit, seeing as it's been several weeks since Durant might have reached Paris, but regardless, we must try. I still stand by the belief that if Circe told him to go to France, that he will stay here.

At any rate, I shall endeavor to write you daily, and I look forward to your letters as well, even if they are late as far as news is concerned. I've taken up lodgings at 22 Rue Geoffroy l'Angevin, Paris. Please direct your correspondence there.

Ever your friend,

Byron Constantine

November 28, 1888

Dear Sir,

I cannot begin to describe the relief I felt upon receiving your letter. I had quite forgotten how much of a delay occurs in correspondence between England and France. Walker and I did manage to communicate frequently enough while he was at school, although we often waited for a response before penning new letters. This shall be an interesting experiment, especially considering that it took a full eleven days for your letter to arrive. It seemed much faster when I wrote Walker.

Hopefully, by the time this reaches Paris, all will be resolved, you'll be safely back in London, and Durant will be in police custody. However, if that isn't the case, I would hate to leave you waiting on the other end of a pen for my response.

I am pleased that my sketch is proving so useful. I only wish that we still had my original portrait of him, as it was much more accurate to his character. If you require any additional help, you need but ask, even if it will be delayed somewhat by our communication method.

Yesterday I finally escaped my prison of a sofa and went on a walk outside. Perhaps "escape" is the wrong word for it, as it didn't take much cunning or intellect on my part or my brother's. Landon fully endorsed and supervised the outing, but regardless of the particulars, it was invigorating! I didn't have the faintest hint of a twinge in my ankle for the entire walk. Perhaps soon I'll be able to keep up with you without the danger of new injury.

On the note of impossible things, I will say that it was always possible for you to regain your memories and your recovery has very little to do with me. I do, however, appreciate the sentiment behind the statement.

Sincerely yours,

Samira Blayse

November 18, 1888

My Dear Miss Blayse,

Our investigation, as predicted, has begun with a lack of leads and minimal support. The fact that Circe has erased the man's existence has posed quite the problem for convincing the French police to help in this matter. I have precious few contacts in this city, but shall endeavor to find each of them in hopes of tracking down a lead of some sort. Durant can't have disappeared from the face of the earth, that much I am certain of. It is some comfort that Fred was allowed to accompany me on this trip. He was a tremendous help with that Great Sheep Panic, as they called it, and he has already proved himself an asset to this venture.

I must admit I feel a degree of disappointment that I haven't received a letter from you yet. Naturally, it will take some time for you to receive my first letter and I shouldn't expect a prompt response. Regardless, I wish I knew how long I have to wait.

Forgive me for the shortness of this note, but it is late in the evening and I need to pay some attention to my journal if I'm to be successful in this investigation. I shall continue to keep correspondence despite the void of postal service between us and hope that I'll hear from you in the next few days.

With greatest respect and fond expectations,

Byron Constantine

November 29, 1888

Dear Mr. Constantine,

It is quite disheartening to hear of the difficulties in working alongside the Paris police. If it helps any, I am an eyewitness to Alexander Durant's existence. Of course, have you considered that Durant could be an alias or a pseudonym? Perhaps the reason he has disappeared is that Alexander Durant was the mask he wore in his dealings with me and my family. Although, it seems an awful lot of trouble to go to just to deceive me. Especially when it would be easier for him and for Circe if they simply eliminated me from the equation altogether. I know that you asked me not to speak of it in such terms, but it is quite impossible for me to forget what he said when I last saw him. There must be some reason why we are still playing this game.

As far as your apology is concerned, I do not accept it, simply on the principle of an apology being unnecessary in the first place. Your journal has been a fast friend of mine these past few months, and there shall be no jealousy on my part in regard to it. As long as I receive some scrap of paper with your name on it to ensure me of your wellbeing, I am content.

Yours ardently,

Samira Blayse

November 19, 1888

My Dearest Mira,

Over the last few days, it has become more and more apparent that "Madam" or even "Miss Blayse" is too formal for the nature of our relationship. I reverted to the former, of course, because those that dictate the culture for the rest of us have some inane notion of what is proper and right. And perhaps they are correct, but it occurred to me just how unorthodox our acquaintance has been up to this point. And so, with your permission, I take great pleasure in calling you Mira and calling you my own. Granted, seeing as I have yet to receive a response from you, that permission will likely not come for a while yet. Perhaps I ought to curtail my feelings and go back to standard practice.

As far as the investigation goes, I've hit multiple dead ends in trying to track down Durant. The police have helpfully put up a perimeter with his description and your sketch, but they only have so many men available to help in that regard, and honestly, I doubt that Durant would be so careless as to be caught in such a trap. I have one more contact to meet with tomorrow, and if that proves promising, I may have some real news for you when I write tomorrow evening.

Sincerely and entirely yours,

Byron Constantine

November 30, 1888

My Adored Byron,

    I too was falling back on practices instilled in me from the first time I picked up a pencil as a child. If my uncle were to read our correspondence, he would likely find it to be full of scandal and impropriety! But as he has approved of our courtship, he must forgive the brief lapses in sanity that allow us to share our true feelings in paper and ink. I like to imagine that you laughed at that last bit, mostly because I miss hearing your laughter in person. I do look forward to your next letter and hope that your contact was as helpful as you thought they would be. The part of me that has more pessimistic tendencies feels that nothing came of the encounter, seeing as you are still in France as I'm writing this letter weeks after you wrote your last note. But perhaps I am wrong and there is some other mystery keeping you there.

    I read in the newspaper this morning that the police have received another letter addressed "Dear Boss," presumably from Jack the Ripper. It indicates that the Ripper has been traveling around England but will be returning to London soon enough. Based on what we found about Circe's involvement there, I almost wonder if someone is finding great fun in messing about and writing fake correspondence.

    In the few society events I've had the pleasure of attending in the past weeks, most people are considering it a game to guess who it could be. I'm only grateful my injury has precluded my attendance at most of these gatherings. Walker and Liza have taken to spending as much time as possible in my company. I think, perhaps, it is because I am a better chaperone for them than Liza's aunt. Or a worse one, as the case may be. Despite their near constant companionship, I do miss your society and pray for your safe return.

Yours ever faithful,

Mira Blayse

November 20, 1888

My Darling Mira,

It seems so strange to me to write these letters out into the void, for though I know you are waiting for their reception and will be writing in response, I have no frame of reference for what you will write.

As it stands, my contact had nothing for us, but promised to keep an eye out. We've decided to take a more systematic approach and go to each arrondissement in Paris to question local bakeries, cafés, tailors, and the like. Even if he is attempting to disappear into the dark recesses of Paris, a man must eat. 'No man is an island,' and all that. There are twenty arrondissements in total, so it may take some time. Unless, of course, we find him in the first one.

I truly hope for that outcome, not only because you cannot be safe until Durant faces justice, but because I can't shake the feeling that something terrible has happened to you in my absence. It seems silly considering how few days I have been away, but I think much of that anxiety comes from needing you present in my memory. There's a fear that if I don't keep you within my thoughts in every waking moment that I will forget you, as I've done in the past, and I cannot allow it. The journal helps, certainly, but it does not assuage the anxiety of not having you near.

Although I would not wish this fear on you, I simultaneously hope that you feel the same way about me. The two feelings are caught in a dissonance of thought, but regardless, I want you to know that I care for you, my dear one, and I hope that you care for me.

Yours affectionately and forever,

Byron

December 1, 1888

My Dearest Detective,

 I wish I could remove the delay between us and converse as if we were side by side, but unfortunately, I have yet to discover that power within me. For now, the void must remain and this letter must travel through time to reach you.

 Have you ever thought it strange that it only takes a day or so of traveling to go between London and Paris, and yet our correspondence takes nearly fourteen times that long to travel that same distance? I suppose it has something to do with the way that letters are handled by their delivery men.

 I believe that your anxiety must be contagious, as I fear the day that your letters cease, whether that be due to some unfortunate circumstance in Paris or due to your memory. As of yet, that hasn't occurred, so I am forced to be patient and believe that all is well with you, even as I worry that something has happened with Mr. Durant that I don't know about.

 But despite this, I am comforted to be reminded of your feelings and intentions once again and hope you find some comfort in knowing that I reciprocate them with all my heart. I also hope that you appreciate the token that I've included in this envelope. Perhaps it will help you to have a constant reminder that I am real, and that I care for you, even if I am not with you.

Now and always your own,

Mira

December 2, 1888

THE RAINDROPS DRIPPED DOWN THE WINDOW, SLOW and steady. Two came closer together, almost combining into a rivulet, but kept drifting apart rather than merging. If they collided, they would pick up speed and beat the rest of the water down to the bottom of the pane. But instead, they kept dancing around each other, never quite touching. Mira rubbed a hand over her arm, bracing against the chill coming from the glass. She leaned back against the frame of the window seat. Her cat, Nero, hopped off of her lap at the motion and moved over to curl up closer to the fire.

"Are you sure you don't want to play a game?" Liza Renaldi asked from where she reclined on a chaise.

"You've asked her twice already, Liza," Walker said. He sat in an armchair across the room, nose deep into a newspaper. His expression mirrored one that she'd seen on her uncle's face time and time again. A soft frown and pinched eyebrows. Mira doubted that either of them realized they made that face each time they read the paper.

"Yes, but she could have changed her mind, couldn't she?"

Mira abandoned the raindrops and turned so she could face both of them. "I am right here, you know, and can answer for myself."

"Yes?" Liza said.

Mira let out a long breath. "What sort of game?"

In truth, she was getting bored with games. Bored with the sitting room. Bored with the house. Landon didn't want her going out into the rain just yet, despite the fact that her ankle was almost healed, because of the slippery conditions. And since Landon was so adamant about her staying indoors, it would be fruitless to ask her brother or uncle to help her convince him to change his mind. She fiddled with the ends of her hair. A bit of it was much shorter than the rest. She had braided a portion and cut it to send to Byron. Hopefully, it would help him remember her despite the distance between them.

Byron had been gone for the better part of November, first for a week out to Berkshire, and then almost immediately to France. She'd scarcely seen him three days together in the entire month. Yes, his exploits in Paris were important—heaven forbid Alexander Durant (if that was even his name) get away clean—but she couldn't help but miss being with her detective. Curse her ankle! If only she hadn't been so careless as to twist it all those weeks back. Not only would it have saved her several unfortunate encounters with Mr. Durant, but the man would likely already be in prison, and Byron would still be in London. Things would be as they ought to be. As it was, she was two weeks behind on the state of the case and getting sick with worry. Had Alexander been caught already? Was Byron on his way back to London?

"Mira?"

"Yes, Liza?" Mira blinked, returning her focus to the conversation at hand.

"You didn't hear anything I just said, did you?" Liza asked, crossing her arms.

"Er," Mira bit her lip. "Not exactly?"

Walker stifled a laugh. "Don't be so surprised, Liza. She's probably thinking about Mr. Constantine again."

A heat rose to Mira's cheeks and Liza smiled.

"Ah, yes. You do seem a bit preoccupied."

"If you want to play something, I'd be up for it," Mira said, trying to change the subject.

Liza hid a smile. "No, it's alright. I can see your heart wouldn't be in it at the moment."

"Can't have you falling into a daydream about Byron halfway through a move, can we?" Walker continued to tease. "Just read your letters. You can't tell me you haven't been eying them all morning."

Mira sighed. Was it that obvious? Part of her wanted to prove her brother wrong. But her heart won out, and she moved over to the mantle, pulling the stack of Byron's letters from behind a vase. She settled into a chair closer to the fire as the trio fell into a delicate silence.

She wasn't daydreaming about Byron, per se. She just was so worried about him. There should have been twice the number of letters in her hands, and yet no dates were missing from the correspondence. He had written her the moment he got to Paris and continued to write her daily. It just took much too long to get to her. Perhaps it was the holidays. Or maybe she was just impatient.

Mira thumbed through the letters, one by one, in case she missed any details about the case. Based on the contents of the most recent letter, they had quite a bit more investigating to do before finding Durant. The next letter should arrive in a few hours, and she could feel her anxiety surging beneath her skin. What if something had gone wrong? Would she even know about it until it was too late? Could she even do anything to help from where she was?

Walker stoked the fire, and the sound brought Mira out of her reverie. She looked around. Liza was attempting to pull something from her pocket without either of them noticing. A pamphlet or something. Walker moved over and plucked the papers from her hand.

"What's this, I wonder?" He danced away as Liza ran after him.

"Give it back!" She lunged for him, giggling. Walker hid the booklet behind his back.

"And what if I don't want to?"

"Then I suppose I'll have to make you." Liza whirled around him, attempting to snatch it from his grasp. He raised it above his head and Liza stood up on her tiptoes, trying to take it back.

Mira smiled at the exchange. If she were a better chaperone, she would get after them for being in such close proximity. But she didn't see the harm in it. Not really. Besides, it wouldn't be long before the two were engaged, that was certain.

"Oh, give it back, Walker," Mira said, but it had no heat behind it.

Her brother acquiesced, dropping it into Liza's waiting hands.

"Thank you." She flounced back to her chair and took a seat.

"What is it, anyway?" Walker retrieved his newspaper, cheeks warm, and not from exertion.

"Nothing!" Liza said, much too fast.

Mira's eyes narrowed. "It must be something. And something you'd rather we didn't know about."

Liza turned bright red. "Promise you won't laugh?"

"Why would we laugh?" Walker asked.

"Because it's a penny dreadful."

Mira groaned. "Not you, too." Her brother had been obsessed with the cheap gothic literature since he first found a bound copy of *Varney the Vampire* in the library when they were twelve.

Walker's eyes lit up, and he leaned closer. "Which one?"

Liza sat back, surprised. "It's called *The Curse of Death*. I've only read a few of this one. You read penny dreadfuls?"

"He doesn't so much read them as devour them," Mira said.

Walker ignored her. "I haven't read that one yet. Did it just come out?" he asked, moving to sit on the sofa next to Liza.

"A few weeks ago. This is number four."

"What's it about?"

"I wouldn't want to spoil it for you," Liza said, turning so he couldn't read over her shoulder.

"I don't mind." He leaned closer.

The door opened, and the two broke apart fast enough that Walker lost his balance and fell off of the sofa from the motion. Professor Burke stepped in.

"Did I interrupt something?" He gave the lovebirds a quizzical look as Walker stood up, attempting to retain his dignity.

"Nothing important." Mira set her letters to the side and smiled up at her godfather. He'd been traveling for the past month. If she were much younger, she would have jumped to her feet and ran to give him a hug. Being twenty-two, she folded her hands in her lap and stayed where she was. "I didn't realize you'd be back so soon. How was your trip?"

"Lovely, my dear." He came and sat across from her, still eying Walker and Liza as they sat stiff as statues next to each other.

As the professor moved, a sickly sweet citrus smell assaulted her senses. She grimaced. "What is that smell?"

"Oh, do you like it?" The professor smoothed down his lapels. "I got it while I was in Cologne."

Mira's nose crinkled. "It is quite strong."

"Yes, I may have spilled a little on my suit this morning. Hasn't quite died down."

"A little?" Walker said. "It smells like a perfumery in here."

The professor laughed. "I must have gotten used to it." He turned towards Mira again. "How's your ankle doing?"

"Much better, thank you."

The door opened once again and Landon came in.

"Dinner is served."

"Oh good!" Walker said, helping Liza to her feet.

"Will our uncle be joining us today?" Mira asked, returning her letters to their place on the mantle.

"I'm afraid he's still reviewing some business affairs," Landon said.

"Perhaps I can persuade him," Professor Burke said. "I'll join you all in a minute."

❧❦❧

CYRUS DID END UP COMING TO DINNER, which was a first for the week, and Professor Burke regaled them with stories of his travels. Usually, these stories would have enraptured her, but her thoughts were set on Byron and how he was faring in France. His next letter was due to arrive within the hour, and she hoped it brought promising news.

After dinner, Liza returned home, and the professor left as well, citing a need to unpack. Cyrus called Walker into his office shortly thereafter to discuss something about Griffon Industries. This left Mira with little to do but sit and stew, waiting for Byron's letter to arrive.

She took up a seat in the parlor and attempted to read with Nero curled up on her lap.

After a few minutes, Landon joined her, dusting the shelves, books, and the painting of her grandparents, mother, and uncle.

"Are you alright, Miss? You hardly touched your food this evening."

Mira stroked Nero's dark fur. "Don't you worry about me. I'm fine. I just wasn't hungry."

Landon nodded. "If you wanted to talk, I'm sure I could find more to dust."

A laugh escaped her, but it petered out. "There isn't much to talk about."

The butler gave her a knowing look. "Are you certain this all doesn't have to do with a certain detective of yours?"

Mira let out a sigh. "I miss him. There's nothing more to it than that."

Landon paused in his dusting to raise an eyebrow at her.

She sank further into her seat.

"Alright. I am also worried that something has gone wrong. And I won't know for certain until he comes home."

More silence as Landon flitted the duster over the shelves and Nero purred under her fingertips.

"And perhaps," she continued, softer this time. "Perhaps I'm a bit concerned about what is going to happen when he does."

"In what way?"

"The only reason either of us has any sort of acquaintance is that I became his secretary. But it's obvious he doesn't need me for that anymore. He's off in France and managing quite well without me."

"I would think that would be a good thing."

"Yes. It is good, certainly. And I'm so happy that he's doing so well, and yet . . ."

Landon gave up any pretense of dusting and sat across from her, his silence prompting her to proceed. She swallowed, not certain how she could explain how she felt.

"I want to keep solving cases with him, Landon, and if he doesn't need me anymore, I'm afraid he won't let me."

Landon twisted the feather duster in his hands. Nero

pounced at it as the feathers moved about, batting it out of his hand. Landon ignored it for the moment, leaning forward and focusing his entire attention on her. "Mira, I think that you're forgetting two important pieces to this puzzle of yours."

"Yes?"

"One, that if Mr. Constantine had his way, you would be at his side in France."

"You can't know that for certain!"

"I suppose not, but that brings me to point two: If you put your mind to it, and decided to join him, I don't think he could stop you if he wanted to." Landon's eyes crinkled as he smiled.

"Says the man who won't let me go out in the rain."

"I still stand by the notion that if you really wanted to be out there, you would have found a way. But that reminds me."

He knelt down in front of her. At this point, she was more than used to the routine, and she helped him to unbutton her shoe for him to check her ankle. He rolled it around, pushed it back and forth, and not a thing he did made it twinge. When he was done, he helped her back into her shoe and stood.

"Congratulations. I give you a clean bill of health."

"Really?" A swell of relief rushed through her.

"I wouldn't give you false hope." His gaze flicked to the window. "And I believe I see the postman coming up the street. Shall I bring the evening post in here, or would you like to retrieve it for yourself?"

"I'll come with you."

After saving the feather duster from a fate worse than housework, they both moved to the entry hall. Sure enough, the postman came to the door as they opened it and passed over the evening's letters. One for her uncle and one for her. She thanked the postman, nodded to Landon, and headed up to her room to read it. Once she lit the gas lamps and sat at her desk, she ran a letter opener along the wax seal of the envelope.

November 21, 1888

My Dearest Mira,

We spent the better part of the day walking around the first arrondissement with no luck whatsoever. Part of that may be because my French is not exactly up to scratch and Fred's isn't much better. We've managed to get by for the most part, but it is making things rather difficult.

If our investigations fall short, there's only one other course of action I could take to track down Durant. But to do that, I will need your help. Just recently, I finished a case out in Berkshire. I'm afraid that I don't remember if I told you about it or not. Fred and I caught some art thieves with the help of the local constabulary.

I need you to go and speak with one of them and ask them about their employer. Her name is Selene Vermielle. Fred tells me that we've worked with her before on a case, but I can't remember. She's the brains behind those thefts, I believe. The thief you want to talk to is named Monty and should still be held in the cells at the Berkshire Constabulary. When you go, ask to speak with Colonel Blandy. Tell him that I sent you, and he should let you speak with Monty.

I know that Vermielle is operating out of France, and I'm hoping that she's in Paris. If she is, she would be aware of the criminal underground in the

area and might be able to give us some valuable leads
on Durant. Send me a letter as soon as you know. At
the current rate, it may take a few weeks to get here,
but it's the only alternative I can think of.
Take care,

Byron

Her heart dropped, knowing that he was forgetting things
again. Although it was only natural that the recovery process
would be a slow one. At least he remembered her.

Selene Vermielle. She tapped the envelope against her hand.
That was the burglar that had helped them catch The Shadow
back at the beginning of October. She'd disappeared without
a trace from the Pit. If Byron was right about Selene being in
Paris, she would probably be their best contact for catching
Durant.

She smiled. It seemed that her remaining in London was
useful after all! Because if she hadn't stayed behind, there would
be no way of them getting the information from the thieves.

Goodness, she'd need to head down to Berkshire the next
day. But with Landon's blessing, at least her ankle wasn't an
obstacle anymore. Perhaps Liza and Walker would enjoy a quick
day trip. They could find a nice tea house, make a mini-holiday
of it. Ever since Byron came back with tales of sheep, parrots,
and stolen art, she'd wanted to take a trip and see it for herself.
Granted, she had hoped Byron would be with her. But at least
this way, she'd be able to help the investigation, even if it was
in a small way.

Could Byron wait another two weeks for the information,
though? She folded the letter and placed it to the side. She

could hire an express courier, perhaps. Someone to take it to him direct. A telegram would get there quicker, but which cable should she use? And would there be an issue with translation between code readers? There was one other option. One she scarcely dared to think.

She could go to Paris herself. The information was rather time sensitive, wasn't it? And they wouldn't want it to fall into the wrong hands, now, would they? The thought of traveling out of the country made her heart thrum. She'd always wanted to go to France, and this was the perfect opportunity.

She pulled out a fresh sheet of paper and prepped her pen. She had a letter to write, even if she reached Byron before it did.

December 3, 1888

"I'VE NEVER BEEN TO READING BEFORE," LIZA said, twisting her gloves in her lap.

"I've heard it's beautiful in the summer." Walker shifted in his seat.

Mira held in a smile at the exchange. They were trying to communicate with Liza's aunt watching their every move. The chaperone sat near the door of the train car, nose deep into her book. Squinting, Mira could make out the title. *Phantasms of the Living*. But if Walker and Liza so much as breathed wrong, her sharp gaze fell upon them.

Mira sighed and leaned back. When she suggested they go out to Berkshire together, Mira didn't even consider that Liza's parents would insist on a real chaperone.

One of Liza's gloves slipped onto the floor of the train, and she leaned forward.

"Oh no, allow me."

Walker beat her to it, gaze flicking up to the aunt before passing the glove over.

Aunt Eleanor made a "harrumph" noise in the back of her throat and the two separated at once, a light blush coloring Walker's face. Mira was grateful that she and Byron hadn't needed a chaperone yet. Or perhaps they had, but one hadn't been assigned, thank goodness.

Eleanor's presence caused more complications than simply dashing Walker's hopes for flirtation, though. Uncle Cyrus, Liza's parents, and Eleanor herself were unaware of their true purpose in going to Berkshire, and Mira would prefer not to explain why she needed to stop off at the constabulary on their day trip.

THE TRAIN LURCHED TO A STOP, AND the group stood and gathered their things. Aunt Eleanor made it a point to stay behind the group as they disembarked and found their bearings.

The atmosphere reminded Mira of Bristol, only with a lack of sea air. A market was set up in the town square with farmers selling the last of their fall produce. The Thames sparkled in the midmorning light, and in the distance, miles of fields stretched out to the horizon. White blotches of sheep dotted the grass as far as the eye could see.

Mira turned to Walker. "Why don't the two of you, and Aunt Eleanor, of course, take a stroll down by the river? I'll go find a tea shop for us, and perhaps talk with some of the locals?"

Walker nodded in understanding and offered his arm to Liza. "What a splendid idea! What do you think, Miss Renaldi?"

"Oh, I would love to."

When Eleanor gave an approving nod, Liza took hold of Walker's arm and the three of them headed off towards the docks.

Mira let out a breath of relief and turned in a circle to examine her surroundings. Where would the Berkshire Constabulary be? She approached one of the women in the market square.

"Excuse me," she said. "Would you know where the constabulary is located?"

"Oh, of course, Miss." The woman pointed down the road. "It's just down there a ways, then you'll turn left and see a park. There's a building real close to there, and that's the place."

"Thank you! One other thing, is there a tea shop near here?"

"Only one in town is just past the market, over yonder." The woman pointed once again.

"Thank you for your help."

Following the woman's directions brought her to a rather nice building near a park with letters carved into the lintel over the door. *Berkshire Constabulary*. She smiled and entered the building. It was much smaller than Scotland Yard and not as impressive, but that was to be expected in a smaller town. She approached the constable on duty at the front desk.

"Excuse me, sir, but may I speak with Colonel Blandy?"

The constable looked up from his paperwork and gave her a suspicious once over. "May I ask who you are?"

"My name is Samira Blayse. I've been sent on behalf of Detective Byron Constantine."

The man paused for a moment. "I'm afraid that Colonel Blandy is not to be disturbed."

"This is of the utmost importance, I assure you," Mira said.

"I have my orders, Miss and there's nothing that would—"

The man was interrupted as a door opened down the hall and a gentleman in an official looking uniform stepped out, approaching them.

"What's the situation, Swaby?" the new man said.

Swaby looked sufficiently cowed as he answered, "This young woman wishes to speak with you, sir."

Colonel Blandy appraised her and gave a small smile. "What can I do for you, Miss?"

"Blayse. Samira Blayse. I've been sent by Byron Constantine. He told me to speak with you."

"Of course. Please, follow me."

He led the way into his office, closing the door behind the two of them. He gestured towards a chair in front of a mahogany desk. Once they both were seated, Blandy said, "Was there something in particular that Mr. Constantine needed?"

"He's in France, attempting to track down a murderer named Alexander Durant. So far, he hasn't had any successful leads. But he believes that if he can find Selene Vermielle that she might be able to help him."

"Selene Vermielle?"

Mira nodded.

Blandy sighed. "I assume that you've been sent to speak with those thieves, then?"

"Yes. Byron suggested that I—"

"Byron?" Blandy chuckled. "The two of you must be close."

A blush rose to Mira's cheeks. "Yes. Well. We are courting."

"I'm even more pleased to meet you then. Byron is a fine man."

"Yes. He is." She shifted in her seat. "Would it be possible for me to speak with Monty?"

"I can arrange it, yes. Both of them are still being held in the cells here. Their trial was pushed off a bit because of some complications." He stood and gestured for her to follow him.

"What sort of complications?"

"We discovered that they deserted the army almost a decade ago during the last conflict in Afghanistan. At the moment, we're determining when a court martial could be held."

"That is unfortunate."

"As far as I can tell," Colonel Blandy said as he led her down to the cells, "Monty, or Charles Montague as I've discovered his name to be, is fairly cooperative. He never really wanted to be a thief in the first place. I get the feeling that the desertion wasn't his idea either, but rather Aaron Dennis, the other thief, roped him into it. I'd be surprised if Monty didn't help you."

He took a set of keys from his belt and fit one of them into the lock on the outside door. It swung open, and two rows of cells on either side appeared behind it. The air was crisp, even though a small stove burned on the opposite side of the room. Two of the cells stood occupied.

One of the men reclined on a cot. He was tall, broad shouldered, and his face was full of stubble. A scar ran down his left cheek, starting at the corner of his eyebrow and ending below his cheekbone. Deep, ragged, and red. She hoped he wasn't Monty.

The other was sitting on his cot. Short, sandy blond hair, and a nervous look about him. His leg was bouncing up and down.

"Hey there, Monty," Blandy said. "You have a visitor."

The tall man sat up and gave her a grim smile. The shorter one turned and stood, moving to the cell bars.

"A visitor?" the shorter one asked. When he caught sight of her behind Blandy, his eyes widened, and he took off his hat.

"Good morning, Miss."

"Good morning. Are you Charles Montague?"

"Yes, Miss."

"I'm here on behalf of Detective Constantine and I—"

"Don't tell her anything, Monty," the other thief said, standing up. He towered above her, and she shrunk back under his gaze.

Colonel Blandy turned a glare on the other thief. "Your court martial will be in a few weeks, Dennis. There isn't much that'd hurt your case more than the actual crimes you committed. Go ahead and ask your question, Miss Blayse."

Mira cleared her throat. "We're needing to track down Selene Vermielle. Do you have any idea as to her whereabouts?"

"What, so you can arrest her too?" Dennis said.

"We didn't ask you," Blandy said.

"And we don't intend to arrest her. Especially considering that we don't have jurisdiction in France." Turning back to Monty she said, "Do you know where we could find her?"

"If you're not wanting to arrest her, then why do you need to find her?" Monty asked.

"There's a known murderer who's escaped to Paris. We need to track him down, but unless we can gain access to the Parisian criminal underground, we don't have much hope for doing so."

"You mean, if I help you, you'll be able to catch the chap?"

"Exactly. And I'm sure Colonel Blandy will let the judge know about your cooperation in that regard."

Blandy nodded. Monty pursed his lips and sat on his cot.

"They're lying. You can never trust the brass, Monty. You know that."

"Shut up, Dennis." Monty said. "Could we go somewhere private?"

Blandy nodded and pulled out a ring of keys. He unlocked the cell door.

"You'll regret this." Dennis said, laying back on the cot as the three of them left the room.

Blandy led the way, ignoring the strange look from his constable as he ushered them into an interrogation room. Once the door was shut and locked, Mira and Blandy took a seat while Monty paced along the side wall.

"Alright. I'll help you. Although, I'm not sure how helpful the information will be. It's been weeks since I saw her."

"Anything you can tell me will be helpful, I assure you."

"Right." Monty rubbed his hands on his trousers before taking a seat himself. "Well. Selene's operating an art gallery. Galerie de Mestra. It's above the board. The government and police in Paris have no idea that it's a front."

"Is that where you sold the stolen paintings?" Mira pulled out a small notebook and pencil.

"Where we would have, yeah." Monty rubbed the back of his neck. "This was a trial run to see if we could manage to steal works from England and sell them in France. John Constable's paintings are growing in interest right now."

"And the gallery is in Paris?" Blandy asked.

"That's right. It's in Montmartre on Rue Véron. There are a few other galleries in the quarter, but if you ask around, you'll be able to find it."

"How is it that the Parisian police aren't aware of it?"

"Not everything there is stolen, Miss. Vermielle has a few artists that come to her with pieces. Some of those impressionists or the like. And the stolen pieces are in the cellar, see? Only the most trusted of customers are allowed down there."

"I see. Is there anything else you can think of that might help?"

Monty's face twisted in thought. "Not that I can think of."

Mira nodded. "So, if we were to pop over to Rue Véron, we would be able to find her?"

"Unless she's moved in the last month or so, I believe so."

"Thank you very much, Monty." Mira jotted down the last detail and closed the notebook. "You've been incredibly helpful."

"I hope so." He turned to Blandy. "And me helping and all, that'll look good for the court martial?"

"It won't hurt anything, I can assure you of that."

Monty sighed. "Well, I suppose that's all I can ask for." He stood as Mira did and inclined his head. "It's been a pleasure, Miss. I liked Mr. Constantine, even if he did lie about who he was."

"I hope things go well for you in your trial."

"So do I."

AFTER LEAVING THE BERKSHIRE CONSTABULARY, MIRA HEADED down to the docks to see if she couldn't track down her brother, Liza, and the unfortunate chaperone. The chill air nipped at her cheeks, and she pulled her coat tighter around her as she searched the riverbank. With no sign of them, she retreated towards the town center and found her way towards the lone tea shop.

Walker waved her over as she entered. "There you are! Did you get lost?"

Mira shook her head fondly at the way he emphasized the word "lost." She sat down, and Walker handed her a cup of tea.

"I think I must have passed you without either of us realizing it," she said.

Aunt Eleanor nodded sagely. "Or perhaps the spirits led you another way." She patted the top of her book.

Liza cleared her throat. "It's gotten quite a bit colder out there. Do you think it will snow?"

"It would be more likely for it to sleet, I think," Walker said. "Would you like some cream, Mira?"

Mira nodded and took the proffered pitcher. "I just hope it all stays in the clouds until we can get back on the train."

"Agreed," Eleanor said, rubbing the joints on her hands. "It is far too cold for this type of outing. I don't know what gets into young people's heads. I'm sure this place is lovely in the summer, but it is quite taxing at this time of year."

"Did you talk with any of the locals while you were lost, Mira?" Walker asked, the tone in his voice revealing the words he dared not say.

"A few." She hid her smile in her teacup. "And their directions were impeccable."

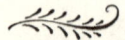

December 3, 1888

Byron,

If my handwriting is irregular, you can blame the train from which I'm writing this letter. I've visited Colonel Blandy at the Berkshire Constabulary and spoken with Charles Montague, or Monty. Selene Vermielle has an art gallery in Montmartre on Rue Véron. The Galerie de Mestra. I'm sending this to you now in case my plans come to nothing, but I intend to arrive in Paris before this letter does. Perhaps I can help you with your French.

Au revoir,

Mira

December 4, 1888

November 22, 1888

My Mira,

We've finished our search in the first arrondissement. Tomorrow we'll start on the second. So far not a single person has recognized the sketch or description of Durant. I worry that he has changed his appearance in some way.

I do hope that you're alright. With the amount of time since I sent my first letter, I know I should have received a response by now. I've tried to ask the postmaster about it, but as I don't know French, it's been next to impossible to communicate with him. The only explanation I can come up with is that I have the wrong address for you, and that can't be right. In *any case, I wish I knew how you were and what was happening on your end. There is so much news that I know I am missing.*

For instance, has your brother found new employment yet? I know how much he wishes to stay in London with Miss Renaldi. I understand his feelings entirely.

Yours now and always,

Byron Constantine

Mira folded the letter and placed it in the back of her sketchbook. She wished she could help Byron feel more at ease. It had taken almost two weeks for his first letter to arrive. That would suggest hers would be delayed as well. There must have been a storm over the channel.

In any case, it was considerate of Byron to be concerned about her brother, but he didn't need to be. After everything had come out about the Sutherland murder, Walker had decided to cut ties with the apprenticeship that Durant urged him into.

But with the merger between Griffon Industries and Emoria-Sutherland several high-profile positions had opened up. Walker had any number of jobs he could choose from. That is if their Uncle Cyrus could convince him.

"I understand where you are coming from, Uncle, but I don't want my success to be determined by other people. I want to make something of myself on my own." Walker paced in front of the fireplace.

"Calm down, my boy. It was only a suggestion." Cyrus lit

his pipe and leaned back. "You mentioned that you wanted to stay in London, and I gave you an alternative to finding apprenticeships in France or on the coast."

Mira kept her mouth shut, focusing on the pencil sketch at hand. When should she ask about her own trip to France? She would need to be careful about the way she asked about it. With her uncle's proclivity towards overprotectiveness, her argument would need to be sound.

Professor Burke sat next to her holding a book that he wasn't paying attention to whatsoever. In fact, he leaned over, examined her sketch and gave a brief nod of approval before turning back to the conversation.

Walker stopped, brow furrowed. "You don't mind?"

Cyrus chuckled. "I had similar inclinations myself as a young man. Thought about joining the military, but my father convinced me to go on a business trip with him to India. Changed my mind entirely about the profession, and I ended up taking over the family business." He tapped the side of his pipe. "Just as well I didn't join the military. I don't think I would have done well there."

"And you never would have met me," Professor Burke said, thoughtful. "And I would never have introduced Rose and Tavian to one another."

"Thank goodness you didn't go into the military." Mira laughed. "Otherwise, none of us would be here right now."

"Strange how one decision affected so many outcomes," Walker let out a sigh and sat in the armchair closest to the fireplace. "I'm not sure what it is that I'm meant to do."

"You'll figure something out, eventually. However, I do want to set something straight: If you were to take a position in the company, it would not be a free ride on my coattails. I would expect you to find your own success using your own merits."

"Your uncle has a point, Walker. And perhaps you could

take a position from the Sutherland side of the branch. No familial connection there. Not really." Burke abandoned his novel to the side table.

"And then you could stay close to Liza. In London," Mira said with a smirk.

Walker's face twisted in thought. "You've all given some excellent points."

"Think it over," Cyrus said. "There's no hurry to come to a decision."

"I think I'll go for a walk." Walker stood and moved towards the door. "Clear my head a bit."

The door closed behind him as Mira erased a few stray smudges from her sketch.

Professor Burke picked up his book again. "I would wager he's heading over to Miss Renaldi's."

"No one would bet against you on that," Mira said. "I think he'll come around to the idea, Uncle."

"Yes. I believe so as well. It would be a great help to have someone in the company that I can trust." His expression darkened. "With all this smuggling nonsense that you and Constantine have found out, I'd rather know the people that work for me."

"Rather difficult to do that when many of your holdings are in France now, isn't it?" Burke asked.

Mira frowned. "France? I thought most of the company's connections were in India."

Cyrus nodded. "They were until the merger. Sutherland's company dealt more with the continent. France. Prussia. Spain. In fact, I just got a letter the day before yesterday from one of my merchants in Paris. Apparently, Sutherland had arranged to help with the transport of goods and materials to and from the Universal Exposition happening there next May. The biggest contract is iron for some tower they are building. Unfortunately, I wasn't aware of it until now and am left in the rather awkward position of figuring out how to accomplish it."

"Did he not have the plans figured out already?" Mira asked.

"Some of the plans had been finalized. They started building the tower in January of last year, and Sutherland has been over the iron delivery. However, the final shipments weren't approved before Sutherland died. I'm going to have to figure it out by the end of the month if I want it to work."

"Yes, I can see why it would be awkward," Burke said. "And that isn't even accounting for the boycott."

"Boycott?" Mira leaned forward.

"Yes," Burke continued. "The exposition is celebrating the centennial of the storming of the Bastille. One hundred years since the dissolution of their monarchy. It wouldn't look good for Her Majesty if England went and supported it, would it?"

"I suppose it wouldn't." Mira frowned. "Is that going to cause you problems, Uncle?"

"The contracts were signed before the boycott was finalized, so I don't think so." He paused a moment, brow furrowing. "At least I hope it doesn't. After all, if we manage to arrange everything, it would be excellent business."

Burke shifted forward in his seat a bit, abandoning his book once again. "I have an idea for you. I'm scheduled to speak in Provence in a few weeks."

"So soon after your last trip?" Cyrus interrupted.

Professor Burke nodded. "I agreed to do a lecture there ages before I planned my trip to Prussia. In any case, I could leave a week early and meet with your people in Paris for you. Assess them and help to figure out some of those arrangements."

Mira froze in place. If the professor was already going to Paris, perhaps she could go with him. Her gaze flicked to Cyrus. He'd gone still with thought. He would probably come up with some excuse for her to stay behind. But there had to be some way to convince him. Maybe he wouldn't allow her to go with the professor. But if her uncle were going, perhaps he'd let her go with him?

"That is an interesting prospect," Cyrus said. "One cannot trust correspondence implicitly, but if you were to go in person, we'd get a reliable idea of what we're working with."

"May I propose an alternative idea?" Mira asked, closing her sketchbook.

"Of course, my dear," Cyrus said.

She took a deep breath. If she didn't word this carefully, it would all come to naught. "What if you were to go to Paris yourself? Walker could take over things here for a week or two. It could give him some good experience with the company and help him make his decision. Think of it as a trial period. You could meet with the merchants in Paris, see the warehouses, make sure that everything is running as it should, and make the final arrangements for the exposition."

Burke furrowed his brow. "Would Walker be prepared to take on so much responsibility in such a short time?"

"We wouldn't be gone long, and it would be a great opportunity for him," Mira said.

"We?" Cyrus sat forward and set his pipe on the side table.

Mira cringed. She hadn't meant to include herself yet. "Well. I was just thinking. We usually give the staff a few weeks off for holiday in December. And while I can handle myself well enough on my own, wouldn't it be easier if I came with you?"

Cyrus pinched the bridge of his nose. "First of all, I haven't decided whether I'm going or not. I haven't had the chance to mull it over, let alone come to a decision. Secondly, if I were to go, there's no reason you couldn't stay here with your brother."

"And there's no reason for either of you to go when I'm already planning on a trip to Paris," Burke said.

Cyrus put a hand up. "No, I do see the sense in me going myself. If you were still willing to leave a week or so early for your trip, perhaps the day after tomorrow, I would appreciate your knowledge of the city."

"It would be my pleasure." Burke grinned. "It's been a while since we traveled together."

"Well. That's settled then." He stood. "If either of you need anything, I'll be in my office making preparations."

He left the room, the door closing without a sound. Mira let out a long breath. Dash it all! It would be impossible to convince him now. Perhaps a telegram would be needed after all.

Professor Burke frowned as he stood to put his book away. "This sudden interest in going to France doesn't have anything to do with your absent detective, does it, Mira?"

Mira furrowed her brow at the tone of the question. "I would hardly call my interest sudden, Professor." She set her sketchbook to the side. "I've wanted to go to France since I learned the difference between a pencil and a paintbrush."

His worry-lines melted away, and he chuckled. "I suppose that is true. And you've begged me for every travel story I know since before then." He paused, gaze resting on the fire for a moment before drifting back to her. "It's hard to remember that you aren't a little girl anymore."

"I haven't been for a good long while."

"No. You haven't. But in some ways, you always will be." He sat in the armchair across from her. The fire crackled in the hearth, punctuating the silence with pops and hisses as the logs settled. After a few moments the professor said, "You know, I think one of my favorite memories was when I returned from Vienna when you were six."

"That was the first time you brought back stereographs, wasn't it?"

Burke smiled. "It was. You sat on the floor and looked at them for hours. I'd never understood what it meant to be a godfather before. But in that moment, I knew that I would do anything to protect you."

"You and my uncle share a similar sentiment in that regard." Mira sighed.

"If you stopped getting into trouble, perhaps we wouldn't worry so much." He stood and stretched. "Then again, I think we would always worry." His eyes sparkled with mirth as he moved over to her. "I ought to be going. If I'm going to France the day after tomorrow, I'd best make some arrangements." He kissed the top of her head and left the room.

Mira tried to go back to sketching, but her mind was whirling with various scenarios. She could just go up to her uncle's office. Knock on the door. Walk in. Explain her reasons for coming with him to France. But based on their history, he would say no, and that would be that. She stood to pace the room. Perhaps if she made it seem like it was his idea, he'd come around to it. But how to go about that?

The door creaked open, and she turned towards the sound. Her uncle stepped in.

"Oh, has Edward left already?"

"Just a few minutes ago."

Cyrus hummed. "A pity. I had a question I wished to ask him."

"I'm sure you'll have plenty of time to talk about it before you leave." She turned her back to him, staring up at the painting of her grandparents, uncle, and mother. So much for hiding her frustration. She crossed her arms across her chest.

Cyrus moved to stand beside her. "I understand why you're upset."

"Do you?"

"You were hoping to see Mr. Constantine."

Mira clenched her fists, nails digging into her arms. "While that is part of the reason I wished to go, that is not why I'm upset, Uncle."

"Why, then?"

"I'll answer that if you can answer a question of mine. Why do you not want me to go?"

"It isn't safe."

"It isn't safe?" A strangled laugh escaped her lips. He was such a hypocrite! "And yet you allowed Walker to study there. You're traveling there yourself."

Cyrus pinched the bridge of his nose. "I have my reasons for wanting you to stay home. Why can't you be satisfied, Mira?"

"Because it isn't fair! Can't you see that?"

"The last time we argued about what's fair and what's not, you convinced me, against my better judgment, mind you, to let you go live on your own. Look what that got you: Death threats and kidnappings!"

"And you think I'm safer here at Swan Walk? London is hardly the safest place on the planet, whether I'm living under your roof or not. And aside from that, Circe knows very well where I am. If they wanted me dead, I would be."

Cyrus' mouth snapped shut.

"How many times do I have to prove myself?" She paced in front of the bookcases. "How many times have I faced death and walked straight back again?" Remembering the professor's words, she paused in front of him, voice breaking. "I'm not a child anymore!"

His frown deepened. "Faced death? What do you—"

She interrupted, face flushed. "Why can't you just trust me?"

"I can't lose you, too!" he yelled.

She blinked at him as he stepped away, sinking into one of the armchairs, head in his hands.

"You've said that before." She drew her gaze back towards the portrait. At this point, the likeness could be her own, she looked so much like her mother. A cold realization trickled into her bones.

"It's because I remind you of her, isn't it?"

Her uncle shook his head. "It isn't that."

"I thought you had moved past that. That you were finally

seeing me, but," She turned towards him. "Every time you look at me you see her, don't you?"

He swallowed. "I couldn't save her."

"Her death isn't your fault."

"But I should have done something."

"You have! You took me and Walker in. You raised us when my parents couldn't!"

Cyrus opened his mouth and shut it again. Mira sighed.

"Just over a month ago you told me and Walker that you were going to try to be better about living in the present. That you weren't going to hold such high expectations for us."

She moved towards the door, pausing to look back as she opened it. "You want to know why I'm upset, Uncle? Because no matter what I do, you will never see me for me. She's gone, but that doesn't mean you have to treat me as if I'm a ghost, too."

"Mira—"

She turned and left, not wanting to hear the platitudes he intended to use against her. Hot tears rose to the surface as she climbed the stairs to her room. Her heart constricted, beating itself senseless against her ribcage.

The worst part of all is that while she meant every word that she said, she didn't quite mean for them to come out in that way. She wiped at a stray tear and collapsed on the bed. For all that she said she wasn't a child anymore, she certainly was crying like one.

A knock came at the door, and she sat up, scrubbing the tears away. "Come in."

The door creaked open and Landon popped his head through. "I have a letter for you, Miss."

She stood and moved to take it. "Thank you, Landon."

He appraised her for a moment. "I'll go make up some tea and biscuits for you."

She smiled as he disappeared down the staircase again. She couldn't hide anything from the butler, regardless of how hard she tried. Moving to the desk, she plucked up a letter opener and ran it along the side.

November 23, 1888

Beloved Mira,

It continues to feel strange to write to you in this fashion. I had thought it would be a simple mission to arrest Durant, but looking back, it was a fool's hope. I should have known that with Circe involved, it would be much more complicated than simply tracking him down. The second arrondissement hasn't proved any more successful than the first.

If you haven't already done so, please contact Monty at the Berkshire Constabulary. It's looking more and more like that lead is the only one we have, and I haven't made any headway on finding Miss Vermielle myself.

I hope you and your family are well. I miss the way you would laugh at the silly things I'd say.

You are forever in my memory,

If only she had kept her head. If she had managed to explain the need for her to go to Paris, that her going could be the line between Durant being captured or getting away, then her uncle might have listened. And yet, she couldn't feel entirely remorseful about yelling at him. She'd been covered by her mother's shroud for years, and it was about time to escape from it.

She pulled out her sketchbook and flipped to the very last page. At the top she wrote *France Preparations*. It would take a bit of doing, but she had savings. She knew the language. If her uncle wouldn't take her, she'd find her own way.

December 5, 1888

*M*IRA TAPPED ON THE SIDE OF HER egg and pulled off the top. A bit of yolk dribbled down the side of the cup, and she caught it with a piece of toast. A yawn escaped her lips. She'd stayed up well into the night making plans for her trip. She needed to leave after her uncle, otherwise he'd find some way to put a stop to it. But she also didn't want to wait too long. If she played it right, she'd be back in London before he returned.

The lack of sleep was making it difficult to concentrate on Walker's ramblings on whether he should take up the position with Griffon Industries.

"What did Liza say when you talked to her yesterday?" she asked.

"It was a bit difficult to decipher," Walker said from across the breakfast table. "After all, her aunt was there, and I didn't fancy discussing things out in the open with her circling the conversation like a vulture." He took a sip of tea, deep in thought. "The good news is that we have determined that Aunt Eleanor has a weakness when it comes to spiritualism. Perhaps we could spook her off somehow. Make up some kind of poltergeist or vision about her premature death, or something."

"Or you could simply get engaged." Mira laughed.

"Oh, no. It would be much easier to feign an encounter with the great beyond. Like this." He placed a hand to his temple. "Oh! I feel it! Something quite terrible shall happen to you if you stay in this house!" He grinned. "I bet she would go quite green about the gills and make a break for it. That is, if she didn't faint clean away."

"The poor woman! She has no idea what she's up against," Mira giggled at the image.

"I haven't convinced Liza of the plan yet. Rather difficult to do it in front of the superstitious aunt. In any case, I think Liza would prefer I stay in London, which is only to be expected." He paused in buttering his toast. "You've been awfully quiet about the whole thing, Mouse. What do you think I should do?"

"I think that it's your life, and it's your decision. Why should my opinion matter?"

"Because you're my sister, and that means I'm obligated to care about what you think."

Mira tore off another bit of toast. "Yes, but you have enough familial opinions to muddle your brain, don't you?"

"I'd like to add yours to the mix. I'm nothing if not thorough."

"Alright." She laughed. "I agree with Liza. I would love for you to stay in London. And I think that there's nothing wrong with getting a head start in the business."

"But it's the very definition of nepotism!"

Footsteps sounded from the hall and the twins became more interested in their toast. "Good morning," their uncle said as he came into the room.

"Good morning," Walker said.

Mira remained silent. Cyrus moved past them and took a seat, but instead of opening up a newspaper, he cleared his throat and turned to Walker.

"I have a proposal for you."

"I'm not quite ready to propose to Liza yet, but thanks for putting one together all the same." Walker smirked and shoved a forkful of egg into his mouth.

Cyrus chuckled. "I was thinking more along the lines of a business proposal. How would you feel about testing your mettle and being in charge of Griffon Industries for a week or so?"

Walker choked on his eggs. "What?"

"I'm going to Paris to check on our holdings there, and it would be good to have someone to keep an eye on things here."

Walker's eyes flicked to Mira for a moment. "You want to put me in charge of the company?"

"For a short time. It will give you more context for making a decision, and if you do decide to take a position with the company, it will help me make an informed choice on where to place you. Allow you to make it in the world on your own merits, as you wanted."

"Right." Walker frowned. "When are you leaving?"

"Tomorrow, I'd say. The sooner the better."

"This is rather sudden, isn't it?" Walker asked. "When did you decide this?"

"Yesterday evening, actually. I've already spoken with the staff about taking an early and prolonged holiday, and Professor Burke has agreed to accompany me."

Mira chewed on the inside of her cheek. He was following her suggestion to a fault. Should she push her luck and ask to come again, or keep planning to go on her own? Cyrus continued to explain the benefits of his trip, with Walker's rapt attention.

"But I would only be able to make the trip if you'd be willing to watch over things while I'm gone."

"Well, when you put it that way, I suppose it would be a good opportunity."

"That settles it. I think if I can get everything arranged, I could leave tomorrow." Cyrus picked up his newspaper and opened it.

The table settled into silence other than the scraping of silverware on plates and the crunch of toast. A palpable tension sat in the air and Walker mouthed, *What's wrong?*

Mira checked to ensure their uncle's preoccupation before mouthing, *Later.* Stacking her cutlery on top of her plate, she stood to leave.

Cyrus cleared his throat. "Mira, would you go to my office? I'd like to speak with you."

She took a deep breath. "Yes, of course, Uncle."

"I'll be there in a few minutes."

A CHILL VEIN OF ANXIETY COILED THROUGH her as she sat in her uncle's office. She wasn't entirely certain what he wanted to speak about. Surely, it had something to do with the argument from the day before. The first time they'd had an argument of that volume, he'd sent her off to finishing school. Granted, he had been doing better at listening since he'd been acquitted of murder. And it wasn't as if he could send her to finishing school again. Or could he?

The minutes ticked by. Cyrus was likely finishing his breakfast and collecting his thoughts. On the desk in front of her lay plans for the trip to Paris. Preparations. Travel arrangements.

She stood and moved closer. Could she use some of the same arrangements for herself? It would be much easier, and if her uncle had already gone through the process of choosing accommodations and modes of travel, they would be reputable. Of course, she couldn't use the exact same itinerary, could she? Otherwise, they'd cross paths. Maybe she should focus on finding notes for when he would be returning home.

His footsteps sounded on the squeaky floorboard outside the office, and she resumed a bored expression in her seat of choice as the door opened.

"Ah, Mira. We have quite a bit to discuss." He crossed the room and took a seat behind the desk.

"Do we?"

"Yes." He positioned his spectacles on his nose and picked up a paper to read from it. "The plan is to leave tomorrow. Around eight in the morning. We'll travel by train to Dover and take a ship across the channel. With any luck, we'll be in Paris before nightfall."

Mira nodded. She had the beginning of her timeline, then. If she left a day later, she'd miss him entirely. But why was he telling her this? Cyrus picked up a new piece of paper as he continued.

"The only issue is I haven't been able to find accommodations as of yet. Edward said that he'd take care of it, but it is rather short notice. I'm hopeful we'll be able to find a boarding house that will take us, at least for one night while we find something suitable for a prolonged stay."

Mira fought the urge to huff. It was one thing to not let her go. But to add insult to injury by laying out the entire trip in detail? She had half a mind to walk out regardless of what he wanted to talk to her about. "That's well and good, Uncle but—"

He held up a hand. "I was wondering if you'd be packed and ready to go in that timeframe."

Her ready-made retort froze on her tongue. "What?"

Cyrus leaned back, a conflicted expression crossing his features. "I've been up half the night thinking about our argument yesterday. You're right. I've been unfair."

"You mean," The beginning of a smile tugged at her lips. "I'm coming with you?"

"Unless you've changed your mind." He paused a moment, a flicker of hope in his eyes.

"No, I'd love to come. But you were so against it yesterday. What's changed?" Her memory drifted back to the dozens of times he had forbidden her to travel before. Did his overbearing nature finally have a crack?

He sighed. "I still don't like the idea. But I realized that this time you'll probably just go off on your own, and at least this way I'll be there with you. And if we need another translator, you know the language well enough, don't you?"

She nodded. "I'd be happy to help. Although," She fidgeted with her hands. "You ought to know that I have another purpose for going."

"Oh?"

"Well, you were right in some regard yesterday. About me wanting to see Mr. Constantine, I mean. You see, he's hit several dead ends as far as Durant is concerned. He asked me to look into some leads here, which is why we took that trip up to Berkshire earlier this week. The information is crucial to the investigation and highly sensitive. It would be best if I brought it myself."

Cyrus hummed. "Yes, I believe that would take precedence."

"Really?" Mira frowned. He was being much too calm about the revelation. She'd expected him to go back on his agreement and say she couldn't come once he realized she was at the center of another investigation.

"What, you think I'd prefer that the murderer of my late business partner got away?"

"Well, no, but—"

He interrupted, picking up some papers to examine them. "Aside from that, you and Mr. Constantine are courting, and it's been over a month since the two of you have been seen together in society."

She knew that he was teasing her now, but a blush rushed to her ears, nonetheless. "Uncle!"

He smiled over his spectacles. "Why don't you go pack?"

She stood and moved over to him, giving him a hug around the shoulders.

"Thank you!"

He froze in place, shocked at her affection. After a moment he reached a hand up and patted her arm.

"Yes. Well." He cleared his throat. "Off you go."

MIRA PULLED HER TRUNK FROM HER CLOSET, opened it up and stood there, stunned. She was going to France! She let out a rather unladylike squeal and flopped onto the bed. And not just France, she was going to the City of Light!

She sat up. What did she need to pack? How long were they going to be there? A week? Two? She set to work pulling out walking dresses, gowns, underskirts, gloves, and undergarments and laid them all out on the bed. Her cat, Nero, hopped up onto the bed and settled atop her wool cloak. Folding each article in a neat stack, she organized them by category and outlined her plan of attack, so to speak. Oh, how she'd much rather stuff it all in the trunk and call it a day!

But her uncle was liable to check her trunk before they left, and she didn't want to give him any reason to go back on his decision to let her come with. Thank goodness she had the entirety of the day free to pack!

A few hours in, a knock rapped at her door. She said, "Come in," without a thought.

"It looks like a fashion house exploded all over your room," Walker tutted.

"I'll clean it up before I'm done." She tucked an old cloth around her travel art supplies and bundled them in the depth of fabric and petticoats.

"What is all this, anyway? Are you running away?"

"Not exactly." She grinned. "Uncle is taking me to Paris!"

"And here I thought you two were out of sorts with each other." He found an unoccupied space on the bed and sat.

"Well. Yes." She sat beside him, voice softening. "We had a bit of a disagreement about his overprotectiveness."

"Sorted it out, then?" He scratched the top of Nero's head. The cat leaned into his hand and moved closer so they both could stroke his fur.

She smiled. "I think so."

"Good."

"You'll look after Nero for me while I'm gone, won't you?"

"I'm sure he'd travel well enough in that trunk of yours." Walker picked the cat up and placed him on the top of the pile.

"I'm not eager to have my dresses shredded, thank you!"

"It would only be fair after what you've done to my clothes in the past." Walker smirked. "But I'll watch him for you."

"Good." She set Nero on the floor and placed the last article of clothing in the trunk. "Because there's no room for him."

"Packing it tight, are we?"

She closed the lid of the trunk and sat on it to get it latched. "I'm not sure how long we'll be staying, and I'd rather be safe."

When the trunk wouldn't close, Walker moved to sit beside her. Between the two of them, they managed to get it closed and latched. "Did Uncle say?"

She shook her head and moved back to the bed. "It all depends on how long it takes to visit each of the warehouses and make the arrangements for the exposition. And aside from that, my plan is to help Byron, and who knows how long that will take?" Nero hopped on her lap, purring away.

Walker laughed. "Oh, yes. I had forgotten about your true reason for escaping the country. It has nothing to do with your lifelong ambition to visit Paris, or the fact that you've been cooped up for the better part of a month. No, it has everything to do with a dashing detective with dangerous pastimes."

"You know it's more than that."

Walker smiled and meandered towards the door. "Well, I think I ought to warn you in any case."

"Warn me? About what?"

He gave a shrug of his shoulders and opened the door, turning back to her. "It's just I overheard Uncle and Burke the other evening. Discussing the two of you." He placed a hand to his temple. "Oh! I think I'm getting a vision! Something hazy . . ."

"Walker! What is it?"

"I see . . . I see a chaperone in your future!"

She threw a pillow at him, which he deflected with the door.

He laughed and left the room. "Good luck with that, dear sister!"

December 5, 1888

My Dearest Byron,

I couldn't help but write you once more. My uncle has agreed to my accompanying him to Paris! I have the information on Vermielle, and I cannot wait to see you again. I can only hope that you've kept the same residence in your time there. Then I'll be able to find you straight away.

Until we meet,

Mira

December 6, 1888

MIRA WOKE BRIGHT AND EARLY THE NEXT morning and rushed to get ready. Paris! She buttoned her shoes in an instant. She was going to Paris! A quick jump positioned each of her colored petticoats inline along her hem. She could cry with excitement! Her hands danced along the hooks of her bodice. Paris!

She took half a moment to appraise herself in the mirror. Each and every hair stayed in place, and her clothes suited the latest traveling fashions. With everything in its proper order, Cyrus couldn't possibly find anything to complain about. With one last considering look, she sped down the stairs.

Walker caught hold of her arm on the second landing, pulling her to a stop.

"Whoa, there! The carriage isn't leaving just yet."

"Right." Mira attempted to compose herself but found she

couldn't contain her grin. "But perhaps if everything is in order, we could leave sooner!"

"So eager to leave me behind?" he teased.

"You'll be fine. Think of all the fun you'll have while we're gone."

"Oh yes. Loads of fun. Working in an office all day. Running a business I know practically nothing about. How could I possibly have more fun than that?"

"You forgot that you'll also be tormenting a poor aunt into thinking she's haunted."

"Oh yes!" Walker leaned back on his heels. "I do have that to look forward to."

She smiled at him. "Thank you."

"For what?" His brow furrowed.

"Staying behind." She leaned over and kissed his cheek. "Uncle wouldn't be going to Paris if he didn't trust you."

With that, she left her stunned brother on the stairs and made her way to the kitchen.

Landon was in the process of arranging plates and cutlery on a tray. Mrs. Pringle, the cook, pulled some hot rolls from the oven and set about removing them from the pan. Mira drank in the scent as she came down the stairs.

The butler glanced up as she made it to the bottom. "Breakfast will be served in a few minutes, Miss Mira."

"I know, and it smells heavenly. I just wanted to say goodbye before everything gets hectic upstairs."

"Are you excited to finally be going to France, Miss?" Mrs. Pringle asked. After Mrs. Hunt, the previous cook, went away to Wales to get married a few years back, Mrs. Pringle took on the position. Mira hadn't even known her name before she had moved back into Swan Walk in September. The cook was a busybody, wanting to know everything that went on above stairs. When Mira injured her ankle, she enabled that gossip by visiting the kitchens to find someone to talk to. Mrs. Pringle was more than willing to talk.

"It doesn't feel quite real yet."

"Probably won't until you're off the train in Dover. Or when you're able to see the cliffs from the other side." She wrapped the rolls up in a soft towel to keep them warm and placed them in the dumbwaiter next to the plates.

"Perhaps. Are you excited for your own holiday?"

"Oh yes. I haven't been back to Scotland in years. My brother'll be so surprised."

Mira turned to Landon. "Where are you going this year?"

"I haven't quite decided." He tugged on the pulley system to move the dumbwaiter to the upper floor. "Your uncle did announce the change in plans rather abruptly and I haven't had much time to consider it."

"I'm sure you'd be welcome to come with me, if you were willing to bear the cold," Mrs. Pringle said. Mira hid a smile. Mrs. Pringle had had her eye on Landon for quite some time. Just the week before, she'd confided in Mira that she often wondered if the butler would ever want to settle down again.

Landon tilted his head to the side. "That is an interesting idea. Let me think on it for a bit." He moved towards the stairs.

Mira paused a moment, letting her smirk take over. "Inviting him to meet your family? That is rather forward of you."

Mrs. Pringle flushed. "Hush now! It's nothing of the sort." She leaned over the counter, lowering her voice. "Do you think he'll come?"

Mira furrowed her brow. "I can't say. But you have a fair chance. In any case, travel safe."

"You as well, Miss! I do look forward to hearing about Paris when you return."

Mira grinned and headed up the stairs.

Landon was setting the table when she emerged into the dining room.

"You're all packed then?" he said without looking up.

"And ready to go!"

"You didn't forget anything?" He set the last plate in place on the table and turned back to the dumbwaiter to move the food from the dumbwaiter to the sideboard.

"If I did, I wouldn't know." She ran her hand along the tops of each of the chairs. "You seem nervous about me going."

Landon hesitated before shaking his head. "Just promise to stay safe."

"I can't promise that, but I'll try."

He gave her a thin smile and closed the dumbwaiter doors. "Why don't we go find your uncle, hm? It's time for breakfast."

They split up in the entry hall, Landon going to her uncle's office and Mira going to the parlor. From the parlor window she caught sight of Cyrus supervising the movements of their trunks onto the carriage. Moving outside, she found Professor Burke standing next to him on the stairs. His trunks were already positioned and tied down.

"No, no! The smaller one can fit there." Cyrus moved to have a more hands-on role in his supervision.

Mira stood next to Professor Burke, catching another strong whiff of floral citrus as he turned his head towards her. He gave her a smile and pointed to her uncle.

"He hasn't changed much from the last time we traveled together. I always wonder why he hires boys to pack the carriage when he ends up doing most of it himself."

Mira chuckled. "I suppose some things don't change. When was your last trip with him?"

He hooked his thumb in his waistcoat pocket and rocked back on his heels. "That's a good question. It's been a couple decades."

"Before I was born?"

"Likely." He sighed. "You're still sure you want to go on a trip with a couple of old curmudgeons like ourselves?"

"You won't talk me out of this."

He laughed. "I don't think I'll even try."

Cyrus concluded his lecture on proper weight management

and moved back towards the steps. A healthy red tinged his cheeks from the exercise.

"Good morning, Mira! Are you ready to go?"

She gave a quick turn about. "I think so. Do I pass?"

Cyrus nodded. "Practical. Sharp. It'll do nicely. Although you need a cloak."

"My waterproof one is in the hall."

"Very good. You'll also want to grab some smelling salts, in case you get seasick."

Mira huffed. "I won't get seasick."

"Yes," the professor said. "But your uncle just might."

Cyrus gave him a withering glare. "I will not."

"Why don't we just use your cologne, professor? It's strong enough." Mira held in a laugh.

"I find it distinguished." The professor straightened his posture, as if posing for a portrait.

Walker poked his head out of the doorway. "What are you lot all standing out here for? Breakfast is getting cold!"

"Oh, is it ready?" the professor said, heading up the stairs. "I'm famished."

AFTER BREAKFAST AND A FEW MORE ROUNDS of goodbyes, they were finally on their way. It was just a quick carriage ride to the station, jostling and jolting over the cobblestones. They paused to ensure the porters received their luggage and that they knew which train to place it on when the time came. Mira took a moment to orient herself as they moved amidst the hustle and bustle of hundreds of strangers all trying to get to their respective platforms. Their train wouldn't arrive for another thirty or so minutes, so they stopped off in the waiting room. A half dozen conversations drifted about over their heads from various groups around the room as they took their seats.

Cyrus pulled out his pipe. "We made good time."

The professor nodded. "I just hope the weather is fair enough at Dover to cross. It's a bit tricky this time of year."

"You mean there's a possibility that we won't get to Paris today?" Mira asked.

"We could be delayed, yes. It depends on the conditions."

"Don't worry too much about it, Mira. Things will turn out in any case," Cyrus said.

Soon enough, their train entered the station, and they boarded, finding their compartment with ease. Mira took the seat across from her uncle and the professor. As the two of them discussed their travel plans, she lost her thoughts to the movement of the buildings outside the window.

Would the buildings be much different in Paris? Or would they only be foreign to her because of their unfamiliar arrangement? She'd seen pictures, of course, and stereographs, but that was much different to seeing them in real life, wasn't it?

What kind of building had Byron been living in for almost a month? Would she be able to find it once they got there? She had brought his letters with her, in part to read over them again during the journey, but also to keep the address close at hand. More letters would be coming to Swan Walk while she was out of the country. She frowned. Hopefully Walker wouldn't read them.

She pulled a book out of her bag and settled in to read for the duration of the journey, hoping that the weather would be favorable upon their arrival.

THE TRAIN SLOWED TO A STOP AND nudged her out of her gentle doze. She blinked a few times, making sense of her surroundings. The sun had traveled far since she last remembered, but it wasn't close to setting just yet.

"We're here, Mira. Grab your things," Cyrus said.

With a quick stretch and a hidden yawn, she picked up her smaller belongings and followed the two men out of the train and onto the platform.

They managed to track down their luggage, directing the porters to settle it on the back of a hansom cab.

"Which dock do we need to get to?" Professor Burke asked, climbing into the carriage.

Cyrus pulled a paper from his pocket and studied it a moment before taking his seat as well. "Claremont Port. It's a new one, I think."

"Aye, that it is," the driver said. "I know the way."

Mira climbed in last, her uncle helping her into the carriage before it moved away from the station.

"It doesn't look stormy," the professor said.

Mira glanced out the window. While it was cold enough that she could see her breath, the sun shone from behind the clouds. The wind was fair, too.

Cyrus frowned as the driver turned the cab away from the ports, going up a hill.

"Are you certain you know where you are going?" he said, voice gruff.

The driver laughed. "Sure as I can see my hands here. It's up at the top of those cliffs there." He pointed.

"Cliffs?" Burke asked.

"Are you hard of hearing, sir? You can see the ships right up ahead."

Mira's eyes widened as she caught sight of a massive blue dirigible attached to a dock near the cliffside. Were they taking an airship? Excitement bubbled under her skin. They were going to fly! As they moved closer, several other dirigibles came into view. Her gaze flicked to her uncle. He hated airships, so why had he booked one?

"There must be a mistake." Cyrus referenced his papers,

flipping through the stack like mad. "We were supposed to take a ship." He squinted at his handwriting. "The *Raposa.*"

The driver pointed again. "That's the reddish-brown one there at the end. Its platform has the flag with the fox insignia on it."

Her uncle's pallor dipped towards a ghostly white.

Burke nodded, noticing his friend's condition. "Is there a way we can switch to an ocean steamer, rather than an air one?" he asked.

Cyrus sunk back in his seat, papers limp in his hand. "I got the tickets with Thomas Cook and Son. I don't think they are transferable."

Mira placed her hand on his arm. It shook beneath her fingertips. Poor man! He had been terrified of airships for almost two decades. "It will all turn out fine," she said, trying to comfort him.

He swallowed. "We can only hope."

THEY STOOD BENEATH THE RUST-COLORED BALLOON, STARING up at it through the scaffolding that held up the dock. Cyrus was rooted to the ground, mouth agape at it. He cleared his throat. "I've, er, never been so close to one before."

"They are quite a different experience than traveling by boat, that's certain." Professor Burke clapped him on the back. "It'll be a new adventure."

"You've flown in one of these contraptions then?" Cyrus said, gaze still on the dirigible.

"Many times. No issue. 'Course, I was a bit wary of them after the, well."

The three fell silent, the wind rushing through their hair. Mira rubbed her arms at the chill. She glanced between her uncle and the professor. Burke's face sagged with grief, looking so much older than he usually did. Cyrus' eyes were clouded and heavy. The balloon swayed from side to side, casting its shadow across them.

The death of her parents cast a similar shadow. She hated the way it hung over them, never letting them forget. Every interaction they had, even the most joyful, suffered from the desaturated coloring of grief. Some days, she wished they could all just forget it ever happened. Why was their absence so keenly felt? Especially after all this time? Why couldn't they be happy in their lives together now?

But to forget that they died would be erasing them, too, and she didn't want to do that. Even with the pain of eighteen years behind her, she didn't want to change it. And yet at the same time she wished for things to be different.

Professor Burke shifted his stance, clearing his throat. "It is a dashed convenient way to travel though."

Cyrus' shoulders tightened. "Right."

Mira took him by the arm. "It's perfectly safe. But we need to board soon. Do you feel up to it?"

He gave a sharp nod. "I'll have to be, won't I? Our luggage is already aboard."

"That's the spirit," the professor said, starting towards the gangway.

Mira and Cyrus followed at a slower pace. She didn't want to push her uncle too much. He'd had an intense fear and hatred for airships ever since the accident happened in 1870. She didn't blame him for being so wary of the machine that took his only sibling. When she had discovered the truth about their deaths, she hadn't known how to tell her uncle that it hadn't been an accident. The Order of Circe had murdered them to maintain their smuggling operation. It was one of the hardest conversations that she had ever had in her life. The same expression of sorrow and shock from that revelation was present on his features as they approached the dirigible.

"I'm sorry that this is so difficult for you," Mira said.

Cyrus swallowed. "I shouldn't be so apprehensive about it."

She squeezed his arm. "I don't blame you for it."

"Yes, but the death of your mother didn't have anything to do with the airship itself, did it? She died somewhere else?" It seemed to pain him to even admit it.

She nodded, letting go of his arm.

He let out a slow, shaky breath as they came to the bottom of the gangway. "And Edward said he's traveled on one."

Mira paused in thought. He was still oblivious to the fact that she and Walker had also traveled by airship. Walker would be against her spilling their secret, but would it help to calm their uncle's nerves?

"Do you want to know a secret?" She steeled herself and stepped onto the plank. "So have Walker and I."

His eyes widened. "You have? But—"

"I know, you forbade us from ever setting foot on one. And yet, we both did. And it was fine. We were safe." She extended a hand to him. "I think it's your turn now."

He considered her statement a moment, then took her hand, stepping onto the plank.

"If you had told me any earlier than this moment, you would be in so much trouble."

She smiled. "I know."

THEY MET PROFESSOR BURKE ON THE DECK of the ship. It was quite similar to the first airship that Mira had traveled on, the *Horizon*. The main difference was in the coloring. The *Raposa* took on a more reddish-orange palette, whereas the *Horizon* favored blues. Glass and wood lined the outer wall. Intricate wallpaper and wood paneling on the inside wall. Lush carpet beneath their feet. They followed the flow of people around the side of the ship to where the observation deck was. From their vantage point they could see the ocean stretching out to their left, and the white cliffs of Dover on the right. Mira moved right to the edge of the glass and peered down. The waves crashed upon the rocks below them, foam tendrils spreading out onto the shore. She stepped back before she grew too dizzy.

Cyrus's complexion paled further. The engines hummed a bit louder and his whole body tightened with anxiety. Mira took pity on him and moved back over.

"That's just the engines prepping to leave the dock. We're already hovering in the air," she said.

"That doesn't comfort me in the slightest."

"Why don't we sit down?" the professor said. "It's easier on the stomach if you're seated."

"I never even considered my stomach," Cyrus grumbled, moving over to a few unoccupied armchairs.

Mira noted that he chose one that faced away from the observation window. The professor sat next to him, and Mira sat across from them both so she could see what was happening outside. She placed her bag by her feet.

A booming voice sounded through the megaphone: "A good day to you all. This is Captain Clessott speaking. We're finishing up some final weather checks, but everything seems to be in order. We should be pushing off in the next five minutes. We'll be traveling directly to Paris, and will arrive in about two hours, if the weather continues to agree with us. If you have any concerns, please speak to a member of the crew."

Cyrus' hands clenched the armrests of his chair, knuckles turning white. Mira leaned forward. "It's going to be alright, Uncle. Do you remember how much I wanted to ride on an airship when I was younger?"

He nodded. "You begged me almost every time you saw one."

"When I took my first flight, I was terrified. I wanted to fly so desperately, but the moment before the ship took off, I had all these doubts and fears flood into my mind. I could hardly breathe." She paused, a small smile forming at the memory of Byron taking her hand and calming her with his gentle voice. That was the first time he had held her hand.

"Once the ship lifted off, it felt like I was weightless. We traveled through the clouds, and everything turned out just fine."

He let out another shaky breath. "I still can't believe you went behind my back."

"I believe it," the professor teased. "Haven't you noticed how rebellious she's become as of late?"

The ship rumbled and broke away from the dock. The exhilarating sensation of flying settled into her stomach as the engines came to full power. Cyrus clenched his fists, eyes squeezed shut. Mira leaned forward.

"It's better if you look out the window."

He kept his eyes firmly closed. "No. I think I'm fine here, thank you."

"If you're certain." She shared a glance with the professor.

He cleared his throat and opened up a newspaper. "By the way, I did manage to find a boarding house. Quite close to where you're needing to do your business."

Cyrus slid one eye open. "Oh?"

"It's quite reputable, too."

"Excellent. That's one thing settled, then."

The ship lurched and Cyrus gripped the armrests of the chair.

"We seem to have hit some rough wind," Burke said.

Cyrus grimaced. "I may need something for my stomach after all."

Mira reached for her bag. "I did bring the smelling salts."

His nose crinkled, and he shook his head. "No, that will only give me a headache." He waved down a steward. "Do you have any bicarbonate of soda onboard? Or at least some water?"

"Of course, sir. I'll find you some straight away." The steward gave a short bow and moved away.

"Phenomenal service." The professor stood and stretched. "Now, I don't know about you lot, but I'm going to take advantage of the observation window while I can."

※◊※

AFTER THE BICARB SETTLED HIS STOMACH, THEY managed to convince Cyrus to look out the window. From that point on in the journey, his anxiety lessened, and Mira was grateful for it. The clouds were few, but beautiful, and it was lovely to see the ocean and shoreline from such a view. She only wished her drawing supplies weren't tucked away in her trunk on the lower level.

The sun had dipped below the horizon by the time the airship touched down on the outskirts of Paris. They disembarked and found their luggage, and soon enough, they were trundling down a new set of cobblestones on their way to the boarding house.

"I do hope it's satisfactory," Cyrus said. "I'm getting tired of traveling."

"It is a bit taxing on the older body, isn't it?" The professor shifted, and his back cracked.

While the journey had been tiring, Mira was still alert, scanning the buildings as they passed them. People busied themselves in the streets, finishing up their errands before returning to their homes. It dawned on her that thousands of people lived in this new city, each of them with their own lives, dreams, and aspirations. And each and every one of them was ignorant of her existence. Except for Byron. If his memory was still holding up.

And Alexander. A chill ran up her spine. In her excitement for the trip, she'd nearly forgotten that he was the main reason for her coming to France at all. The thrill of being in a new city dissipated as a deep-set anxiety took hold of her thoughts. That murderer could be anywhere in the city. They could have passed by him in the street. He couldn't know that she was in France, but what if he did? Would he follow her to the boarding house?

She clenched her fists, trying to ground herself. It was silly to be so worried. Byron didn't even know she was there, how could Alexander? She swallowed. Circe could know, couldn't they? And they could inform him of her location. After all, if Circe had some reason to need her alive, logic would dictate they would keep tabs on her whereabouts. Except, that wasn't the full truth, was it? It wasn't just Circe. Number Three wanted her alive. Who was Number Three anyway?

Professor Burke leaned forward, brow furrowed. "Are you quite alright, Mira?"

She forced a smile and a laugh. "Oh yes! I just am a bit overwhelmed, I think."

He nodded. "I remember my first time going out of the country. It was actually when I first met your uncle. I was on my way to India to join the Indian Civil service. Met your uncle on the train. And of course, once we got there, my worldview changed entirely. Wouldn't you say, Cyrus?"

A faint snore was the only response. Her uncle was fast asleep, his head cushioned by the wall of the carriage. Mira and Burke stifled their laughter as the carriage continued on towards the boarding house.

"I HOPE THEY HAVE ROOMS AVAILABLE," MIRA said, hiding a yawn. "I think I could fall asleep standing." She stretched outside the carriage door, looking up at the glowing windows of the boarding house.

Cyrus stepped out next. "I'm feeling strangely energized, myself."

The professor shared a conspiratorial glance with Mira. "Can't imagine why that might be."

With the driver's help, they retrieved their trunks and stacked them on the pavement. Cyrus rapped on the door. A minute or so passed, and the door opened, revealing a well-dressed, middle-aged woman.

The woman's eyes widened in surprise. "Cyrus?"

Mira's mouth fell open, and she turned towards her uncle. Did they know each other? His mouth wobbled open and shut, but no sound came out. The professor stepped forward.

"Loretta, how lovely to see you! It's been years."

Mira frowned. The professor didn't seem surprised at all to run into an old friend. Granted, he had been the one to make the accommodations. Did he set this up on purpose?

"Edward?" The woman, Loretta, looked between the two men. "What are you both doing here?" Her gaze fell on Mira, and she frowned. "And who is this with you?"

"I did some research and found that this is the best boarding house in this quarter," Burke said. "We're in Paris for business, you see. And this is Mira."

Mira inclined her head. "A pleasure to meet you."

"You as well," Loretta said, confusion still coloring her features.

"Are there any rooms open?" Burke asked.

Loretta came out of her stupor and nodded. "Yes, there are. Mssr. Marsden and his family moved out last week. That leaves four open rooms, so you could have your choice."

Cyrus found his words. "We wouldn't want to trouble you. We could always—"

"No, it really isn't any trouble," she interrupted. "We're

friends, aren't we? I wouldn't want to send you back out into this chill. Just let me get my boys, they'll help with your luggage."

"Thank you so much," Mira said.

Loretta gave her a tight smile and called into the house in French.

"*Georges! Jean-Marie! Come here please!*"

A few moments later, two boys came into the foyer. One rather short, about fifteen, and the other a bit taller and older, perhaps nineteen or twenty.

"*Would you help them with their luggage please? Second floor, where the Marsden's were staying?*"

"*Yes, mama,*" the older said. "*Come on, Jean.*" He nodded to the group as he moved past to get the trunks.

"Please, come in," Loretta said.

With a glance at her uncle, Mira did so, relishing the warm interior. The professor followed, and after a few moments, life seemed to come back into Cyrus, and he stepped in as well.

"I-it is wonderful to see you again, Lettie," he stammered.

A blush rose to Loretta's cheeks, or perhaps it came from the heat of the room. The light of the flickering gas lamps made it difficult to tell. "And you."

A softness came to Cyrus' eyes that had Mira reeling. She glanced at the professor. He shrugged with a small smile.

"I heard that you, well, had married. Two children?" Cyrus asked.

"Four, actually. Clarisse is my youngest. She's asleep upstairs. And Emilie is my oldest, but she's living with her employer at the moment. She works for Madame de Bonnemains."

Cyrus nodded. "Four."

"I hadn't heard that you had married. Your daughter is beautiful."

Mira blinked. While she and Walker had been mistaken for Cyrus', or even the professor's, children, it hadn't happened in years.

"Oh, no. I never did end up tying the knot." Cyrus gave a nervous chuckle.

A sharp crease came to Loretta's brow. Mira froze, her chest tightening. Cyrus hadn't denied that Mira was his daughter! What must Loretta think? She rushed to say, "I'm his niece!" before any improper conclusions were made.

Cyrus' cheeks flushed, but before he could say anything, the boys made their way back in with the first trunk and clunked their way up the stairs.

The professor clapped his hands. "While I would love to continue this little reunion, we have been traveling all day and I would appreciate a good bed."

"Of course! Right this way." Loretta lit a lamp on the side table, picked it up, and led the way to the stairs, where her boys were coming back down to get the next trunk.

The house was quite well kept, with beautiful wallpaper, woodwork, and ornaments. The expense that went into the house was evident, which made Mira pause to wonder why it was a boarding house at all. If they had the funds for such a fine house, why would they need to rent it out?

On the second landing, Loretta stopped to point out each of the bedrooms, lighting the lamps on the walls as she went. Cyrus took the one closest to the stairs, the professor taking the one opposite him.

"I think the one at the end of the hall will please you," she said, skipping over several rooms. She opened the door and led Mira inside. She went to each of the gas lamps on the wall and lit them one by one. As the flickering light illuminated the place, Mira gasped. The walls were a beautiful, muted blue with gold wainscotting. A round peach, blue, and gold rug took up most of the space, with a bed, dressing table, and writing desk filling out the room but not overcrowding it.

"Oh, it's beautiful!"

"It was my daughter's before she left to work for Madame

de Bonnemains." A fond smile came to Loretta's features as she closed the curtains. "And it suits you as well."

"Thank you." Mira paused. "Would you rather I call you Loretta or Mrs. Lavigne?"

"Loretta, if you will." She picked up her own lamp and moved to the door. "Everyone here calls me that."

"Thank you, Loretta." She had so many questions but would it be improper to ask them? Especially since they had only just met?

But before she could make a decision, Loretta said, "Goodnight," and swept out of the room. Mira frowned. It could have been a trick of the light, but she was certain that Mrs. Lavigne wasn't wearing a ring.

December 7, 1888: Morning

*M*IRA WOKE REFRESHED EARLY THE NEXT MORNING, and opened the curtains to let more light in. Frost had eased into the corner of each pane, making the view misty and ethereal. The trees outside her window still clung to some of the last leaves of the season.

After unpacking her trunk, she changed into attire suitable for the chill weather and stepped out into the hall. She made her way down the stairs, following the promising smell of breakfast. As she approached what seemed to be the dining area, a conversation from an adjoining room caught her ear. She paused when she recognized the professor's voice.

"You need to tell him. He has a right to know."

"It would only hurt him," Loretta said. "And it's been so long."

So long since what? Since they met? And were they talking about her uncle?

"I'm growing tired of keeping secrets, Lettie," Professor Burke said.

"Is that why you came? To force this?"

Mira leaned closer to the door, straining to hear.

A moment of silence passed before the professor said, "I thought you would be happy."

"How can I be? It's been almost thirty years. Things have changed."

"Have they?"

A rustling of fabric and hurried footsteps hustled towards the door. Mira took a few steps back to avoid being caught, pretending to be coming down the stairs for the first time.

"I have to see to breakfast!" Loretta said as she exited the room. She was quite red, but when she saw Mira, she composed herself in an instant. "Good morning, Mira! Did you sleep well?"

"I don't know if I've stayed in a room more comfortable!"

"I'm glad to hear it! Sorry that I can't stay to chat. I don't want breakfast to boil over in the kitchen." Loretta stormed off in that direction leaving Mira quite baffled.

Only a few weeks ago, her uncle had told her that he'd been in love once. With a girl he met in India. He had told her that it hadn't worked out because she had been in love with another man.

From the few interactions with Loretta that she had seen, she had determined two things:

One, Loretta was a likely candidate for that woman.

Two, Edward Burke could very well be the other man.

But she couldn't imagine the Professor being so tactless as to bring them all together all these years later to talk it out. And if the other man was the professor, then why had Loretta married a man named Lavigne?

She was missing something. Perhaps she'd know more once she met the husband.

As she moved towards the dining room again, Professor Burke peeked his head out of the sitting room.

"Oh! Good morning, Mira."

"Good morning, professor." She raised an eyebrow at him. He chuckled and closed the door behind him.

"You're probably wondering why I would be in a room alone with Mrs. Lavigne, aren't you?"

"I am a bit curious, yes." She folded her arms.

A sly grin crept onto the professor's face, and he came closer, lowering his voice. "Promise not to tell your uncle?"

"That all depends on what you are about to say."

"Fair enough. Well, I was apologizing for coming without contacting her first. You see, when I went looking for lodgings, her last name caught me as odd. Tickled a faint memory of her being married to someone called Lavigne. Did a bit of digging, and sure enough, it was our Loretta! Thought it would be a nice surprise."

Mira frowned. Based on the reaction of the evening before, it was certainly a surprise. She wasn't sure if it was a nice one based on her uncle's blustering. And that still didn't explain the conversation she had just overheard. "And how do you two know her?"

"We all met in India some thirty years ago. I think I mentioned that I wanted to join the Civil Service there?"

Mira nodded, and he continued. "I ended up working for her father instead. Your uncle and grandfather were down there doing some business for Griffon Industries, and I suppose the rest is history, as they say."

He started off in the same direction that Loretta had disappeared to.

"I see." Mira mulled this new information over. It was plausible, but her gut instinct said that something was amiss.

As she entered the dining room behind him, she noted Georges and Jean-Marie were already at the table eating some

porridge with fruit. A young girl sat at the table with them, presumably Clarisse. Mira noted that her uncle and Loretta were
absent from the group.

As they entered, the boys both nodded to them. Clarisse
lifted her head.

"*Good morning!*" she said, in French.

Mira smiled and moved into the room, answering back.
"*Good morning.*"

Clarisse's eyes widened. "*You speak French?*"

The professor pulled out Mira's chair and sat next to her.
"*We both do.*"

The little girl grinned. "*But you also speak English?*"

Mira nodded.

"*May I practice?*"

"Of course," Mira said.

Clarisse swallowed a bit more porridge and paused before
attempting some English. "You are my mother's friends?"

"We were, a long time ago," Burke said, serving some porridge for himself and Mira. She thanked him as he handed her
the bowl.

Clarisse nodded. "Then you are my friends, too."

Mira couldn't help her smile. Clarisse seemed to be about
twelve and had beautiful golden hair and dark brown eyes. She
looked like a little copy of her mother.

"You must be more careful who you make friends with,"
a new voice said. Mira turned to see an older woman coming
into the room. Her silvery hair was pulled into an updo, and
she wore an intricate wrapper covered in lace and colorful floral
designs. She stalked over to the table and sat at the head of it.
"You never know who you can trust." Her accent wasn't quite
French, but Mira couldn't place it.

"Hello Mrs. Ivan-Iva . . ." Clarissa stumbled over the name.

"Ivanovna," Loretta said as she came from the kitchen,
carrying another large pot of porridge. "Edward, Mira, this

is Svetlana Ivanovna. She's another one of my boarders." She served herself a bowl of porridge and sat next to Clarisse.

"Please!" the woman said. "Call me Klasha!" Her gaze became quite distant. "No one ever calls me Klasha anymore."

"It's nice to meet you, Klasha," Mira said.

"You are English! How nice to have you here."

"Where are you from?" Mira asked.

"Russia. And I would be there still, but, no." She smiled at Clarisse. "Keep asking your questions, and then you can decide if you are friends."

"Klasha told me that in Russia, there is lots of snow," Clarisse said. "Are there lots of snow in England?"

"Is there much snow in England," her mother corrected. Clarisse made a face.

Mira considered the question. "Sometimes, yes. I love it when it snows."

"It doesn't snow much here. And it never sticks," Loretta said.

Clarisse turned back to Mira. "Staying long?"

"*Are* you staying long," her mother corrected again.

Clarisse nodded. "Are you staying long?"

"It all depends," the professor said. "Cyrus has some business meetings to attend, and I have a lecture next week."

Loretta nodded. "You may stay as long as you like."

"Thank you," Mira said.

"As long as you do not overstay welcome," Klasha said. "I have overstayed by several years." She laughed.

Georges stood and picked up his bowl, kissing his mother on the forehead as he made his way to the kitchen. They exchanged a few words in French. "*I'm off to work,*" he said. "*I'll be back around six.*"

She caught his hand and squeezed it. "*Stay safe.*"

Jean-Marie stood next. "*I ought to be going too.*" He kissed his mother on the forehead and followed his brother into the kitchen.

Cyrus came in, a palpable tension with him. He had visible bags under his eyes and moved in a rather sluggish manner. Mira frowned.

"Are you alright, Uncle?"

"I found it hard to fall asleep last night, that's all." He took the seat to her right.

"I hope the bed wasn't uncomfortable," Loretta said, gaze set on her porridge.

He rushed over his words. "No, it was quite comfortable. I just had some things I needed to work out in my head."

Klasha stood, bringing an abrupt halt to the conversation. "I shall be in my room if anyone needs me." She leaned towards Clarisse. "I may just open my old trunk."

Clarisse's eyes widened. "May I go see, mama?"

"Of course, dear, just take your bowl to the kitchen."

The little girl stood, gave a quick curtsy to the group, and picked up her bowl to take to the kitchen. Klasha stayed standing by her chair.

Cyrus chuckled. "Your children are wonderful."

Loretta had a soft smile on her face. "Yes, they are my greatest joys."

"Your husband's, too, I wouldn't wonder." Cyrus picked up a spoonful of porridge.

Klasha huffed. "He would if he weren't dead."

Cyrus choked on his porridge.

Loretta gave a chiding look to Klasha who just shrugged. "It is the truth, yes?"

"I like to think he loved them." Loretta sighed. "He died about eleven years ago."

Mira's brow furrowed. That would explain the absent wedding ring, but did the professor know she was a widow? His expression betrayed surprise, so maybe he didn't.

Cyrus managed to catch his breath. "I had no idea. I'm so sorry, Lettie."

"Me, too. He was a good man, despite everything, but he did leave us quite a bit of debt."

"Is that why—" Mira stopped herself before she asked anything indelicate.

Loretta swallowed. "Why I'm running a boarding house? Yes. I couldn't bear to leave this place, but it is expensive to keep up. All the children chip in, too."

Clarisse came out of the kitchen and ran to Klasha, taking her hand. "Do you think I could try on one of the dresses?"

Klasha laughed as she led the little girl out of the room. "We shall see."

After a moment, Cyrus said, "You've raised them well."

Loretta nodded, a shine coming to her eyes. "Yes, well. I've tried, at any rate." She stood and brushed off her apron. "I'd best get a bowl of this up to Mssr. Antoin. He's old enough he doesn't really leave his room. You can leave your bowls where they are. I'll come clean up in a bit."

She served up another bowl of porridge and left the room.

The professor leaned back in his chair. "You okay, old boy? Sounded like you breathed some of your breakfast earlier."

Cyrus crumpled. "She looks exactly the same."

"A bit of grey hair, here and there, but yes. I'd agree."

The way her uncle looked at Loretta would suggest that he loved her. But that was only a suspicion. She bit her lip. There was one way of knowing for certain. A breach of decorum, but perhaps that was necessary.

"She's the girl from India you told me about, isn't she?" Mira asked. "The one you were in love with?"

Cyrus gave a shaky breath and nodded. "I just didn't realize that I was still in love with her."

A strange feeling came over her. Like she was intruding on something in her uncle's past that he never intended to share. Some secret that he wanted to forget.

But the professor knew this secret. It was clear from their

interactions. And perhaps he had his own hidden past that was connected to it. Regardless, she couldn't push off the feeling that this secret, whatever it was, was quite grave. But before she could apologize, or ask more questions, Cyrus turned to her.

"What are your plans for the day, Mira?"

"Oh. Erm." She set her bowl to the side. "I was hoping I could track Mr. Constantine down. It's early enough, he may still be at his residence."

"Hm. I thought as much," Cyrus said.

"Is that alright with you?"

"Perfectly. We just need to discuss how we want to go about this. I need to get to my business meeting as well. Perhaps the three of us could travel to the warehouses together, and you two could go on from there."

Mira frowned. "Us two?"

"You and Edward."

Confusion took over her mind. Why would the professor need to come with her? Sure, close proximity in the carriage would give her an opportunity to figure out what was happening between him and Loretta, but what reason could he have for accompanying her to Byron's?

Burke took pity on her. "I believe what your uncle has neglected to say is that I've been assigned as your chaperone."

Mira's mind went blank for a moment. "Chaperone? But we've never needed one before."

"I beg to differ," Cyrus said. "You've needed one all along. And now that you are officially courting, you need one more than ever."

"But—"

"I'm afraid you aren't getting out of it, Mira. Now, go get your things. We ought to be going as soon as possible."

꙰

Mira brooded on the ride over. Perhaps it was the appropriate thing to do, but they really didn't need one. Did her uncle think that her and Byron were being indecent when left alone? Hardly. Their relationship was almost entirely professional.

Well. It was. Back when she first started working for him under their trial agreement.

Come to think of it, she had never been paid, had she?

But that aside, that was then, when she was only his secretary. Now things were complicated. Or were they? She loved him, and he loved her. That was simple fact.

Perhaps her uncle had a point.

As they approached Cyrus' stop, an enormous half-constructed tower came into view rising high above the buildings in the distance. It was the tallest structure that Mira had ever seen before.

"What's that?" she asked.

Cyrus leaned over to see. "It's that project I was telling you about, for the exposition. Heaven knows what Sutherland was thinking when he made that contract, may he rest in peace."

The carriage slowed to a stop, and Cyrus exited.

"Are you certain that you'll be alright on your own?" Mira asked.

"I'm sure I'll manage. Have a good day!"

The carriage started up again, on its way to 22 Rue Geoffroy l'Angevin, Paris. She'd written it so many times before, it was blazoned on her memory.

"That Klasha certainly was an interesting character," the professor said. "I wonder what she's doing in Paris."

"Could be for any number of reasons, I'm sure," Mira said, unenthused. Here she was, on her way to see Byron for the first time in a month, and she felt like a leashed dog.

The professor seemed to catch onto her mood, and he sighed. "I know this isn't the arrangement you were hoping for, but your uncle was insistent."

"Yes, I know." Mira turned towards the window.

"I'll try to give the two of you some space. I know you've got your case to solve."

"Right." It had been two weeks since the events of the last letter she'd received from Byron. What if he'd already found Alexander? What if he was on his way back to London as they jostled to and fro in this carriage? What if—

Was that Byron? There he was, walking in the opposite direction on the pavement outside. They passed him before she had the sense to shout, "Stop the carriage!"

She opened the door before the wheels were stationary, and the only thing that stopped her from running was her fast-dissolving resolve to be self-disciplined.

As she got closer, she called out, "Byron!"

He turned towards her in confusion.

"Do I know you?"

A cold force gripped her, and she stepped back, flushing. Her mouth gaped open as she realized that it wasn't Byron at all. In her excitement she didn't even pause to think that it wasn't him. Up close, she could see her mistake. And his accent was decidedly French.

"I am so sorry! I thought," she paused. "It doesn't matter what I thought. I cannot apologize enough."

He shook his head and lifted her hand to his lips. "I wish I was the man you thought I was. Good day, mademoiselle."

"Good day, sir."

He swept past her, and she paused a moment to compose herself. How stupid of her! She moved back towards the carriage, where Professor Burke was still sitting. He had a small smirk on his face as she sat across from him.

"Do you make it a habit of rushing strange men like that? I'm just wondering, since I'm going to be your chaperone, what I ought to be prepared for."

"No, I do not make it a habit." She crossed her arms and

leaned back, even if it was unladylike. "That was a singular occurrence."

"Oh, good."

They traveled the rest of the way in silence, as Mira turned the words over in her head. *"Do I know you?"* Harmless when used with acquaintances and strangers, but she had heard them far too many times from Byron. What if he'd forgotten her again? He'd been writing to her daily, but the last letter she received was sent weeks before. What if he had stopped? Could his memory really have improved so much that he would still remember her?

By the time they pulled up to number twenty-two she had worked her way into an anxious fit.

"Mira, you're shaking," the professor said.

"I'm fine." She stepped out of the carriage and surveyed the building, if only to delay the inevitable. It was a large, white-brick building with small wrought-iron balconies at each of the windows. It was six stories tall and seemed well kept.

The carriage drove away behind them as the professor stood next to her on the pavement.

"Are we going in?"

"I suppose we ought to." She took a long breath to brace herself, went up the stairs, and knocked on the door with the big metal knocker.

A few moments later, the door opened, a friendly face appearing with a smile.

"Why, Samira Blayse, you astonish me!" Frederick Wensley said, opening the door more.

"I wonder why," she smiled, her anxiety ceasing for the moment. Something about Fred's demeanor always made her feel at ease, regardless of what they were up to. "Is Byron around?"

Fred laughed. "You mean you didn't come to visit me?"

"Of course, I came to visit you!" She leaned closer and

lowered her voice. "But I do have some information that our detective friend could use."

"Come on in from the cold, and I'll see if I can't track him down."

She and the professor stepped in, rubbing at their arms as the chill air was replaced with warm. Fred closed the door behind them and called up the stairs.

"Byron, you have a visitor!" He glanced back at the professor and amended his statement. "Make that two visitors."

His voice echoed through the small entry hall. The wood flooring was bare, with no carpet to dampen the sound in the main foyer or going up the stairs. Each step was steep and narrow, but they seemed serviceable enough.

"Why don't you two come into the sitting room?" Fred led the way into a small side room with a fireplace, several chairs, and a small window overlooking the street.

The professor made himself comfortable close to the fire, but Mira chose to remain standing, resisting the urge to pace.

Footsteps sounded on the stairs, moving to the hall, and within moments, Byron appeared at the door, journal in hand, and hair messy.

"Who might these visitors—" his voice cut out as he caught sight of her.

His eyebrow raised in a question. Confusion, maybe? Mira swallowed and glanced away. He'd forgotten her. Again. She opened her mouth to ask if he had read his journal yet, but he beat her to it.

"Mira?" He laughed, bold and bright and wonderful, and her heart leapt.

She smiled, taking a step closer to him. "Hello, Byron."

"Why? What?" He laughed again, running a hand through his hair and looking to his friend for answers. Fred shrugged and Byron moved closer to her, seeming to not know what to do.

"I'm pleased to see you, of course I am, but what are you doing here?"

"You asked for information on Selene Vermielle?" Mira said. "I thought it would be more efficient to deliver it in person."

He reached for her, taking her hand in his. The professor cleared his throat and Mira stepped back.

"You've met Professor Burke, of course."

Byron tilted his head to the side. "If I have, I don't remember." He turned back to Mira. "I've found my memory is still not the most reliable thing. Fred has had to help me out of a few scrapes because of it. But I do trust you when you say we have met."

Professor Burke stood and offered a hand. "Good to meet you again for the first time or twentieth. It is always a pleasure."

Byron shook the proffered hand and furrowed his brow. "Might I ask why you accompanied Mira on this trip?"

She flushed as the professor shot a look at her.

"It would seem that her uncle believes you are in need of a chaperone."

Fred snorted, then attempted to cover it up with a feigned cough.

Byron blinked. "A chaperone?"

Mira bit her lip. "Seeing as we are courting? It is a delicate time in our relationship, or so I've been told." Rouge couldn't make her cheeks any redder.

His eyes lit up. "We're courting?" He flipped his journal open and scanned the pages, searching for answers. "I should have liked to remember that . . ." He traced his finger down one of the earliest pages. The journal was new, started after the last one suffered brutal immolation at the hand of Alexander Durant. "Ah. Here we are. I must have missed it in my skimming."

Mira frowned. "I thought—"

"I remembered you this morning." Byron was quick to calm her fears. "Properly, of course. But I still have details that slip through the cracks. Even if they are paramount." He sighed. "It's better than it was."

She nodded. "I'll do my best to fill in what's missing."

"You always do," he grinned. "Now, what was this about Selene Vermielle?" He gestured for the group to take a seat.

"I spoke with Charles Montague. Monty, as you called him." Mira pulled her notes from her bag.

"Oh! I rather liked Monty," Fred said. "Didn't get to talk with him much, but he seemed a decent sort."

"Right," Byron said, turning his attention back to Mira. "What did he tell you?"

"She owns a gallery on Rue Véron." She consulted her papers. "Galerie de Mestra."

"We passed by that just a few days ago, didn't we?" Fred asked.

Byron shrugged. "I didn't write it down at the time, so don't ask me. Is that where the stolen paintings are taken?"

"According to Monty, their stint in Berkshire was a trial run. I'm sure they have stolen goods already, though. Monty mentioned a secret cellar where they took particular customers."

"Excellent work, Mira."

"I did nothing but ask the questions you sent me."

"But you did it marvelously." He stood and paced before the fireplace, drumming his fingers on the mantle. "Unfortunately, I'm not sure if it's needed anymore."

"Not needed?" Burke said. "She came all the way from London and you don't even need the information?"

"It's alright, Professor." Mira sighed, shoulders slumping. "I had wondered if that would be the case."

Byron moved towards her. "I didn't say it wasn't useful. If anything, it brought you here, didn't it?" He glanced towards the professor then left a considerable amount of room between himself and Mira on the sofa as he sat down. "As far as I'm concerned, that's the most important part."

She blushed and changed the subject. "Did you find another lead, then?"

Byron nodded. "We hit a break, day before yesterday, actually. We've been investigating in the fourteenth arrondissement—"

"And it's been raining cats and dogs and the rest of Noah's menagerie, I'll tell you what," Fred interrupted.

"In any case," Byron continued, "we were questioning some of the locals in a bakery there. We had passed around your sketch, expecting once again to have no recognition whatsoever. Sure enough, it came back around to us, but then one of the bakers asked to see it again. Apparently, he has a new customer who looks quite like the sketch, except he has a mustache."

"But it's been over a month since we last saw Durant. More than enough time to grow a mustache," Fred said. "So, we went down our list of possible aliases with him, and he recognized a name."

"So, he *is* using an alias!" Mira said. "I thought he might be."

"Did I forget to write to you about that?" Byron frowned. "He's used five that we know of, other than Alexander Durant. He switched them out as he traveled." He opened his journal and flipped through the pages. "So far, we've got him down as Francis Warwick, Oliver Huffman, Theodore Owens, Leslie Sayers, and Edmund Leroux."

He snapped the journal closed. "That last one is the one he recognized. So, yesterday we asked the landlords in the vicinity if they had recently leased out any apartments to an Edmund Leroux and showed them the sketch. We found one, Pierre Bonnet, who leased an apartment a few weeks ago to a man with the same name and description, and he gave us the address."

"That's excellent news!" Mira said. "Why, that means you could arrest him today!"

"It's likely. We had already arranged for the other members of our team from Scotland Yard to investigate in the seventeenth arrondissement today, so I'm not sure we'd be able to track them down. Fred and I had just decided to go meet with the Police Prefect to discuss our next steps this morning."

"I do have one question," the professor said. "How certain are you that this is the address Durant is staying at, and not something to throw you off the trail? I don't know much about the man, but it seems he would be more careful about covering his back than this."

Byron frowned, a distant look coming to his eyes. "Hm. You may be right about that. And if we show our hand too soon, it might force him into disappearing again. Changing more of his appearance and his alias again."

"But how could we know for certain if we don't investigate it?" Mira asked.

"I suppose we won't know until you do," Professor Burke said. "And since you don't have any other leads, that's your only option."

Fred stood. "Except we do have another lead." He pointed at Mira. "Selene Vermielle! Maybe she isn't working with Circe anymore, but she's bound to know something."

Byron nodded. "In that case, let's stop by the Galerie de Mestra before we head to the police prefecture. Are you coming with, Mira?"

"Of course." She turned to the professor. "Are you coming as well?"

He straightened his lapels. "Are you questioning my dedication to my role as chaperone?"

"Is that a yes?" Fred asked, laughing as the group stood.

"Indeed it is. Besides, I'm curious to know what it's like being part of an investigation. I haven't had the opportunity before."

"You'll find it quite fascinating, I'm sure," Mira said as she made ready to enter the cold winter air again. "I think you may prefer it to lectures."

"You may be right." Burke wrapped a scarf around his

neck. "Speaking of which, would you mind if we make a quick stop on the way? I need to send a telegram to the University in Provence about my speaking engagement next week."

"We'll have time," Byron said, opening the door.

"Good. I meant to take care of it this morning, but it slipped my mind," the professor said.

Byron nodded. "It will give us some time to discuss how we want to approach Miss Vermielle."

Fred waved down a carriage, and soon enough, they were on their way to the Galerie de Mestra.

RUE VÉRON WAS A LITTLE SIDE STREET in the southwestern part of Montmartre, just a few streets away from a cemetery. The street was a bit narrow, with shops and residences on either side. The Galerie de Mestra was about halfway up the street and stood out from the rest because of the bright red canopy set over the window. The name of the gallery was painted across the front of it, and when the wind blew, it could be read as Mestra, Era, or Met depending on the way the folds moved. They paused outside the gallery.

"Now, you're certain that I should be the one to do this?" Fred asked.

"She would recognize both me and Mira," Byron said.

"And she won't recognize me?" Fred ran a hand through his hair. "I worked with her no less than four times. And aside from that, my French is absolute rubbish."

The professor cleared his throat. "I seem to have missed something when I popped in to send my telegram. Why do we need her not to recognize us?"

"Seeing as we are entering unknown territory, it would be best if we had a better idea of what we were dealing with," Byron said.

"Ah. But since she'd recognize the three of you, it would be rather difficult to scout. I see."

Mira paused. Yes, Selene was certain to recognize all of them. Except . . . "She wouldn't recognize you." She looked up at the professor. "And you know the language."

The professor took a deep breath, pinching the bridge of his nose. "If I'm to be a proper chaperone, I really shouldn't leave the two of you alone."

"We wouldn't be left alone!" Mira said. "Fred will still be here."

The professor paused, considering Fred. "Mr. Wensley, if I were to leave, would you ensure that nothing untoward happened between these two?"

"I'd do my best, sir."

"I suppose that will have to do." He turned to Byron. "What would you like me to do?"

"Act like you're interested in some of the paintings. Walk around a bit. See how many people are in there and if there are any guards. And then leave and come out here again. We'll make a plan from there."

The professor nodded. "Straightforward enough. I'll be out in a few minutes." He approached the gallery door, opened it, and stepped inside.

The wind was quite frigid, and Mira turned the collar of her coat up to avoid the chill on her neck. Byron took a step closer to her, seeming to examine the canopy again. Fred turned away from them. Just as Mira was about to ask why Fred had turned away, Byron laced his fingers with hers, and pulled her into a warm embrace. Her longing, built up through the weeks spent apart, melted away under his touch. She set her head on his shoulder, the winter wind long forgotten.

"I see why the two of you need a chaperone."

Mira sharply pulled away, but Byron kept hold of her hand. Fred smirked, and it caused a flush to creep into her features.

"Don't tease, Fred. Or I'll tell her about the time down by Healey's well."

"You forget that I have an equal number of embarrassing stories about you. Perhaps even more. But I'll stop teasing if you stop holding hands before the real chaperone comes back."

Byron gave her hand a squeeze before letting go. "I do wonder what's keeping him."

"Maybe the gallery is bigger than we thought?" Mira said.

The door opened, and a man stepped out. He was tall and thin with a feathery mustache that quirked upwards as a slow grin appeared on his face. He approached, tapping a finger against his cheek as he surveyed them.

"*So, you are the detectives Selene has told me about, eh?*" he said in French.

Byron turned to Mira. "What did he say?"

Before Mira could translate, the man from the gallery spoke up, this time in English. "Ah, forgive me. I forget that not everyone speaks my beautiful language." He stepped forward and took Mira's hand. He switched back to French, speaking only to Mira. "*But it would seem you understand the language of romance.*" He kissed the back of her hand and let her go.

"Who are you?" Byron asked, stepping between Mira and the man.

The man narrowed his eyes. "My name isn't important, but my employer is. And Mademoiselle Mestra is quite upset that you didn't come up to see her yourself." He moved to the side and gestured to the door of the gallery. "Please. We wouldn't want to keep her waiting."

It felt like a trap, but most things involving Selene did. Then again, Selene couldn't have anticipated them coming. Mira took the first step forward, and soon their group found themselves in the warm, dark interior of the gallery.

December 7, 1888: Afternoon

*P*AINTINGS LINED THE WALLS. THE ONES CLOSEST to the front were lit by the light coming in from the window. But further back you could only see them by the oil lamps hung from the ceiling. It seemed like it had been converted from an old house. Graying wallpaper hung behind the paintings. Pillars held up the ceiling in places where walls had been removed.

"This way, please," the man said. He led them to the back where a staircase stood. They climbed the stairs after him and came to a little sitting area with a hearth, and a little bay window overlooking the street. Professor Burke sat in one of the armchairs, adjusting his tie, gaze flicking to the burly man standing next to him. A woman perched like a cat on the armchair closest to the fire. She wore an extravagant dressing gown, with silver embroidery and beading. The woman turned towards them as they came to the top of the stairs, and Mira's eyes widened. It was Selene Vermielle! She almost didn't recognize her in all the finery, but sure enough, it was her. The burglar smiled at them as they approached, but it did not reach her eyes.

The man that led them into the gallery moved over to Selene, and she lifted her hand as he came close. He kissed the back of it, a softness coming to his features.

"Thank you, Theo," Selene purred.

"Of course, *mon chéri.*" Theo moved to stand behind Selene's armchair, and the thief focused her attention back on the newcomers.

"You know I do not take kindly to spies," she said, her slight French lilt evident in her consonants. A moment of silence passed between them before she spoke again. "But for the detective and his secretary, I suppose I will make an exception."

Mira caught the gaze of the professor who seemed stiff.

"I'm sorry," he said, gesturing to the window. "She had already seen us in the street, and well . . ."

Selene said, "Come, sit. Tell me why you have deemed it necessary to send this one to spy on me."

A single sofa stood across from where the thief and the professor sat. Fred looked between Byron and Mira, and then promptly sat in the middle of it, forcing the other two to sit with him between them. Mira sighed, but sat on the edge of the sofa, nonetheless. Byron moved closer, but remained standing.

"We've come to ask a favor of you, Miss Vermielle," he said.

"Hm. It seems that is all you ever come to me for, detective." She reclined with a half-concealed yawn. "I do wish you'd come for something more interesting."

"Like what?" Mira asked.

"Oh. Perhaps apologizing for the harm he did to my business last month." She shot a glare at Byron.

"I'm not sure what you mean," Byron said, maintaining eye contact.

"You mean your memory has allowed you to forget the sheep panic that cost me seven, no, eight paintings, paintings that could have been loved here in Paris?"

Byron smiled. "Oh, yes. The paintings your people stole?"

"Rescued," Selene insisted. "Before you sent them back to the prisons you call houses."

Mira covered her mouth so as not to laugh at the exchange. Selene had her own way of looking at the world.

"In any case, we do need a favor," Byron said.

"Ha!" Selene stood and moved towards him. "You ask me for this after you have tried to undermine my business?"

"We could always not mention this gallery to the police," Fred said.

Selene laughed and turned to Fred. "You would stoop to petty blackmail? Like that Pennington man? Let them come! Let them search!" She spread her arms in one direction and then the other. "They will find nothing here that would suggest illegality."

"So, you won't help us?" Mira asked.

Selene turned away. "I didn't say that." She stalked back to her seat and perched upon it, pulling her legs up beneath her. "Tell me what the favor is, and perhaps I'll consider it."

Byron said, "We're looking for a member of Circe. Alexander Durant."

Selene frowned, picking at a stray thread on the armrest. "I am no longer affiliated with Circe. And this Alexander Durant? It must be an alias, as no one uses their real names in such a business."

"We have a list of his aliases if that would help," Fred said. She put a hand up. "No."

"I'm sure you have an ear to the criminal circles here in Paris. It would be bad business not to," Byron said. "Any information you have on Durant would be useful."

Selene's gaze flicked to each of them in turn, landing on the man standing guard over the professor. She waved him off, and he moved to a door adjacent to the staircase, leaving the room. Theo ran a hand along Selene's shoulders as he moved to stand in front of the stairs, blocking their only way out.

"I may be able to help you, but if I do, then you owe me a favor, detective." She leaned forward. "A favor which I will collect at any time."

"Agreed." Byron finally settled on the other side of the sofa, pulling out his journal to take notes.

She settled back with a sigh, rubbing at her temples. "You remember when you came to me that last time in Scotland Yard? When you asked me to help you find the Shadow?"

Mira nodded. "That was when you agreed to bring us to the Pit."

Selene averted her gaze, looking out the window. "The man you are searching for, Alexander Durant, he came to me just after. I'm not sure if he bribed the guards or if someone just let him in. He threatened me for going against Circe. I don't know how he knew, but he did. He showed me the Symbol of the Charger and had me tell him everything I knew. That is why Circe knew that we would be going to the Pit. And why the Shadow was able to recognize you."

Byron lifted his pen from where he scribbled and looked up. "What did you mean by 'the Symbol of the Charger?'"

Selene paled for a moment before covering it up with a laugh. "Oh, you should know by now that Circe thrives off symbols and codes. It is no matter."

"What does it mean?" Mira asked.

Selene swallowed. "What do any symbols mean? It could be interpreted in many ways, couldn't it?" She stood and gestured to a painting. "This artist uses many symbols throughout, but it is up to the viewer to determine what it truly means."

Mira stood and moved to stand next to her, examining the painting. It was a dark piece depicting a shoreline, a blackish ocean, and several ships in the distance. The only light in the piece came from a full moon obstructed by clouds, casting its eerie moonlight onto the water. The brushstrokes were masterful, and it gave Mira a sense of unease just looking at it.

"Yes, but within an organization, symbols mean something concrete," Byron said. "He had a purpose for showing you that symbol."

Selene wrung her hands. "Are you certain you do not wish to purchase a painting? That may be far more useful to you than this nonsense."

Mira reached out and placed her hands on top of Selene's to still them. "This information won't leave this room, and it will help us catch him. You'll be safe, I promise."

Selene took a deep breath, pulling her hands away. "Promises like that are difficult to keep in a business such as this. You cannot know for certain how far or how fast information can spread."

"Please," Mira pleaded with her. "Durant is dangerous. You know this."

Selene moved back to her seat. "Very well. But first tell me what you know about Circe. I would not like to repeat things you already know."

"Their organization has been around for at least a few centuries, although it is difficult to track," Byron said. "I haven't gathered as much information as I would like, but based on the movements and actions that I have been able to catalog, I believe that there are three sections to it. Thieves, smugglers, and mercenaries. We also know that one of the leaders is known as Number Three, which would suggest that there are at least two other leaders."

Selene blinked. "You know quite a bit, then."

Mira took one last look at the painting on the wall and moved back to her seat. "One can gain quite a bit of knowledge by listening in on others' conversations."

"Right." Selene seemed to relax by a fraction. "In that case, I do not think it would hurt for you to know a bit more in this regard. Your hypothesis is correct, Monsieur Detective. There are three guilds in Circe. The Guild of the Crossroads, smugglers and their many methods of transport. The Guild of the Crescent, thieves, like myself, that work under the light of the moon. And last of all, the Guild of the Cypress, killers that fill the underworld with their victims."

"You mean to say, there are names for each of them?" Byron flipped to a fresh page in his journal.

"Oui. And you are also correct about there being three leaders. They are known to most as Three, Two, and One. Together they are known as the Trio. But they each have a more sophisticated title as well."

"I'm sorry," Professor Burke said. "I'm a bit confused. What does all of this have to do with Alexander Durant?"

Selene's gaze flicked to him, jaw clenching as she sat straighter in her chair. "You have asked me for information, and that is what I am giving."

It occurred to Mira that they had never spoken about Circe in front of the professor before. The poor man had no frame of reference for the conversation whatsoever.

"The Order of Circe is the organization that Durant is working for," Mira tried to explain. "Any information about Circe could help us catch him."

The professor's frown deepened, but he said nothing as Selene continued.

"As I was saying, they have other titles that they go by. Number One is known as the Hound. They are the most ruthless of the three, as is fitting for their role as the head of the killers in Cypress. Two is known as the Serpent, slippery and cunning, leading the thieves in Crescent. And the last, Number Three. The Charger, a swift horse that guides the smugglers in the Crossroads."

Mira swallowed. "So, if Durant showed you the symbol of the Charger, that means he was working for Number Three?"

"Exactly," Selene said.

"We already knew that." Byron tapped his pen against the page. "Is there anything that you can tell us about Durant since he came to Paris? Anything that you've heard?"

Selene considered the question, looking down at her hands. After a moment she nodded. "He has been seen in the city, yes. Operating south of the Seine."

"How do you know that it is Durant?" Fred asked.

"It is difficult to escape from Circe. Even now, I worry that somehow, they will find me. And so, I keep sharp, and I ensure that my people are sharp as well. As Durant was known to me, I asked them to keep an eye out for someone matching his description, in case he followed me. Of course, that may have been unnecessary. After all, I was a rather small player in Circe, and it seems that Durant is here for some other reason."

"What reason?" Mira asked.

"H-how am I to know?" Selene stuttered. "All I know is that he has not bothered me here, and he has been in the city for weeks."

Byron narrowed his gaze. "But you have a suspicion?"

Selene stood and moved away, hand to her forehead. "I'm getting tired of your questions."

"We'll do everything in our power to protect you, Selene," Mira said. "But the best way of protecting you is by catching Durant. Surely, you see this?"

"There are more dangerous people than Durant in Paris," Selene said.

Byron ignored the statement. "Why is he in Paris?"

"I only hear idle gossip." She paced over to the mantle. "I doubt it would help you in your investigation."

"We won't know until you tell us," Byron said.

She let out a string of fast, muttered French that Mira

couldn't catch before going silent for a few moments. "The revanchists," she said without looking up from the fire. "I heard something about them."

"Care to elaborate?" Byron asked.

Selene averted her gaze. "I've probably told you too much in any case." She examined her nails, taking on an air of boredom. "If you find my body somewhere, you'll ensure that I'm buried well, won't you?"

"Hopefully it won't come to that." Byron stood. "Thank you for the information."

"I wouldn't thank me until after you've returned my favor. Don't worry. It may be many years before I ask you for it."

She moved over to him, extending a hand. Byron furrowed his brow for a moment, before taking it and placing a kiss on the back of it. Selene moved past Fred to stand in front of Mira. She took Mira's hands and pulled her to standing, turning to the others.

"You ought to be going. I have customers coming in a few minutes."

"Legal customers?" Byron asked.

Theo stepped away from the stairs. "Madame Mestra's clientele is none of your concern," he said. "This way, if you would."

Selene smiled, and linked her arm with Mira's, keeping her in place as the men were ushered down the stairs by Theo. Once the men were out of sight, she leaned over and whispered in Mira's ear.

"Circe is dangerous, and you are already known to them. You may wish to consider your own happiness before you become more entangled in this."

Mira pulled back, a tense coldness flooding her body. But the guise of earnestness had already left Selene as she guided Mira towards the stairs to join the others.

"Thank you for your help," Byron said, tipping his hat.

"Do not call on me again if you can help it," Selene said as Theo opened the door for them to leave. "I do have a reputation to uphold."

With that, they found themselves standing once again on Rue Véron. Mira wrapped her cloak tighter around her shoulders as an icy gust of wind swept down the street. She turned to Byron.

"That wasn't helpful, was it?"

Byron sighed, his breath forming a cloud of vapor in the chill December air as he walked. "She confirmed that he is working south of the Seine. And that's where we thought his apartment was."

"And that bit on the revanchists might be useful. It could help us to figure out who he's working with here in Paris," Fred said.

"Who are the revanchists, anyway?" Mira asked.

"They are people who believe that France should have won the Franco-Prussian war and want to take revenge somehow," Byron said. "We've met a few campaigners since coming to France."

Mira frowned. "How do they expect to take revenge? By starting another war?"

Byron nodded. "Wouldn't that put Circe in the perfect place to profit?"

Alexander had mentioned a war when she had last seen him, hadn't he? That was why Circe had tried to frame the ambassador for murder. And when that didn't work, they kidnapped him to delay the treaty. A war was Circe's current objective, no matter the cost.

The meaning behind Selene's words became quite clear in Mira's mind. This situation was much more complicated than she had known before. Did she really want to be involved in this? In any other circumstance, her first trip to France would have been full of sight-seeing and painting. She would have gone to museums, and perused galleries, not to talk to thieves, but to appreciate the masters.

But that reality was impossible now, wasn't it? After everything that had happened between her and Byron, she couldn't go back to her old life.

The professor cleared his throat. "Perhaps we can continue to discuss this somewhere a bit warmer? We've been at this for hours now, and I'm getting a bit peckish."

Byron paused, checking his pocket watch. "Yes, that took longer than I thought it would."

Fred nodded. "I could use a bite. Didn't we pass a café on the way in?"

AFTER A LATE LUNCH, THE GROUP HEADED to the Police Prefecture. It was a large yellow brick building with a towering archway over the entrance. It was as grand a building as Mira had ever seen, and the interior bustled with activity. An officer stopped them near the entrance.

"Good morning, detective. Constable." He nodded to Byron and Fred. "Who are these with you?"

Byron smiled. "Good morning, Dupont! This is Miss Blayse, my secretary, and her chaperone, Professor Burke." He gestured to each of them in turn.

Dupont frowned, seeming to mull the words over in his head. Mira extended a hand and switched to French.

"*Thank you for allowing us to visit. I've come to help Mr. Constantine with his investigation. My name is Mira Blayse, and this is my chaperone, Professor Burke.*"

Dupont's eyes lit up, and he kissed the back of her hand. "*It is a pleasure to meet you, Miss. I'm sorry for the delay. I've been assigned to ensure that we check everyone who enters the prefecture. It's procedure.*"

She inclined her head. *"I am happy to follow procedure. May we pass?"*

"Of course. Where are you heading?"

She turned to Byron, whose surprise was evident on his face. "Who are we meeting with?" she asked.

"Er. I believe we need to speak with Prefect Lozé."

Dupont nodded, switching back to English. "You know the way."

Byron nodded to him again and led the group up the stairs and down the corridor. Soon they stood in front of a desk with another constable on duty. He glanced up at them as they approached.

"You're here to see Lozé?" he asked, his English much more polished than the constable at the entrance.

"Yes. Is he available? We have some news," Byron said.

The constable consulted a list on the desk, then stood. "He should be. Let me check."

He knocked on the door to the office and waited a moment before popping his head in. After a short, muffled conversation he turned towards the group.

"Please, come in."

The office was quite large. One might even classify it as a sitting room. The usual office furnishings sat along the far side of the space. Bookcases and files stood against the walls with a desk in the middle, just before the window. Closer to the door, a fire raged in a hearth and warmed the armchairs, sofa, and table that sat nearest to it. Adjacent to this sitting area was an end table suitable for holding tea things and liquors as needed.

Lozé, or at least who Mira presumed was Lozé, stood at the back of the office, holding a curtain to the side so he could look out the window onto the street below. He turned as they entered, offering them a smile. He was a rather short man, with a full beard and an impressive mustache. Spectacles hung from a chain attached to his lapel.

"It has been quite a few days since we last spoke, gentleman," he said, moving towards the armchairs at the front of the room. "And this time you brought a lady with you." He reached for Mira's hand and kissed the back of it. "I am delighted to meet you, Mademoiselle Blayse, was it?"

Mira nodded. "It is good to meet you as well."

Lozé gestured for them all to take a seat, which they did. "Would anyone like anything to drink?" He gestured to the end table.

When they all answered in the negative, he continued. "LaGrande tells me that you have news for me."

Byron leaned forward, opening his journal to the relevant information. "We've found Durant's apartment. It's on Rue Lacaze and was rented out to his alias, Edmund Leroux, a few weeks ago." He flipped a few pages forward and laid the journal flat on the table. "We observed it, discreetly, yesterday and determined that the apartment had only two exits that he could use."

He drew a quick, vague diagram of the building. "The front door of the building, or through a window in his rooms. There is no fire escape on the building, and his apartment is on the third floor, but there is a possibility he could attempt to leap to the roof of a neighboring apartment and escape over the rooftops."

Lozé nodded, stroking his beard. "Do you think he'll try to run?"

"He has a history of it," Mira said.

Byron capped his pen. "I think it would be best to start with someone already on the rooftop of the nearest building, one in the alleyway, and another near the entrance in case he gets past those that attempt to confront him at the apartment door." He tapped each location with his pen as he spoke. "I have two other men that came with us from Scotland Yard, but they're out investigating in arrondissement seventeen."

"I can arrange for my men to help you," Lozé laughed. "It's amazing that just a few weeks ago, I thought you were insane for going after a man who didn't exist."

Byron narrowed his eyes. "Right." He checked his watch. "It's almost three now. Do you think we could be ready to arrest him by five? Based on what movements we've managed to pin down, he should be there around then."

Lozé stood and walked to his desk. "That's reasonable. I believe that Inspector Grandpierre should be available to help you. I'll have him and a few of his men meet you at the park near Montsouris at half-past four."

THEY STOPPED BY BYRON AND FRED'S LODGINGS so that they could finish their preparations. Before they left, Byron retrieved and loaded his revolver, just in case.

Around four o'clock, they waved down a carriage and headed off towards the Montsouris neighborhood.

"Are you sure you want to go with, Mira?" Burke asked. "It seems rather," he cleared his throat, "dangerous."

"I've been in situations more perilous than this before, professor," Mira said.

"Well, your uncle should be getting back to the boarding house soon and perhaps we should be there when he returns."

Mira's gaze flicked over to him. His leg was bouncing, and he fiddled with the buttons on his coat. He'd seemed shaken ever since Byron came down the stairs with his revolver. She frowned. "You don't want to go, do you?"

"It isn't that at all! I just haven't done anything like this before."

She raised an eyebrow. "If you want to go back, there's nothing wrong with that. But I need to see this to the end."

Burke straightened his lapels. "No, if you are staying on, then I shall as well."

Mira placed a hand on his arm. "There's nothing to worry about."

In truth, her stomach was turning itself in knots. Her last memory of Alexander Durant was not the most pleasant. In fact, she almost wished she had Byron's memory, so she could forget the entire experience. What if Alexander was armed? Would there be a struggle? Someone could get hurt, die even.

She caught Byron's gaze on her, and he smiled as their eyes met. Her anxiety lessened by a fraction. Byron would be there, and they could figure it out. They always did.

AFTER MEETING UP WITH THE POLICE TEAM in the park and discussing their assignments, they moved into position. One constable entered the building to the right and made his way to the roof. One stayed in the alleyway. Fred was assigned to stay on the street in case he managed to escape out the front door. Inspector Grandpierre frowned upon realizing a woman would be joining them, but said nothing as he led the way into the building. Byron and Mira followed behind with the professor taking up the rear.

When they reached the apartment in question, Grandpierre stood on one side of the door, Byron on the other, revolver at the ready. Mira stood out of the way and Professor Burke blocked the stairs.

Inspector Grandpierre knocked on the door.

Silence.

He knocked again.

Mira could hear her own heart beating in her ears, but no sound came from the apartment. No footsteps coming towards the door. No creaking floorboards. No shouts telling them to come in or stay out.

Grandpierre stepped back, readying himself to break down

the door. Byron held up a hand to stop him, then tested the handle. It was unlocked.

The hinges squeaked as Byron pushed the door open. The room was dim, the sun's dwindling light catching on dust specks in the air. Other than the dust, the room was stripped bare and abandoned. The group froze for a moment, before Mira moved past the men and into the apartment.

Byron rushed after her, grabbing her hand to pull her behind him. "Careful, Mira. We don't know if he's still here."

She turned in place. "No. He's gone," her voice echoed in the room. "If he ever was here."

After lighting the gas lamps, the group checked each of the small rooms in turn, not finding Durant or any sign of his belongings.

Once they were all in the main room again, Inspector Grandpierre said, "Next time, I would appreciate not being sent on a goose hunt, eh?"

"Our information said—" Byron started.

"No," the inspector interrupted. "I will not be made to be a fool. I am taking my men, and you can deal with your own false information. Good day, sir." Grandpierre slammed the door behind him.

"Well," Professor Burke said. "That was rude."

"Could we have chosen the wrong apartment?" Mira asked.

Byron's gaze remained steady, his lips forming a thin line as he dismissed the notion with a wave of his hand. "No. It's the right one. Either the landlord was bribed to send us off the trail and Durant was never here in the first place, or somehow, he knew we were coming and left." He ran a finger along a shelf. "I believe it's the latter based on the dust patterns. He cleared out in a hurry."

"There has to be something of use!" Mira said, moving through the apartment again to attempt a more thorough search.

As she moved to the window in the bedroom, she heard something crinkle under her feet. She stepped back and crouched. There, dropped between two floorboards was a small slip of paper. She pulled it free.

The ink was smudged, but the writing was legible enough to see what it was: a tailor's receipt with a date and an address. "I've found something!" Hope thrummed within her as she rejoined Byron and the Professor in the main room, receipt in hand. Byron stood near the desk, holding a piece of paper. The professor stood near the window.

She moved to Byron, who folded his paper and placed it on the desk as she approached. "What's that?" she asked.

"Durant left something." Byron's eyes were icy, his posture stiff.

"So that means he was here," Mira said.

The professor moved over to them. "What did he leave?"

Byron ignored the professor, his lip curling. "What did you find, Mira?"

Mira's brow knit together. It wasn't usual for Byron to deflect in that fashion. And his tone was so cold. Her gaze fell to the paper on the desk, but Byron planted his hand on top of it. What could Durant have left? A list? A plan? Surely anything they found in the apartment wouldn't be trivial. But what would have made Byron react in such a visceral way?

She took a breath and held the receipt up so that Byron could see it.

"It's for a tailor in Rue de la Paix. And see?" She pointed to the date listed. "It was written up just last week."

Byron nodded, the tension in his shoulders relaxing by a fraction. "The tailor should be able to tell us whether the receipt belonged to Durant, or someone matching his description. And being a tailor makes one naturally observant."

"Now, what did you find?" Mira asked, careful to keep her voice soft and warm.

He stiffened again, but picked up the paper, nonetheless. "You aren't going to like it."

"What is it?"

Byron took a breath and handed it over.

My Dearest Mira,

How kind of you to come to Paris for me. I apologize that I'm not there in person to greet you and your pet detective. I'm afraid I had some other business to attend to that precluded my being caught. Please forgive me for that.

My love for you burns as fierce as ever. I know that you do not share the same sentiment, but I must assure you that I am not the monster you believe me to be. If you could but understand the world that Circe is trying to create. Under different circumstances, I'm sure you would have agreed with our ideology. You would have seen the beauty in it.

As it is, I would suggest that you turn your attentions elsewhere, for your own safety. You would not want yourself, or your companions, to suffer the same fate as those who have dared cross me in the past. Yours, in eternal devotion,

Alexander Durant

She read the note again. Hands shaking, she folded the page in half and placed it back on the desk. Mira looked up at Byron, a sense of dread and revulsion settling over her. Burke's brow furrowed, and he snatched the paper up, reading over its contents. As he read, he became quite still. Mira swallowed, turning away. Byron came to her side.

"Are you alright?" he asked, all traces of frigidity gone from his voice.

She pressed a hand to her temple with a shake of her head and moved over to a chair, feeling quite ill.

Alexander Durant knew she was in Paris. And though his note was filled with flowery words, she knew that it wasn't meant to be a love letter. No. It was a threat.

December 8, 1888

*A*FTER SHE AND THE PROFESSOR HAD RETURNED to the boarding house the night before, Mira went straight to bed, not having much of an appetite. But she also couldn't sleep. Images of her last encounter with Alexander Durant, etched into her memory, came to the forefront of her mind, tormenting her.

His sneer as he ridiculed her about her relationship with Byron. The manic glee as he burned Byron's journal right in front of her. She ran a hand over her neck, still feeling a ghost of a sensation where he held her in place, stealing a kiss from her lips and a key from her pocket.

Alexander knew she was in Paris. He knew she and Byron were tracking him down. And once again, he was taunting them.

When she finally managed to doze off, she had nightmares about being locked in a room with nowhere to go. Being unable to run, unable to breathe. She dreamt of Alexander, and she woke in a cold sweat.

Needless to say, she was in a sorry state early the next morning, but for as much as she wanted to stay in bed, she couldn't lie about all day. No, they had a lead, and if all went as it should, they would bring Alexander to justice once and for all.

Once she was more presentable, she went down to the dining room. She was earlier this time. The children hadn't woken yet, and Loretta was just setting the table.

"Can I help with anything?" Mira said.

Loretta jolted, quite nearly dropping a saucer before she righted herself. "Oh! I didn't see you there!" She placed a hand to her heart and smoothed out her apron. "No, dear. But if you set yourself down, I'll get you something."

Mira nodded and took a seat. Loretta continued to set plates and saucers out, the only sound in the room being the subtle clink of each piece as she placed them down. Mira cleared her throat.

"How long have you lived here?"

Loretta halted a moment, straightening some silverware before answering. "We moved here just after we were married. His father received it during the revolution, and Charles inherited it before we met."

"It's beautiful," Mira said.

"It is old," Klasha came in with her usual ostentatious style and took her seat. "And there is nothing, as you say, beautiful in being old." She jerked a thumb towards Loretta. "Is the breakfast still clucking, or is it ready?"

Loretta's lips curved into a slight smile and she left for the kitchen, shaking her head. As soon as the door had closed behind her, Klasha leaned over the table, glancing around.

"She is acting quite odd since you came here," the old woman said. "Very odd. How many are with you again?"

"Just me, my uncle, and a family friend."

Klasha nodded, with a knowing glint in her eye and tapped the side of her nose. "I have lived here for six years and never has she acted this way. She knows you?"

"Not really. But she knows my uncle and the professor."

"Hm."

The door to the dining room opened and Professor Burke came into the room, taking a seat next to Mira. "Good morning to both of you lovely ladies!"

Klasha ran her tongue over her teeth, grimacing. "Niceties that are not meant are not flattering, you know."

"I meant it in earnest," Burke said.

"Eh," Klasha said.

Loretta came back in with a tray of food. "I'm going to go wake Clarissa. Do any of you need anything?"

"No, thank you, Lettie," Burke said with a smile.

Loretta's brow furrowed, and she left the room. Klasha reached across the table to serve herself some eggs.

"See?" she clicked her tongue. "Odd."

Her uncle came in much later than the rest of the party. Mira frowned. She didn't remember seeing him being so disheveled in the morning. Maybe being in the same house as Loretta was more taxing on him than she had thought. And it was obvious to everyone watching, even Klasha, it seemed, who knew next to nothing about the situation. With conversation so stilted, especially when the two were both in the room, Mira couldn't have been happier to escape by the time breakfast ended.

"Where are you off to today?" her uncle asked while they trundled along in the carriage towards the warehouses.

"We're going to talk to Durant's tailor," Mira said.

Cyrus nodded. "Good. Good."

He was miserable, that much was certain. She glanced at the professor. "I've been thinking," she said. "Perhaps it would be advantageous for us to find other lodgings here in Paris."

"Oh?" Cyrus cleared his throat. "Why would you think that?"

She gave him a look, and he sighed, turning towards the window.

"The rent is reasonable. It's close enough to my business. I don't see what the issue is."

"The issue is you and Loretta," Mira said, outright. It was evident that the subtle approach wasn't going to work. "I can see how difficult this is for you."

Cyrus bristled. "I don't know what you mean."

The carriage came to a stop, and Cyrus kissed her on the forehead. "Stop worrying so much, dear." He nodded to Professor Burke and left the carriage.

Mira folded her arms. "You see it, too, don't you?"

Burke settled back in his seat. "Of course I do. But I'm afraid the only thing to do is wait it out. They'll come around to each other in time."

Mira frowned, remembering the conversation she had overheard the day previous.

"Professor, you weren't ever in love with Loretta, were you?"

Burke gave a sharp bark of a laugh. "Me?" He laughed some more. "Heavens no, Mira! Whatever gave you that thought?"

She shrugged. "I just wondered."

❧❦❧

THEY REACHED RUE GEOFFROY L'ANGEVIN AROUND NINE o'clock. Professor Burke knocked on the door. The sun was bearing down through the clouds, and Mira wished it would clear up so it could be a bit warmer. At least it wasn't raining. But if it had to be cold, couldn't it snow? She thought of little Clarisse, and hoped for a grand snowfall before Christmas.

The door opened, and Byron's face broke out in a smile.

"Good morning, Mira. And Professor, it's good to see you again."

"You don't need to lie on my account, Mr. Constantine," Burke said, teasing. "I know you'd prefer it if I wasn't here."

Byron sucked in a breath. "Perhaps. But I don't begrudge you for following propriety. Do the two of you want to come in for a moment to warm up, or shall we just get going?"

"Isn't Fred coming?" Mira asked.

"No, I sent him to go make amends with the Parisian police for yesterday's fiasco," Byron said. "So, I believe it will just be the three of us going to the tailor's."

"Then let's go."

RUE DE LA PAIX WAS NESTLED WITHIN one of the more prestigious parts of Paris. Extravagant clothing and jewelry shops lined the thoroughfare that led up to the Garnier opera house. The receipt showed that the tailor's name was Yves Martin. His shop was near the end of the street in a smaller space than most. A window displayed new fabrics and some ready-made accessories. Mira admired some beautiful purple silk as they approached. A little bell rang as they opened the door.

"*I'll be with you in a moment,*" a man called in French. A workbench sat at the center of the room, all manner of fabrics, pins, and papers spread across it. Various fabrics sat on shelves on both sides of the room, arranged by color and type. A folding screen stood at the back, a long mirror propped against a wall near it. The owner of the voice—a short, thin, wheedly sort of fellow, with a long nose and receding hairline—came out from the back room, grimacing when he saw them.

"*Why is it that all the customers come now, when I have no openings!*" Martin let out an exaggerated sigh, pulling the sewing tape from around his neck and placing it on the workbench. *"I must apologize, but you'll need to find your clothing elsewhere."*

Byron looked once again to Mira, giving a slight shrug to his shoulders. She sighed and answered, in French. *"We aren't here for your services, but we do have some questions for you. Do you speak English by chance?"*

Martin rolled his eyes. "You are English, and you are wasting my time?" He turned back to his workbench. "I have so many orders to fulfill, and not easy ones, mind you. No! Someone wishes to be an elephant! Another a swan. How am I to keep up with this with you asking such questions?"

Byron moved forward, offering the receipt. "We need to know if you can tell us about this receipt and the man you gave it to. Nothing more."

Martin narrowed his eyes at the group, but snatched the receipt up, nonetheless. He dug through the papers on the desk and brought up a pair of spectacles to look through.

"Ah, yes. Mssr. Leroux." Martin pulled a box out from under his workbench, opened it, and rifled through the things inside. After a moment, he produced a paper and read from it.

"Height, weight, neck, shoulders, arms, I have it all here." He waved it above his head before handing it over to Byron.

Martin continued. "Leroux, now there is a customer who understands. He ordered his costume much earlier than the rest. More than enough time to complete it. Was there an issue with the garment?"

"No, not at all. What were you saying earlier? Something about elephants and swans?" Mira asked.

"Oui, mademoiselle. There is a masquerade on Monday, next week. It is said to be in honor of General Boulanger, and everyone in the high society is wishing to go. And so, I have lions, and elephants, and swans taking up my entire shop! And masks, too! I am a French tailor! Not Venetian!" He sighed. "It is so much of the same. But Mssr. Leroux was the first to commission me, and his was the first I completed."

"How long did it take you to finish it?" Byron asked, handing the measurement slip back over.

Martin puffed up his lips as he thought. "A week. If that. It was ludicrous, how simple it was. Men's costumes are always much faster. But the women," he glanced at Mira and looked to the heavens. "I think I may swear off women altogether. All the feathers and ruffles and pleats. Boh."

"It sounds like it was an excellent costume though," Mira said. "What did it look like?"

"No, I won't spoil it. If you have come here to determine who he is by his costume, I will not. That is not the point of the masquerade!" He frowned. "What are you here for, anyway?"

"I'm Byron Constantine, and I'm a detective investigating Mr. Leroux. This is Miss Blayse, and our chaperone Professor Burke."

"A detective?" He squinted at him. "I've never had a detective in my shop before."

"What else can you tell us about Mssr. Leroux?" Byron asked.

"He always pays extra. I don't understand it, but he does." Martin sat behind his workbench, pinning white feathers onto a bodice. "And he doesn't come to me often. The last time he asked for a suit was about nine months ago. I think he is English, but he tries too hard to be French. I don't question it, though. He pays well." He shrugged.

"Do you know where the masquerade will be held?" Mira asked.

"The Trocadéro Palace, I believe. They are holding it in one of the wings, a museum, I think."

"And could you describe Mr. Leroux for us?" Byron asked.

"You have seen his measurements, what more is there to know?" Martin threw up a hand, before choosing more feathers. "He has a darker hair color. Last I saw him, he had a mustache. It didn't suit him. I put him in grey suits to bring out the gold in his eyes, eh?" He frowned. "You are wasting my time with these questions."

"Is there anything else you can tell us?" Byron asked.

"Hm. That is all I know. Now leave. I have work to do."

As they turned to leave the shop, Mira caught sight of a mask and costume set aside. She picked up the mask. It had a blue feather plume attached between the eyes and a beak-like nose.

"Is this for one of your clients?"

Martin clenched his fists as he moved over. "It would be, except that they canceled! Can you believe it? I have other orders to fill, but no. I spend valuable time working on a costume that won't be used. Perhaps I will repurpose the mask."

"How much?"

✦

BYRON TAPPED HIS PEN AGAINST THE SIDE of his cheek. They had returned to the Lavigne Boarding House and were in the sitting room.

"Based on the height and description that Mr. Martin gave us, I would be surprised if Durant did not appear at that masquerade," Byron said.

Mira tied off a line of stitches on the hem of one of the sleeves of the jacket. "Byron, can you try this on again?"

"If only he had told us what Durant was going as. That would make it much easier to find him."

Mira sighed. He was in that wonderful state of mind where he didn't pay attention to anything around him. "Byron?" she said again.

"Hm?" He looked up and saw her holding out the jacket to him. "Oh. Yes." He stood and slipped his own suit jacket off, trying on the altered costume. She had taken it in a bit on the sides and adjusted the collar and sleeves to fit him better. The coat tails of the jacket resembled blue feathers.

Mira moved around him, tugging here and there to check the fit, but it seemed to work fine. The professor made a noise, and she stepped back, turning to him.

"Is something wrong?"

"You were just getting a bit close there."

"Do you want to make the alterations?"

"Heavens, no." He turned the page of his book. "I am wondering what we're going to do for our own costumes, though."

"One thing at a time, professor." Mira stopped in front of Byron. "You'll want to wear a white shirt and vest for the party." She picked the mask up from the table and positioned it on his face.

"How do I look?" Byron turned to the side.

"Like a splendid blue jay. And I'd say that I've done the best I can on that jacket."

"Good." Byron slipped out of it and back into his other one. "Being a mannequin is exhausting."

Mira rolled her eyes and sat back on the sofa. "I don't think we need to be so concerned about which costume Durant is going to wear. I know I'll be able to recognize him, regardless."

"You're certain?" Byron said.

"I'll have to be, won't I?"

The door opened, and Cyrus came in with a newspaper. He paused upon seeing them. "Oh. This is where you all are. Good evening, Constantine. Good to see you."

"You as well, sir."

Cyrus moved into the room, taking up residence in an armchair nearest the fire. He gestured to the mask. "What's this, then?"

"We're going to a masquerade, Uncle."

"A masquerade?" He turned to Byron. "She hates parties. How did you manage to convince her?"

"There may or may not be a murderer in attendance," Professor Burke said, not looking up from his book.

"We have evidence that Durant will be there," Byron elaborated.

"And you all need to go?" Cyrus frowned. "Couldn't the police handle it?"

Byron grimaced. "We aren't on the best terms with the Parisian police at the moment. We're going to have to make do with the team from Scotland Yard."

"Hm. And how are you going to find costumes on such short notice?"

Mira's shoulders slumped. "That is where the issue lies. I'm afraid we only have one costume at the moment. But I'm sure we can figure something out."

The professor slipped a piece of paper into his book to mark his place and leaned forward.

"May I be relieved from my chaperoning duties, Cyrus?"

Cyrus furrowed his brow, but nodded. "Do you have somewhere to be?"

Burke stood. "Nowhere in particular, but I think I'll go see if I can track something down. Can't be that hard to find a costume in Paris, can it?"

"You heard the tailor," Mira said. "Durant's costume took at least a week to make."

Burke shrugged. "Might as well try. Besides, I wouldn't mind some time on my own. I'll be back soon."

He set his book on the side table and left the room. Cyrus opened his newspaper. The fire crackled.

"I think he doesn't like this chaperone business any more than the two of you do," Cyrus said.

Mira felt her ears burning, but Byron smiled at her, laughter in his eyes.

"Thank you for altering the suit," Byron said.

"Of course." She folded it into a neat square and placed it back on the table.

Cyrus turned the page of his newspaper.

"Would you like to stay for dinner?" Mira asked.

Byron hesitated, a thoughtful expression crossing his features before he shook his head. "I wouldn't want to impose. Besides, I need to fill Fred in. He'll be wondering where I wandered off to." He gathered up the newly altered suit and placed it in a bag with the rest of the costume.

Mira chuckled. "Don't let me keep you."

"Shall I see you tomorrow?" Byron stood, gaze flicking over to Cyrus.

"I'd like that," Mira said, standing as well.

Cyrus continued to read his paper.

An awkward silence settled over them. Mira couldn't decide if it was the time spent apart or if it was the presence of a chaperone in the room with them that made conversation so stilted, but she didn't know what to do next. After realizing that they'd been standing there for rather a long time, she said, "I'll walk you to the door," and Byron nodded.

Her uncle said nothing of the exchange and they made their way to the door. Once in the relative privacy of the front hall, Byron stopped and turned to her.

"I don't think I mentioned this yesterday, but I am so glad you've come to Paris, despite everything."

"I am too. I missed you."

His face softened. "I missed you too. And isn't that such a wonderful thing?" He took her hands in his and kissed the back of them. "I remembered you enough to miss you."

She smiled, a warmth spreading from her cheeks down to her toes. "It is wonderful. In fact, I don't think I could be happier!"

He gave both of her hands a squeeze, then pulled away,

grabbing his things from the hooks on the wall. "I'll see you tomorrow then."

"Tomorrow."

As he slipped into his coat and wrapped his scarf around his neck, Mira realized just how much she wanted him to stay. While she knew that she loved him, and he her, something about this was different. As he reached for the door, she caught his hand. He turned towards her, and she reached up on her tiptoes to kiss him on the cheek.

"Do be careful, won't you?"

He raised a hand to cup her face. "Only if you'll be careful too."

She nodded, and he pulled away.

"Goodnight, Miss Blayse."

"Goodnight, Mr. Constantine."

December 9, 1888

SOMEHOW CYRUS HAD MANAGED TO TRACK DOWN one of the few Anglican churches in the whole of France. So, Mira sat in a pew beneath the gothic vaulted ceiling, listening to the minister as he read Isaiah from the lectionary. Around her were other visitors from England and more from America.

Unfortunately, she was having a hard time paying attention. It was the Second Sunday of Advent. Christmas was in just a few short weeks and yet it didn't feel like it. She wanted to think it was because she was in a foreign country. After all, the only other time she'd been away from London for so long was when she went away to school. And even then, she had come home for the holidays. It could be because it hadn't snowed an inch yet, but it didn't always snow before Christmas.

No, her anxiety stemmed from the anticipation of the next day. The masquerade and Alexander Durant. There were so many ways that it could go wrong. She wrung her gloves in her hands. Durant knew they were searching for him. It was doubt-ful that he meant to leave the receipt behind, but he could still suspect that they would follow him to the masquerade. And what then? Would he not come? Or would he be there, hiding in the shadows? Or for that matter, he could be hiding in plain sight, a masked face blending in with a hundred other masked faces.

They'd spent enough time together, surely she'd be able to recognize him, wouldn't she? But what if she couldn't, and he got away again? How would they find him again?

Her uncle reached over and placed a hand over hers, stop-ping her from destroying her gloves further. She tried to bring her thoughts back to the service. Loretta and her children sat to her right. Her uncle and the professor to her left. The choir was singing. The pew was cold. The stained glass windows filtered colors into the room.

What was she going to wear to the masquerade?

THE CHILDREN RUSHED TO GET OUT OF their Sunday things the moment they returned to the boarding house.

"Thank you for inviting us," Loretta said as she rehung the coats that had fallen in haphazard fashion to the floor in her children's haste. "I haven't been to an English-speaking service in years. It was lovely."

Cyrus nodded. "I'm glad you came. It was nice to have the company."

They stood there a moment more before Loretta broke eye contact, swallowing. "I'd best get to work on lunch. Emilie is coming to visit."

She left for the kitchen. Mira cocked her head.

"Emilie. That's her eldest daughter, isn't it?"

Professor Burke nodded. "That's my understanding. It must be her day off."

The trio moved into the sitting room. Cyrus stoked up the fire and stood in front of it, warming his hands. Professor Burke picked up his book again.

Mira sat next to the professor. "Did you end up finding a costume yesterday?"

"Costume?" He looked up. "Oh, yes. I wandered around a bit and found a theatre. They had some costume pieces that they were throwing out. Do you want to see it?"

Mira nodded, and the professor left the room. She turned towards her uncle.

"You've been rather quiet today."

He shrugged and shifted his position. "I have rather a lot on my mind."

"Do you want to talk about it?" Mira stood and moved over to him.

He offered her a wan smile. "You don't want to hear the ramblings of an old man."

"You're not an old man. And even if you were, I'd listen."

The door opened again, and the professor came back in, looking quite pleased with himself. He held the bag out to Mira. "Here it is!"

Mira hesitated, but her uncle gestured for her to move over. They'd have to talk later. She took the bag from the professor and sat down to go through it. She pulled out a white mask and frowned, turning it over in her hand. A crack ran through the side of it, up into the temple.

"Is this meant to be a horse?"

The professor reached over and pointed to a strange indent that Mira hadn't noticed. It was right in the center of the forehead. "A unicorn, but the horn came off. I was thinking we could fix it up. And," he pulled a white suit and vest from the bag. "Maybe with a bit of black paint, I could be a zebra?"

"A zebra?" She laughed. "And ruin a perfectly good suit?"

"They were getting rid of it for a reason. Besides, zebras are 'the most elegant of quadrupeds.' Haven't you read Pennant?"

"No, I haven't. But if you can get me some black paint, I'll spruce it up for you. Although I'd best make the alterations before we paint it."

"You are a marvel, my dear." The professor grinned and placed his costume pieces back in his bag. "I'm sure you've figured your costume out already."

Mira leaned back with a sigh. "I'm afraid I haven't. And we don't have much time to put things together."

"Maybe Lettie has something you could borrow," Burke said.

"It's strange to think about how little I know about her life," Cyrus said, quiet enough that Mira was certain he didn't mean to say it out loud.

"It's been nearly thirty years," Burke broke the silence that had settled over the group. "That's only natural."

Cyrus remained silent, his gaze set on the fire.

Mira excused herself to get her sewing things, deep in thought. The situation with Loretta affected her uncle in a way she had never seen before. It wasn't dissimilar to the way he grieved her mother, but at the same time it held a different sort of melancholy.

It made sense, in a way. She couldn't imagine finding out that Byron didn't love her. And if they parted ways and met again, by chance after decades of being apart, she wasn't sure how she would react, either.

When she reached the stairs, she paused. Her uncle wasn't the type to fall head over heels for someone. He was much too pragmatic for that. Even if he had a different temperament as a young man, she couldn't imagine he'd lose himself altogether if he didn't suspect a hint of reciprocation.

And yet, if the story he told her was correct, Loretta said that she didn't love him at all. Something didn't make sense.

She thought over different ways of breaching the topic as

she made her way through the dining room and pushed open the door to the kitchen.

Loretta stood at the stove, stirring some soup.

"That smells heavenly, Loretta," Mira said as she came in. "Is there anything I can help you with?"

Loretta looked up. "No, that's alright. Thank you for the offer, though."

Mira nodded and moved to lean against the counter. "Of course." She bit her lip. "Does Emilie visit often?"

"Every few weeks." Loretta glanced up. "Madame Bonnemains doesn't give her many days off."

"I'm excited to meet her. She's around my age, isn't she?"

"A little older." Loretta moved to cut some carrots. "She'll be twenty-eight in May."

Mira fiddled with her hands. "I didn't come to ask about Emilie."

"I had wondered." Loretta pushed the carrots into the pot with the edge of her knife. "What did you come to ask?"

"Did you ever love my uncle?"

Loretta dropped the knife into the pot and swore under her breath in French as she tried to fish it out. Mira grabbed a towel for her to dry her hands with.

"I'm sorry, you caught me off guard." Loretta laughed. "I hadn't realized that you knew."

"I'm afraid I don't know that much. Just that he loves you."

Her eyes widened. "Present tense?"

Mira cringed. She should learn to keep her mouth shut. "I hadn't meant to share that secret."

Loretta's smile softened, her gaze unfocused. "No, no. I'm grateful for it." A blush crept onto her face. "Yes. I loved him. Quite dearly, in fact."

"But—"

"I can't explain my reasoning," Loretta interrupted. "But I can tell you that in many ways I don't regret it." She sighed.

Mira's brow furrowed. "You don't regret breaking his heart?"

Loretta went quite still, voice softening. "If I could have prevented it, I would have. And perhaps there was a way for us to be together. One I didn't think of. But no." She looked up at Mira. "I don't regret it."

Mira left the kitchen more confused than when she had entered. Loretta had seemed like such a kind woman. Before that conversation, she understood why her uncle could have loved her.

If Loretta loved her uncle too, how could she not regret breaking his heart? Something didn't add up, and yet Mira detected no dishonesty or lie in any of her statements.

With these thoughts swirling in her mind, she retrieved her sewing things and returned to the sitting room to work on Burke's costume until lunch.

About an hour later, a knock came at the front door, but before someone could come to answer it, a young woman let herself in. She stopped by the door of the sitting room, peering in. Her golden hair, much like her mother's, was coming out of its style, and her clothes were wet with the rain. She seemed quite exhausted, but her green eyes were still sharp and alert as she took in the occupants of the room.

"You must be the new boarders my mother told me about," she said in English. "I'm Emilie."

Mira stood and moved closer. "I'm Mira. This is my Uncle Cyrus, and our friend Professor Burke." She gestured to each of them in turn.

Cyrus stood, eyes fixed on the woman, almost as if he was seeing a ghost.

Professor Burke moved over and offered his hand. "It's a pleasure to meet you."

"You as well." Emilie smiled and shook it. "I'd better go find my mother and say hello."

THE TABLE WAS AS FULL AS MIRA had ever seen it during lunch. Emilie sat between Clarisse and Jean-Marie, smiling wide as they talked in hushed French. Georges leaned in from the other side. Klasha sat to Mira's right, watching with an approving eye. A few other residents, who Mira did not know the names of, sat further along, whispering amongst themselves. The professor and Cyrus sat to Mira's left, with Cyrus becoming noticeably uncomfortable as he realized that he'd be sitting next to Loretta.

"It is always nice when Em comes to visit," Klasha said, stabbing at a bit of potato in her soup. "There is more happiness to be had when she is here."

Mira smiled and nodded. "It's always nice to be together as a family."

"You have much family?" Klasha asked.

"Just my uncle and my brother. Do you?"

Klasha shrugged. "Not anymore."

Loretta came in with another tureen of soup, setting it on the table. "Is there enough for everyone?" she asked, smoothing out her apron.

"There will be as long as you sit down and have some yourself, Maman," Emilie said with a knowing smile.

Loretta laughed and took her seat, her amusement petering out as she saw Cyrus. She cleared her throat and served herself. "I just wanted to be certain."

"You could feed the street with this much soup," Klasha said. "Eat."

The side conversations started up again and Klasha leaned over. "Strange," she said. "Loretta is not usually so stressed with Emilie around." The woman scrunched up her face, studying Mira for a moment before returning to her soup.

Mira glanced over at Loretta and frowned. She did seem oddly stiff, even as she tried to engage with her children. The professor cleared his throat between spoonfuls of soup.

"So, Emilie. Your mother tells us that you work for Madame de Bonnemains."

Emilie's smile faltered. "Oh, well, yes. I'm her lady's maid."

Loretta spoke up. "You might not know this, but Madame de Bonnemains is quite an influential woman in Paris. It's one of the more prestigious positions that she could have taken."

"That is impressive," Cyrus said.

Emilie drew into herself. "Well, she was influential before the divorce. She was married to Viscount de Bonnemains until earlier this year."

"Yes, but weren't you telling me that General Boulanger has come to visit several times?" Loretta said.

Emilie flushed. "He has visited a few times, yes."

"Working for a former viscountess must have its challenges," Professor Burke said. "I've heard that members of royalty can have some interesting quirks."

A small smile appeared on Emilie's face. "Yes, Madame can be quite particular in how she likes things. She despises green colored dresses and comments on them whenever she sees a woman wearing one. Every day she goes for a walk at three-thirty and every night she expects a cup of hot milk steamed with lavender at exactly nine-thirty. And there's a necklace she always wears." Emilie giggled. "She says that it gives her good luck."

"How would a necklace give her luck?" Clarisse asked.

"That is the question, isn't it?" Emilie ruffled her sister's hair. "It's this ghastly pendant that hangs down on a long chain under her dress. Thank goodness for that, because otherwise it would be quite difficult to style. She's going to a masquerade tomorrow, and she refused to take it off during the fittings."

"Why, that must be the masquerade that we're going to!" Mira said.

"You're going to a masque?" Loretta asked.

"Ooh!" Clarisse said. "What are you going as? Can I guess?"

"I'm afraid I haven't found a costume yet. After lunch I thought I'd go look at my dresses and see what I could come up with. Would you like to help?"

Clarisse nodded her head with enthusiasm, then looked to her mother.

"Of course, you can help," Loretta said.

"There is no need," Klasha said, putting a hand up. "I have dress you can borrow."

Mira turned to her. "You do?"

AFTER LUNCH, KLASHA LED THE WAY UP to her room on the first floor, Mira, Clarisse, and Emilie in tow. She stopped in front of the door for a moment before throwing it open.

"Welcome to my abode, please do not touch anything."

Clarisse and Emilie entered without a second thought. Mira paused in the doorway, taking in the room.

Shards of colored glass hung by thin threads attached to the curtain rod, making the light filter into the room in shades of blue, red, and orange. A vanity stood against one wall, all sorts of perfumes, powders, and strange colored bottles spread across it. The walls were covered in pictures, postcards, and notes. The shelves in the room had little knickknacks on it made from porcelain, glass, and metal. A good portion of the room was taken up by a four-poster bed with red velvet drapes and silk bed-clothes.

Klasha moved over to the enormous trunk that sat at the foot of the bed. Clarisse clambered onto the bed, kneeling at the edge for a better view.

"I think I have just the thing for you, if you can find a proper mask." Klasha pulled a key from a chain around her neck and fit it into the lock. It clicked, and the older woman pushed the trunk open.

The top was full of delicate fans, gloves, and purses of varying types. A box that was sure to hold jewelry took up the other side of the divider. Klasha pulled the section out, revealing the dresses underneath.

She moved the various fabrics around until she found what she was looking for. "Ah. Here we are." She pulled out a beautiful, deep blue evening gown and held it up. It had a wide, round neckline with short puffed sleeves. The bodice was beaded in golds, greens, and purples. It seemed to be an older style.

"Why, it's beautiful!" Mira said.

"Of course it is," Klasha said. "And I know you will worry about it being old-fashioned. But I have a way!"

Klasha handed the dress to her and went back to rummaging through her trunk. A moment later she pulled out another bundle of fabric. It was even more exquisite than the original dress. It most resembled a cape, but it slipped over the arms and draped down the back. Blue, green, and purple fabrics cascaded down where the bustle would sit, and at the bottom, a beautiful array of peacock feathers spread out in a train.

"If you place this over the top of the dress with one of your bustles, it will be in the correct style. You only need a mask."

Mira held the dress up to her and moved over to the mirror. "Wherever did you get this?"

Klasha smiled. "When I was a young girl, my mother commissioned a tailor to create this dress for me. My mother loved the original that you are holding, but the tailor, he was forward thinking. He designed the train to be attached to the dress. But my mother despised it. Said it was too flashy. She allowed me to wear the dress, but not the train. But I have kept it all these years, hoping it could be of use."

Mira had never seen anything like it before. The stitching was so even that the beads appeared to be hovering over the fabric. She blushed just thinking of what Byron would think of her in that dress. But she wasn't going to the masquerade to impress anyone, least of all Byron. She wasn't going for the dancing or the food or the socializing. She was going to catch a murderer.

Mira sighed and came back to face the older woman, holding the dress out to her. "I can't possibly wear it."

"Why?" Clarisse asked. "Do you not think you will fit?"

"Hush now, Issy," Emilie said. "That's not polite."

Mira laughed. "No, it's alright. Even if it fits," she turned back to Klasha. "I wouldn't want to ruin it."

Klasha held firm, pushing the dress back into Mira's hands. "I do not care if it never comes back to me, as long as I know it was worn together, one last time. And this is the perfect opportunity."

"Are you certain?"

"How many times do you want me to say it? I wish to spite my mother. Wear the dress. Go to the ball. Be Cinders Ella. I do not care. The dress is yours now."

"Are you going to try it on?" Emilie asked.

"Oh, would you?" Clarisse asked, bouncing up and down from her perch on the bed.

"I suppose we ought to see if it fits." Mira smiled, already working on unbuttoning her bodice.

Between the four of them, it was quick work to get Mira out of her day dress and into Klasha's incredible evening gown. It took a little more finessing to make the train and bustle work together, but in the end it was stunning.

Mira turned from one side to the other, trying to get the full picture in the mirror. "I don't think I've ever worn anything so extraordinary in my life."

"It suits you well," Emilie said. "Although Madame de Bonnemains would hate the green."

Mira burst out laughing.

"Can I try something on, too, Klasha?" Clarisse asked.

The older woman smiled and pulled a tiara from the trunk, settling it upon the ten-year-old's head. "Now you are a princess. Do you want something as well, Em?"

"Oh no, I'm fine."

Clarisse tugged on Emilie's sleeve. "You should!"

Soon enough all of them were wearing something from Klasha's trunk. Emilie had a red velvet gown on with long white gloves, Klasha wore her mother's old shawl, and Clarisse wore several pieces of jewelry, a hat covered in feathers, and a cloak.

Emilie pulled out a necklace from the trunk and held it up to the light. "Where did you get this one, Klasha?"

The old woman smiled and took it from her. "That was from Artur. He was my first love."

"Oh, I love love stories!" Clarisse said. "Tell us about him?"

Klasha tapped the side of her nose. "A lady never tells her secrets."

A knock came at the door and Loretta poked her head in. "I just wanted to see how you were getting on." She turned and saw Mira, her jaw dropping. "Why, that's beautiful! Is that what you're wearing to the masquerade?"

"Well—" Mira started.

"Yes. That is what she is wearing," Klasha said, leaving no room for argument.

"We just need a mask!" Clarisse said.

Loretta tapped her chin. "I think I have something that might work down in my room."

"Do you want us to come with?" Emilie asked.

"You better. It might take me a bit of searching." Loretta turned and led the way out of the room, the group following after in a line. Mira took up the back to not bother anyone with the train. She hadn't had so much fun in years! Was this what having sisters was like? She was careful coming down the stairs, looking more at her feet than anything to avoid tripping on the gown and tumbling down into the entry hall.

"Mira?"

She whipped her head up and all but fell anyway, coming face to face with Byron Constantine. He stood near the door and seemed to be in the process of getting out of his coat and hat. This endeavor had come to a complete standstill as he stood staring at her. She took the last couple steps to the bottom.

"Hello, Byron." She tucked some of her hair behind her ear. "I-I had forgotten that you were coming." If only she had one of Klasha's shawls! While the dress was modest enough, she still felt quite exposed wearing an evening gown in the middle of the day.

"Er, yes." He seemed to find himself again, fidgeting in place as he realized he still had his hat and coat in hand. He hung them on the hooks and said, "I came to see if you wanted to go for a walk."

"I'd like that very much," Mira said. "But I'd need to change first."

"Is that," he cleared his throat, "is that your costume, then?"

She turned to the side. "Do you like it?"

He nodded. "You're beautiful."

A giggle came from the right, and Mira flushed, realizing that they weren't alone. Emilie, Klasha, and Clarisse stood in the hall, not even attempting to pretend that they weren't listening.

"Loretta was going to lend me a mask, and we were just going to get it," she rambled, feeling the need to explain herself.

"Of course," Byron said as he rubbed the back of his neck. "I could come back. Or I suppose I could wait."

Loretta came back into the entry hall. "I found it! It just needs a bit of work but—" She cut herself off upon seeing Byron.

"Good afternoon." Loretta glanced between the two of them. "I didn't realize that we were expecting company."

"Oh, yes," Mira said. "This is Mrs. Lavigne, she runs the boarding house. And this is Detective Constantine my," she trailed off. How should she introduce him? He was technically her employer, but he was so much more than that.

"We're courting," Byron said.

"Oh!" Loretta smiled. "In that case you are more than welcome. Will you be staying long?"

"I'm not sure, yet. I was hoping to take Miss Blayse out for a stroll?"

"You'd need to speak with her uncle about that. I believe he's in the sitting room."

"Ah." Byron hesitated. "I suppose I'll go talk to him."

He stood there a moment more, before breaking his gaze and moving towards the door of the sitting room. Once the door had closed behind him, Mira let out a slow breath and turned to face the others.

"He's quite handsome." Loretta smiled.

"And did you see the way he looked at her?" Emilie asked.

"Definitely in love." Klasha nodded.

Mira moved towards them, a blush rising to her cheeks. "Hush now, he'll hear you!"

"Do you love him?" Clarisse asked, ignoring her.

"Of course, she loves him," Emilie said. "Otherwise, they wouldn't be courting."

"You don't need to court to be in love," Klasha said knowingly.

"Did you find the mask?" Mira turned to Loretta.

The woman took pity on her and handed the mask over. "It needs to be repainted, but I think it will work."

Mira turned it over in her hands. It was an old Venetian mask with swirls and curly cues. It had ribbons that tied in the back. The colors were wrong, but with a bit of work, it would be stunning with the dress.

"Thank you. This is perfect."

Byron walked out just then, a smile on his face. "What's perfect?"

She lifted the mask to her face. Byron nodded in approval.

"That should work out quite well indeed."

Mira moved over to him. "What did my uncle say?"

"He said yes, as long as we find a chaperone. It seems the professor is otherwise occupied."

"I will chaperone," Klasha said.

Mira turned towards her, surprised. "You will?"

"Yes. You go change. I'll talk with your uncle."

Loretta moved over. "And I'll work on the mask while you're out."

Mira stood there a moment, dumbfounded, before Emilie took her by the arm, leading her towards the stairs. "Come on. I'll help you."

KLASHA WAS BY FAR THE BEST CHAPERONE that they could have asked for. At first it seemed that she would be eavesdropping on their every word, but after a few blocks, she slowed her pace to keep a distance behind them. As a result, they were able to talk as they pleased for the first time since Mira came to France.

"I received the most wonderful thing this morning," Byron said as they entered one of the parks. It was cold and grey, but the trees were beautiful in their own way.

"Oh?"

"A letter. From you."

Mira laughed. "It's taken this long for it to arrive?"

He smiled. "Yes, I did think it was rather funny that I finally received a letter from you, two days after you came yourself."

"I don't even remember what I wrote."

"You mentioned that your ankle was doing better. I had

worried about that, you know. Leaving you in London with an injury like that."

"It wasn't much of an injury. More of an inconvenience than anything."

"And it's alright now?"

"I'd challenge you to a race if we weren't under supervision."

He laughed. "You'd win, too, I'm sure."

"Perhaps. What else did I say?"

He cocked his head to the side as if parsing through his memories. "You mentioned some things about the case. I assume those bits were you responding to my first letter."

"I'd imagine you are right about that."

"And then you wrote something ludicrous."

She frowned. "Did I?"

He stopped and turned to face her, an intensity to his gaze that she had rarely seen before. His eyes were so blue and earnest. "You said that you had nothing to do with my memory improving. And I wish to challenge that statement."

"But Byron, I hardly—"

He leaned forward, his expression softening. "No, Mira. You gave me something worth remembering. And for that I will be forever in your debt."

A warmth spread over her, despite the December chill.

"But you remembered all on your own. You didn't need me."

He pulled away with a laugh and ran a hand through his already messy hair. He looked up at the sky's dwindling light.

"Did you know that I used to hate sunsets?" Byron said, starting to walk again. The abrupt change in conversation caught Mira off guard, but she followed at his side, nonetheless.

"I don't think I did."

"Every day, I'd wake up not realizing how much I had lost. I'd go about my day until something would show up that didn't make sense. Autumn leaves on the trees when I remembered it being Spring. Groceries I hadn't bought. That sort of thing. I don't think I had a single day where I didn't discover that I was missing memories. And reading my journal made it clear enough that the memory loss came every time I slept."

He stopped walking again, gaze still set on the sky.

"Sunsets were a sign that I would forget. That the person I was that day was about to die."

Mira placed a hand on his arm. "I'm so sorry. I didn't know."

He glanced her way, eyes soft. "You of all people have no reason to apologize. Especially since you are the reason I love sunsets again."

A blush rose to her cheeks. "I am?"

He smiled. "My memory still isn't perfect. I thought I'd remembered everything that day in October. That I'd remembered everything about you. And yet each day I spend with you I realize how much I don't know. There are still so many gaps, Mira. Blanks where I know you should be. And yet, I remember walks like these, just at dusk. The sun going down, the orange light sparkling on the Thames." He turned towards her. "And you."

He took her hand in his and placed a gentle kiss on the back of it. "Sunsets are a reminder that tomorrow will come, and you'll still be with me."

She swallowed, happy tears threatening to fall. Byron reached over and wiped one away, his smile fading.

"What's wrong?"

She shook her head, smiling. "Nothing at all! I just love you."

"Ah, ah, ah!" Klasha said, her hand coming down between them. Mira hadn't even seen her approaching. "That's enough with the lovey dovey. I gave you time alone, but now the sun sets and the devil comes."

Mira and Byron burst out laughing, but stepped apart.

"I suppose I'd best get you home, Miss Blayse."

"Please do."

And so, they walked back to the Lavigne boarding house, the sun setting behind them.

December 10, 1888: Afternoon

"Let's go over this again," Byron said, tapping the page as he paced with his journal. Mira, Byron, Professor Burke, Fred, and three other constables from Scotland Yard were all at Rue Geoffroy, going over the details of their plan. Everyone else was seated in the small sitting room, sipping tea. A crude map of the Trocadéro Palace was laid out on the table in front of them. Byron moved over to it, setting his journal down and leaning over to point at the map. "Jepson, Simons, and Hayworth will take positions on the outside of the palace, near each feasible exit point, here, here, and here. Unfortunately, Durant is certain to be in disguise, but just keep an eye out for anyone suspicious leaving the building."

Fred turned to the other Scotland Yard constables. "Do you think you three can recognize him based on the sketch?"

They all nodded.

"Very good," Byron said. "Meanwhile, Miss Blayse, Professor Burke, Wensley and myself will all enter the masquerade in costume, invitations courtesy of Fred's investigations yesterday."

Fred bowed his head. "All in a day's work."

Byron continued. "I'll be dressed as a blue jay, Miss Blayse as a peacock, Wensley as a musketeer, and Burke as a zebra. So, if you see any of us in pursuit of someone, you'd best join us."

"Understood," Simons said.

Constable Hayworth frowned. "What if more than one person dresses in those costumes?"

"I doubt that anyone else would be chasing down a criminal, regardless of what they are wearing," Byron said, turning back to Mira. "Once we are in the main room, we'll split up and walk the perimeter of the room. I'll go left with Fred and you and the professor will go right. Look for any signs of Durant, but do not approach. If you do see him, keep an eye on him as you make your way to the back of the room. Wait for me, and we'll determine our next course of action from there."

"But what if we don't recognize him?" Mira asked.

"We'll have to adjust our plans."

"Hm." Professor Burke leaned over the map. "This is a rather large wing. Multiple rooms too. We'll likely need to do a couple of rounds before we'll sight him."

Byron nodded. "It's possible."

"I think we ought to have some way of signaling one another," Simons said. "If each of us had a whistle, if we saw something we could sound it to alert the others."

"Wouldn't it also alert Durant?" Fred asked.

Simons sighed and leaned back. "Right. It would, wouldn't it?"

Mira set her teacup down, chest tight. Countless variables were at play. And the most uncertain of them all was Durant. None of them could predict his actions. They couldn't know whether he would use one door or another. And they didn't have a clue as to what he would be dressed as. This might be their only chance to catch him, and if they muffed it, then where would they be? Right back at the beginning with no leads or chance to arrest him.

"Any other questions?" Byron said. When no response came, he rubbed his hands together. "Right. We all ought to get ready. Everyone needs to be in position by five."

Fred and the constables all stood and made their way out of the room. Mira went to stand as well, but Byron motioned for her to stop.

"Are you alright?" he asked once everyone—barring the professor, of course—had left the room.

"Just nervous is all. There are so many ways that this could go wrong."

"There are also quite a few ways it could go right. Let's focus on them." He winked.

Mira couldn't help her laugh. He moved over to her and took her hand to help her up, glancing at the professor to ensure it was alright. When the professor nodded his approval, Byron turned back to her.

"I'll come to pick you up around four-thirty, if that's alright."

"I'll be ready."

MIRA PACED IN THE SITTING ROOM OF the boarding house. It was far too early to get ready for the masquerade, and yet she felt like she needed to do something useful. She'd already been chased out of the kitchen by Loretta after she'd scrubbed several plates into oblivion. She'd tried reading and painting and all the usual activities that kept her mind off of things. None of them worked.

A dissonance of emotions warred within her. On one hand, she just wanted to get the whole masquerade over with. It was torture to not know if they would succeed. But on the other, she wanted to delay as long as possible. While staying in a state of limbo was agonizing, it was preferable to the possibilities swirling in her mind. One thing was certain: Durant was dangerous. She couldn't shake the feeling that they were playing a game without rules.

By the time the clock struck three, she couldn't stand it anymore. She marched up the stairs to Klasha's room and lifted a hand to knock on the door.

Klasha opened it. "Why are you not getting ready?" the older woman asked. "Come, come, come."

Grateful, Mira allowed herself to be ushered into the room. The dress and train were already laid out on the bed.

"Do you have shoes?" Klasha asked.

Mira frowned. "I think I have some that will work."

"Go get them."

Mira nodded and left, heading up to her own room. After retrieving the shoes and returning, she was surprised to see Loretta had joined Klasha.

"I thought I'd come to help." She smiled.

Klasha and Loretta helped Mira get into the dress and arranged her hair. Somehow, they managed to coax her curls into submission. In the end, her hair was styled into a rather intricate rose on the back of her head, with tight curls cascading beneath it down to her shoulders. A few curls framed her face. Klasha lent Mira some of her costume jewelry to wear with the dress, and the colored glass shone in the light from the gas lamps.

"Now for the final piece," Loretta said, handing the mask to Mira.

Loretta had painted the delicate swirls of the mask with a blue to match the dress, and Klasha had given her one feather that had fallen off the dress to place at the center of the forehead.

"Perfect," Klasha said.

Mira examined herself in the mirror and let out a long breath. "Thank you." She turned to them. "Thank you both."

"Just go to your detective," Klasha said. "I think I heard the boys let him in a minute ago."

Mira smiled and left the room, holding her skirt with one hand and the railing with the other as she came to the base of the stairs. Byron stood in the entryway, looking every bit the handsome blue jay he was supposed to be. His mask did make his nose look rather big, though.

He smiled as she approached him.

"You look rather dashing," she said.

He gave a light chuckle and offered his arm. "I pale in comparison to you."

The door opened, and Fred stepped in. He wore a tabard with a feathered hat, cape, and saber, along with his mask.

"I've gotten a cab to stop. Are we all ready?"

"Hold on!"

Mira turned towards the professor, who was coming out of the sitting room and having a terrible time getting his mask on. He turned his head this way and that before he was able to fit it on his face. Shaking his head, a bit to get his bearings, he moved over.

"Chaperone, reporting for duty." He gave a mock salute.

Mira giggled and turned to Byron and Fred.

"Shall we go, then?"

A LONG LINE OF HANSOM CABS WERE pulling up to the Trocadéro when they arrived. Men and women came out of each dressed in silk, brocade, satin, or taffeta with all the trimmings. Light streamed from the windows of the palace, leaving bright squares of yellow on the pavement.

When their cab slowed to a stop by the curb, Byron exited first before helping Mira down. The feathered train flowed down around her ankles as she took his arm and followed the movement of the crowd to the entrance. Professor Burke and Fred stayed close behind.

Fred handed the invitations off to the steward at the door, who nodded to each of them before allowing them to enter. After dropping off their coats, they were ushered past the foyer of the concert hall and through two large doors on the south-western side. Other couples were already dancing in the center of the large, curved room. Exhibition cases that were normally in place for the museum had been moved against the walls. A full orchestra was stationed off to the side so as not to block the entrance to the next room, but up on a raised platform so they were easy to see.

Byron leaned over to whisper in her ear. "Good luck. Stay safe."

She nodded, and he gave a slight bow, moving around the left side of the room with Fred, gaze set on the dancers at the center. Mira made eye contact with the professor before starting around the right side of the room.

She searched the visible features of every man she could see, trying not to get distracted by the bright colors and unusual textures. The orchestra plucked their final notes at the end of their piece, and the dancers nodded to each other and moved towards the edges of the dance floor once again. Quite a few of the couples seemed to be wearing matching costumes. Perhaps that could help them find Alexander? She couldn't imagine that he would be here with someone else. The tailor hadn't mentioned making an additional costume for a lady. So, they needed to find the gentlemen who didn't seem to be attached to anyone in particular and narrow it down from there.

Mira glanced back to make sure the professor was follow-ing her, which he was, before continuing to walk along the wall and scan the crowd. A King and Queen of Hearts stood near the orchestra, matching without a doubt. A woman dressed as a white cat, held onto the arm of a gentleman black cat and set her head on his shoulder. A butterfly and moth whispered and giggled to each other as the music started up again. And then as a new waltz began, the couples moved as one onto the dance floor to twist and sway once more.

She bumped into a woman dressed in silvers and blues. Her gown emulated the night sky and the moon. Next to her was a man all in gold, with a collar that suggested the sun.

"*I'm so sorry,*" Mira said in French, stepping away.

"*As you should be. Wearing such a color.*" The woman took in her ensemble and turned her nose up in disgust. The man ushered her away, leaving Mira speechless. She glanced down at her dress and train. What was wrong with the color? She often wore jade tones such as blue and purple. And green. Mira suppressed a smile. Had she just stumbled into Emilie's employer, Madame de Bonnemains?

She stared after the couple for a moment before deciding to continue her path around the room. She didn't have time to speculate.

In her next examination of the crowd, she picked out five men that didn't seem attached to anyone. One was dressed as a hedgehog, innocuously round and wearing a spiky hat. Another was dressed as a wolf, with a painted mask and fur cape. The third, a lion with a golden mask and a cloak of yellow fur that looked like a mane. The fourth was a knight with a shield, and the last was dressed in the Egyptian style complete with staff.

The Egyptian and the hedgehog were much too short to be Alexander. She could tell as much, even from the distance she kept. So, she crossed them off of her mental list and went back to observing the wolf, the lion, and the knight as she came to the back of the room and stopped to wait for Byron.

The professor leaned over. "Have you seen him yet?"

Mira's shoulders slumped. "I didn't realize how difficult it would be to recognize him with all the masks."

She caught sight of a blue mask making its way through the crowd. Byron stopped next to her.

"Where's Fred?" Mira asked.

Byron smirked. "A young lady masquerading as an elephant mistook Fred's intentions of moving past her to be an invitation to dance." He pointed the couple out and Mira bit back a laugh at the sight. A strange combination: an elephant and a musketeer.

"Perhaps we could join him?" Byron extended a hand to her.

Not even looking at the professor for permission, she took Byron's hand, and he swept her onto the dance floor.

For a moment she closed her eyes, letting him take complete control. It felt like she was floating, flying. His touch on her waist and hand was feather soft, yet she knew the exact direction that he wanted to take her in. Her anxiety about Alexander and Circe melted away as she spun under the lights and music of the masquerade. She opened her eyes again to find Byron with a soft smile on his face. A light blush colored his cheeks.

She raised an eyebrow under her mask. "What are you thinking?"

"I love you," he said without hesitation.

Her stomach fluttered, and she laughed. His smile brightened. "Is that so funny?" he said.

"No, of course not." She leaned forward, lowering her voice as if offering a secret. "Because I love you too."

He spun her out, her skirts swinging around her ankles. She laughed again as he drew her closer to him, his steady hand warm on her back. Her heartbeat quickened at his touch. His blue eyes sparkled with mirth.

A harsh cough sounded beside them. The professor was dancing with a woman dressed as an asparagus. He gave them a harsh look that had them taking a step away from each other.

Mira's chest tightened, a heat spreading over her face. She'd forgotten that anyone else was around and allowed herself to be carried away by the music. Her spirits fell further as she remembered their reason for being at the masquerade at all.

Byron frowned, brow furrowing.

"Now, what's the matter?"

"Durant's still here, somewhere."

Byron let out a sigh. "You're right. We shouldn't let our guard down. After all, that's why we're here."

"I wish it wasn't," Mira said. "I wish we could just keep dancing."

"Well, maybe we can do both." He spun her again. "Did you see him while you were going around the perimeter? Or anything else worth noting?"

She bit her lip. "Nothing definitive. Although I think we can ignore the couples in matching costumes. It seems that the knight, wolf, and lion are unattached, though."

Byron scanned the crowd as they danced. "That's reasonable enough. I picked out a jester and a raven that seemed suspicious. We should keep them in our minds as we search the other rooms."

The dance ended, and Byron led Mira back towards the far wall. The professor met them there. After one last glance over the crowd, Byron led the way through the doors that opened into the next section.

When the door closed, Mira fought the urge to breathe a sigh of relief. This room was much quieter than the first, and she was grateful for the reprieve. It had a similar layout to the previous, with the exhibit cases having been moved to the sides of the gallery. Couples were perched on various sofas and benches that were scattered about the place. Others hovered near a table with refreshments and water that stood at the center of the room. Caterers moved with trays to pick up stray glasses and offer desserts to couples who would rather be left alone.

Mira scanned the occupants of the room, but none seemed to deserve her suspicion. The group moved over to the refreshment table, to not remain idly standing in the doorway. Byron picked up two glasses of water and handed one to Mira. She sipped at it, grateful for the coolness on her throat. The heat of the previous room had been stifling.

The door opened, letting sound from the orchestra drift in. Fred entered as well, looking a bit more disheveled, along with a few others. When he caught sight of the water, he made a beeline for the table.

"Next time, remind me why I don't like balls," he said, before downing the water in one go. He took his hat off and handed it to Byron. "Hold this a moment, will you?"

Byron let out a fond sigh and held onto it, sipping at his water. Fred lifted his mask to run a handkerchief over his face and then took the hat back.

"Have you seen any sign of him yet?" Fred lowered his voice, scanning the few people in the room with them.

Byron shook his head and, seeing that several people were approaching the refreshment table, ushered the group to the side of the room to talk in a more private setting.

"Mira thinks we'd best keep our eye on unattached gentlemen. Like that man there," Byron gestured to where the lion was sampling some small pastries.

"Or that one dressed as a military officer?" Fred asked, with a subtle point to a man in the corner.

"Exactly."

Fred leaned up against the case. "Doesn't really narrow it down much, does it?"

A man dressed as a bat entered the room and raised his voice in French.

"*The museum chair wishes to make his speech now, in the main wing.*"

Mira translated for Byron and the others.

Byron adjusted his jacket. "I suppose we better go see what this whole masquerade is about."

The main room was even more packed than before. The orchestra had stopped for the time being, and a man stood at the center of the podium, waiting for the crowd to finish moving about. He wore a silver ensemble with a silver mask. Once things had calmed down enough, he shouted out in French over the ballroom. Mira whispered a translation to Byron as he spoke.

"*Apologies for the breach in masquerade propriety by revealing my identity in this way, but I felt the need to thank you all for coming. Your generous donations are what is keeping my museum from falling into ruin. I hope that during your celebrations this evening you are able to enjoy the artifacts that my explorers have brought back from the Americas.*" He gestured to the cases along the walls. "*But I must also acknowledge that you all would not be here without the most important man in Paris, so allow me to introduce, General Boulanger!*"

The crowd erupted in cheers and claps as the museum director stepped down and a new man stepped up. He preened under the attention, grinning beneath his golden mask at the thunderous applause. He wore a white suit with the emblem of the sun at the center and a long golden cape. Mira recognized him from earlier. Her gaze drifted to the side and found the woman she had bumped into. Madame Bonnemains? In any case, the woman applauded up at him, a look of adoration beneath her starry mask. After a few moments, Boulanger placed his hands up to quiet his audience.

"*My friends, I must thank you for an incredible evening,*" he spoke in French. "*I knew that the supporters I had in Paris would never sway in their loyalty, but this is overwhelming.*" He let out a laugh, and the room fell into laughter with him. When it quieted down, he continued. "*In the coming months, with the election and all that follows, I hope that you may continue in your loyalty. When Mssr. Dubois and the museum first approached me, I felt impressed that I must support this masquerade. There is almost nothing more important than the preservation of the arts and sciences. And we all know that with the upcoming grand exposition, that France, and Paris, shall continue to be a leader in these fields for many years to come."*

The room once again exploded with cheers and applause. He bowed before disappearing off of the podium to be accosted by more of his adoring fans.

People filed out of the room again, towards the rest of the museum and the walls so that the dancing could resume. The knight was dancing with a lady in red. Mira couldn't tell what she was meant to be. The wolf was in the corner, talking with some other gentleman. The lion followed the flow of people back into the other galleries.

Byron moved over to her. "Let's move back into the center room. It's too noisy to talk in here."

She nodded and followed, Fred and the professor close behind. Once they were back against their wall in the relative silence of the room, she said, "All three of the men I was watching are still here. But it's impossible to know if any of them are him."

Byron frowned. "If Durant was here to attend Boulanger's speech, there isn't much of a reason for him to stay longer."

"Maybe there are other members of Circe here?" Mira asked, remembering the other men the wolf was speaking to in the first room. "And they'll need to talk?"

"Have we checked the far gallery yet?" Professor Burke asked.

"I'm on it!" Fred said and left towards the last double doors at the end of the room.

Byron's brow furrowed. "I don't like Fred going on his own. You two check the first gallery again while I go after him."

Mira grabbed his arm. "What if we find him?"

Byron paused. "Right. Well." He turned towards the professor.

"Burke, I know you're trying to chaperone and all, but is there any way you'd be convinced to split up from Miss Blayse?"

"Why would that be necessary?" Burke asked.

"If the two of you stay together, and manage to find Durant, you'll be more vulnerable, as you'd need to send one of you to find me or Fred, whilst the other keeps Durant in their sights. If one of you went with Fred, and the other with me, we wouldn't have that issue, as we could arrest him then and there."

"I see the issue." The professor let out a long slow breath, turning to Mira. "I don't think Cyrus would be as upset if you were alone with Wensley."

"Alright." She nodded, anxiety gnawing at her stomach. "Be careful."

"You as well," Byron said.

She broke off from the two of them and moved towards the back of the gallery to find Fred.

As she opened the door, she was met with a similar scene to the first gallery. Another orchestra setting the scene with another dance floor, with only two differences: a myriad of alcoves that led to smaller rooms—offices from the look of it— and an exit that led to the outside. Someone had propped the door open to allow some of the cold December air to circulate. It was still hot where she was, though. She scanned the room for Fred, making her way along the wall.

It was strange. She could have sworn that the lion had entered this room earlier, and yet her cursory glance showed no sign of the bright yellow fur anywhere. Perhaps he was on the other side of the ballroom. If it was Durant, she hoped he hadn't escaped out the open door. Although if he had, Simons would have had the opportunity to catch him.

Still no sign of Fred, either. Of course, the yellow was much easier to see than his subdued musketeer's attire. Had he already swept the room and left while she was making her way around to the back?

A tap came to her shoulder, and she turned, shoulders relaxing as she recognized Fred's feathered hat and ridiculous mask.

"There you are!" she said, the knots in her stomach loosening. "I've been looking for you everywhere." She turned back towards the dance floor, and he came to stand beside her. "Have you seen anything suspicious?"

He shook his head, and Mira sighed, scanning the room. "Neither have I. It's hard to see anything through all the fabric."

Fred offered his hand, gesturing to the dance floor with the other. She looked between him and the dancers. Dancing would give them a better vantage point to look for Durant. And it would disguise their conversation. Although, she'd much rather be dancing with Byron.

She took Fred's hand, allowing him to lead her out onto the dance floor. He fell into a waltz and it was easy to follow his subtle directions as they twirled across the floor, her train swooshing behind her. As they moved, she kept a keen eye out for Durant or Byron, while Fred kept them in line with the other couples.

"If I had known it would be this easy to sweep you off your feet, I would have done it much sooner," he said, pulling her close.

Mira faltered a step, a chill sweeping up her back. Slowly, she brought her gaze up to meet his cold, hazel eyes.

December 10, 1888: Midnight

"Do you like my costume?" Alexander Durant smirked down at her.

"What did you do to Fred?" she asked, pulling back.

He tightened his grip and forced her closer as they continued to waltz.

"Your constable friend is safe. Probably will have a headache tomorrow morning, but otherwise, perfectly fine. Although I must say I'm a bit put out that you didn't recognize me sooner."

Yes, now that she was paying closer attention, it was difficult to see any resemblance between Frederick Wensley and Alexander Durant. His costume didn't fit quite right and his mustache was ginger, not brown. And even if she could put that down to her own distraction, he was at least three inches taller. She was so focused on finding him on the dance floor, she didn't consider he was standing beside her. How could she have been so foolish?

She tried to pull away again, but he kept her in place, leaning forward to whisper in her ear.

"Now, you wouldn't want to cause a scene, would you?" Alexander tutted, breath hot on her cheek.

"What do you want?" she asked, glancing around for any signs of Byron or Professor Burke. They would have to come to this room sooner or later. Unfortunately, all they would see was her dancing with Fred. There had to be some way to alert them to the situation.

"You."

She scowled, but he interrupted before she could protest. "I know, I know. That's the one thing I can't have, so I've settled for seeing you one last time. One last dance. I am, if not anything, a romantic after all."

Her jaw tightened. "You're a murderer."

"A murderous romantic then." His teeth gleamed in a dangerous smile, even as his eyes softened as he took her in. "I am glad you came, though."

An icy chill fell over her. "How could you have known I would be here?"

"I didn't, truth be told. I was here, ensuring some connections, and stepped out to have some refreshments. In a moment of pure, idiotic luck, I happened to glance over as your friend, Wensley, pushed his mask up to relieve some of the dreaded heat."

He led her into a spin then pulled her back into his grip. "I don't blame him. This costume is frightfully hot, and I came from wearing the equivalent of a lion's pelt across my shoulders for the entire evening."

"So, you were the lion."

"Good girl. Glad to see Constantine's observational skills are rubbing off on you in some ways."

She glared at him.

"I have my own detective skills, you know," Alexander

continued. "After Wensley's little masquerade faux pas, it was simple enough to deduce that if he was here, the forgetful detective was as well. And if he was here, why then you mustn't be far behind. And considering that you were the only lady in their company, I knew exactly who you were the moment I saw you."

He leaned closer, gaze flicking over her features, one by one, lingering on her lips. "Although, I think I would have recognized your exquisite beauty anywhere, even without help from Wensley."

The orchestra gave a final swell of strings and the couples pulled apart from each other, heading back to the walls for conversation and refreshment. Alexander cocked his head to the side before releasing her waist. He kept hold of her right hand as he led her off of the dance floor and into one of the alcoves. The shadows darkened his features further.

She swallowed, heart hammering in her chest. "What do you plan to do now? You've revealed yourself to me, and if you think that I will let you get away, then you are quite mad."

He grabbed her by both of her arms and leaned in close. "And what could you possibly do to me?"

"I could scream," she hissed.

He let out a dark laugh and pulled away. "And it would be most effective, I'm sure. Alas, I believe our time is coming to an end." His eyes tracked something out in the main ballroom.

She followed his gaze and caught sight of Byron and the professor entering the room. Hope blossomed in her chest. While she was distracted, Alexander pressed a kiss to her cheek, and she flinched.

"I do wish we had more time together, beloved," he said. "And that you would change your mind. But I suppose that's too much to ask, isn't it?"

He didn't wait for an answer, moving away towards the crowds, and more importantly, the door to freedom. Panic flooded through her. Byron was still too far away, and she couldn't let Alexander reach the door. She slipped the peacock train off from around her shoulders and left it, and her mask, in the alcove, praying that they would stay safe, and that Klasha would forgive her. In the next moment, she was behind Alexander, reaching out and taking his hand.

He turned towards her, surprise evident in his expression, even with the mask.

"Perhaps it isn't too much to ask. I just don't understand," she said, trying to push as much earnestness into her voice as possible.

His face softened, and he took both of her hands in his. "I know what you are doing, my love. And it won't work."

Her jaw tightened as he raised her hands to his lips, pressing a gentle kiss into them before releasing her and disappearing into the crowd before she could react.

She took a step back, gaze darting from side to side, trying to catch sight of him again. A hand touched her shoulder, and she jolted, turning to see Byron and the professor at her side.

"Where's your mask?" Byron asked, brow furrowed. "And was that Fred? Where's he off to?"

"Thank goodness you're here. That was Alexander!" She grabbed his hand and pulled him in the direction of the door, weaving through the dancing couples.

"What?" he said, following after her.

"He knocked Fred out and took his costume. We have to catch him!" she called out over her shoulder.

They reached the door, the cool December air nipping at Mira's exposed arms. She paused at the top of the stairs, letting go of Byron's hand. Spread out in front of them was a garden with paths lined with trees and bushes. The enormous, half-constructed tower covered in scaffolding stood in the distance, only visible because of the barren branches, bereft of leaves. The quarter moon above illuminated the paths, but it was impossible to tell which way Alexander had gone.

She moved to the bottom of the stairs, turning her head from side to side, looking for any sign of him. As she moved, a glint caught in her periphery. She moved towards it.

A saber, hidden beneath a scrubby bush. Alexander had shed his costume.

"There!" The professor pointed to where a shadowy figure moved through the trees on the left path. Byron didn't waste a moment, pulling out his revolver and running in that direction. Sparing one last glance at the party behind her, Mira hiked up her skirts, heart pounding as she followed.

Gravel scattered beneath her feet as she tried to keep pace. The wind stung her cheeks as they weaved through the trees. She focused in on Alexander, fists clenching in her skirts as she picked up speed. He would not be getting away again. She wouldn't let him. Circe would not win today.

Alexander left the safety of the shadows as he exited the garden up ahead, the moonlight catching on his white shirt as he moved across the road and towards a bridge beneath the tower.

Mira pushed herself to her limit, lungs burning. She passed Byron, reaching the edge of the gardens a moment after. They were so close!

As she reached the bridge, she found Alexander standing at the middle, near the right balustrade. His back was towards her, shoulders heaving with exertion.

Mira gulped down a few breaths herself, cautious as she approached. Why had he stopped? The answer lay at the other end of the bridge. While the tower was still quite a distance away, the construction materials and debris blocked the other side of the bridge. He had no escape route.

Byron slowed to a stop beside her, the professor behind him.

"It's over, Durant," Byron said, winded.

Alexander turned his head towards them. A mask still covered his face. "Is it now?"

"You're under arrest for the murder of Vincent Sutherland," Byron said, revolver raised.

"And for your involvement with Circe," Mira added.

Alexander laughed, moving over to the edge of the bridge, staring over the water. "Oh, if you could only see, dear one. The world I wish to live in, the world Circe is building." He reached a hand up and took off his mask, looking back at her. "Why, you'd be perfect for it."

"Circe is burning the world, and you with it," she said, voice cracking.

His eyes glinted in the moonlight. "So, you do care."

She clenched her fists, cool rage flickering beneath her skin. "I never said that."

"And yet, you aren't denying it." He dropped his mask, and it fluttered to the ground.

"Leave it alone, Durant," Byron said, seething. "You can come willingly, or we can take you by force."

A low chuckle escaped Alexander as he turned towards them fully. The moonlight reflected off of the gun in his hand. "I didn't take you for the jealous type, detective."

"Mira, get behind me," Byron said, taking her hand with his free one to guide her. She took a step back.

"I understand, you know. She is exceptionally attractive. Smart, too."

Alexander's eyes bored into her, even as he spoke to Byron. Every muscle in her body tensed, a headache pounding behind her eyes. Professor Burke put a grounding hand on her shoulder. She took a few deep breaths, and the professor stepped to the side.

"We're at a standstill now, aren't we?" Durant examined his gun, keeping it aimed right at Byron's chest. "I'm unable to get away. You need to capture me. But now we both have guns pointed at each other. And we both have one shot. The question is, how good is your aim?"

"Neither of us need to shoot," Byron said.

Professor Burke nodded, stepping forward. "Put your weapon down. We can talk."

"I will, if Constantine puts his weapon down first."

Byron fell silent.

"See? It's a matter of trust." Alexander said, taking a step away from the balustrade. Byron tracked his movement with his revolver.

Alexander continued. "I don't trust you. You don't trust me. In fact, there's only one person I trust here, and that's Miss Blayse."

"Me?" she scoffed.

"I trust that you'll be the one that helps me escape," Alexander said.

"I would *never* help you." She stepped forward, nails digging into her palms. Byron turned his gaze on her, moving in front of her again.

Alexander cocked a smile as he moved his finger over the trigger. "My dear, you already have."

A LIGHT SNOWFALL DRIFTED DOWN, AS THE echoes of the gunshot died out. Moonlight shone onto each flake as they fell to the ground. Snow settled on Edward Burke's chest as he gripped it and stumbled over the balustrade. Reflections danced on the ripples in the water. The snow smelled of sulfur and citrus.

Mira rushed to the edge, fingers gripping the cold stone. Water flowed beneath the bridge, snowflakes melting into the surface. Sharp crystals clung to her hair. She drew her eyes up to the sky. The flurries seemed to stand still in the air. Unmoving. Silent. The world had gone still.

Was she even breathing? She must be, as her throat stung

with each inhale, vapor standing in the air when she breathed out. Her gaze slipped to the dull stones of the bridge. A mask stared up at her. Another shot. Footsteps running. Blurs of movement dashed by her periphery. Yelling. Time was out of order. The clouds covered the moon.

"Mira?"

She crumpled beneath the weight of her name, hot tears running against cold cheeks. Two arms caught her before she collapsed to the ground. Hushed words came to her ear. A warm hand brushed against her back, rubbing in slow circles as sobs wracked her body.

Byron gave orders to the constables as they arrived, still holding her close, but the words came as a vague buzzing in her ears. The tears subsided as the snow did, leaving a numbing sensation where her heart should have been. Byron bent and picked her up, carrying her away from the edge, away from the bridge, away from where the professor fell.

"Where's Durant," she asked, voice hoarse even as she whispered.

"He got away."

December 11, 1888: Morning

*T*HE MORNING LIGHT TRICKLED THROUGH THE GAPS in the curtains. Mira sat, a blanket draped across her shoulders and her fingers wrapped around a cup of tea. The warmth had long since left the porcelain, but she held it close to her anyway as if it could offer some comfort. She didn't know what flavor it was. Her face was stiff—sticky. It felt like if she moved it would crack.

The sofa shifted, and she blinked. The wallpaper was the wrong color. So was the carpet. She wasn't at the boarding house. Where was she? The blanket fell from her shoulders, and two warm hands put it back in place. She turned. Byron sat on the sofa next to her. They were at Rue Geoffrey. When had that happened? Her eyes were so heavy. Had she slept? Had Byron? His entire body was tense and ready to move. He caught her gaze.

"Are you with me?" he asked.

She gave a quick nod.

"Do you remember what happened?" His voice was soft and hesitant, as if he wasn't sure how to speak. Mira was in a similar state. She knew the words, but her tongue refused to work.

Yes. She remembered. It was impossible not to. But she'd been ignoring the memories even as they burned themselves onto her mind. She had stepped forward. Byron had looked at her. Durant had taken aim and fired. And Professor Burke stepped between them, taking the shot. He'd tumbled over the edge of the bridge and into the Seine. And she had stood there, frozen. The professor was gone.

Durant had escaped.

She opened her mouth a few times, and Byron was patient with her, just sitting there in the quiet while he waited for her to speak. At last, she managed some sound.

"I-I don't remember what happened after." She swallowed. Her voice was thick and unfamiliar to her ears.

"Durant turned and ran towards the tower. I shot at him, but I think I missed. I ran after him but he had disappeared into the scaffolding, and I couldn't leave you."

Her throat burned. "I helped him, then," she said, averting her gaze. "Just like he said." Durant had choreographed every movement, had planned a precise escape route, disappearing unscathed. She played right into his hand. And that wasn't the first time, either. How could such a man know her better than she knew herself?

"Don't think like that," Byron said, his voice firm.

"It's the truth."

He slipped off of the sofa, crouching in front of her so that he could look her in the eyes. He took the teacup from her and set it on the table, then held one of her hands in both of his. "Mira Blayse, you are nothing but brave and loyal. I don't care what he said. What happened was not your fault."

Tears threatened at the corners of her eyes, and she turned away. It was her fault. All of it. If she had only kept Alexander from leaving the masquerade. If she had listened to her uncle. If she had heeded the threats and stayed away. If she had never gone back to that café.

She looked up at Byron again. If she had never met him, the professor would still be alive.

He tucked a stray hair behind her face and rubbed his thumb against her cheek.

"It's going to be alright."

The torrent of tears escaped, and she fell into his arms. He sat back, cradling her there on the floor, her dress billowing about them in an ocean of blue.

"I'm so sorry, Mira. It wasn't supposed to happen like this."

"It wasn't supposed to happen at all." She sobbed, holding onto him as if he was the only thing keeping her grounded.

The door to the sitting room opened, but Mira didn't bother looking up.

"So, this is where you've hidden yourselves away," Fred said. "I wake up, head pounding mind you, in my shirt sleeves, and find that the masquerade had ended hours ago."

"Fred—" Byron said.

"No, you listen here! I thought we were tracking down Durant. And when I go looking around, I find this!" He threw Mira's peacock train towards them and it fluttered to the ground in a heap. "And I come back here and find the two of you like this!"

He sighed and slumped into an armchair, setting her mask on the side table. "Don't tell me that the music of the evening had you shoving off your chaperone and canceling the whole thing?"

An anguished sob wracked Mira's body again, despite her attempts to stop it. Byron held her closer.

"Fred, would you be so kind as to shut up?" he snapped.

Silence settled over them, and after a moment, Mira wasn't even certain Fred was still in the room. She managed to take a few slow breaths and stop crying again, pulling away from Byron. Her eyes were puffy and tired, and she just wanted to sleep. Byron had deep bags under his eyes and his hair was sticking out all over the place. She couldn't imagine that he didn't feel the same.

She glanced over at Fred, who was still in the armchair, looking equal parts baffled and concerned. He had a rather large bruise forming on his forehead.

Mira took another breath and attempted to stand. A hiss of pain escaped her as something jabbed into her arm.

"Are you alright?" Byron asked.

Mira shook her head, running a finger over her corset. One of the bones had pushed through the fabric and flossing. It must have broken through in all the commotion. She pushed it back in. She'd have to fix it later. "It's fine."

This time, with Byron steadying her, she stood and gazed out the window. Little dots of white snow caught the first rays of sun.

"What happened?" Fred asked, much more somber than before.

Mira turned back towards the men, rubbing at her arms. Byron looked between the two of them and fell into the sofa with a sigh.

"Durant killed Professor Burke, and in the ensuing panic, he got away," he said.

Fred sat up. "Killed?"

Mira nodded. "It was my fault."

Byron whirled on her. "It was *not* your fault."

"But if—"

"Mira, there are any number of ways an 'if' can take you. None of them can help you now, in this moment."

She fell silent and turned away again, staring at the ceiling in an attempt to keep the tears back. A log crackled and shifted in the fireplace. Sounds came from the entry hall, and Fred rose to see who it was.

Mira moved over to where the train had fallen and picked it up, careful of the feathers. It didn't seem damaged at all. In truth, the dress she was wearing was just a bit dirty, but that could be taken care of. She had been so concerned before the masquerade about keeping the dress pristine. But it didn't really matter, did it? The dress she could fix, but she couldn't save her godfather. She folded the train and placed it on the arm of the sofa.

Fred returned, constables Simons, Hayworth, and Jepson following behind. They were soaked from head to toe. Hayworth limped as he entered the room.

Simons stepped forward. "We've been working with the Parisian police. I'm afraid we couldn't find a trace of Durant, and," he paused, with a hesitant glance at Mira before continuing, "they won't be able to dredge the river until it's warmer."

Byron nodded. "Thank you for letting us know. Go get some rest."

"I hope you will as well, sir." The constables each filed out of the sitting room and up the stairs. Fred stood there a moment longer before Byron waved him off. Soon enough, his footsteps echoed on the stairs above them as well.

Mira moved back to the window, the chill bringing a strange comfort. She felt, rather than saw, Byron moving behind her. He wrapped his arms around her, and she leaned into his warmth.

"We can stay here as long as you need," he said, pressing a kiss into her hair.

If the professor were there, they wouldn't be allowed to be so close. But if he were there, she wouldn't need it so much. Of course, regardless of her feelings, her uncle would be assigning a new chaperone and—

"Oh." A pit of nausea welled up inside her, and she twisted

in his arms, turning to face him. "How are we going to tell Cyrus?"

A strange emotion flickered in Byron's eyes, before he said, "We'll just tell him the truth."

IT WAS CLOSE TO NINE O'CLOCK BY the time they reached the boarding house. Mira shivered on the pavement, holding the peacock train and mask close to her chest. Her coat was long forgotten at the Trocadero Palace. Byron paid the driver and escorted her up the steps and into the house.

The door had scarcely closed behind them when Cyrus came barreling into the entry hall, rage etched into his every feature.

"What the devil do you think you're doing coming back at this hour?"

Byron pinched the bridge of his nose before leaning over and whispering in Mira's ear. "Go get changed. I'll talk to your uncle."

She nodded and started for the stairs.

"Stop right there, young lady!"

Mira froze on the first step and turned around.

Cyrus looked between the two of them with outrage. "When I agreed to the two of you courting, I thought that we were going to play by the rules of society. Yet, here you are, out all night, and you have the audacity to come back without your chaperone."

"Sir," Byron tried.

"I don't want to hear your excuses! The fact that—"

"Sir!" Byron said with more force behind his voice. He set a firm hand on Cyrus' shoulder. "Let's take this to the sitting room." He turned his head towards Mira, voice softening. "Come join us after you've changed."

With a nod, she headed up the stairs, ignoring her uncle

yelling after her. Once in her room, she shut the door, leaning against it. She closed her eyes and took a few deep breaths.

She could only imagine what was happening downstairs. Byron had to be telling her uncle that his best, and longest, friend was dead. Had the shot killed him outright? Or had he drowned? She opened her eyes again. Why was she fixating on that? It wouldn't help anything.

She had seen her uncle grieve, but never just after the news. No, when he had found out about her parents, she and Walker had been sent away from the room. Cyrus had been staying with them at their estate while their parents were away for business. The professor was the one who told him, having just come from identifying the bodies. Then, Burke had left the room, plastered a smile on his face, and came to keep herself and Walker occupied until Cyrus could compose himself. She didn't see Cyrus for several days.

At the time, she had wondered why it had been so long since she'd seen her uncle, and why the professor was staying for so long. His usual style was to come for dinner and leave an hour or so after. And yet, he came and stayed for days while Cyrus was shut up in his office or his room. But he came up with such lovely games, she didn't think too much of it. And she didn't think too much about the strange, pained looks he had every time she asked whether her parents would be coming home soon. It all fell into place once her uncle had finally come out and told them what had happened, and that the twins would be under his care from then on.

She didn't remember how she reacted to that news. It was as if those memories had been locked away. Forgotten. A gap of several years that she couldn't access. But, unlike Byron and his missing memories, she didn't want to remember them. Especially if they were as painful as the emotions she was feeling now.

In truth, she almost didn't know what emotions coursed

through her. It seemed as if she felt everything at once, and she wanted it to stop. She clenched her fists and squeezed her eyes shut again. The swirling mass of emotions coalesced into a concrete, singular sensation.

Anger.

Anger at herself for allowing this to happen. Anger at Byron for doing nothing. Anger at the professor, of all people, for stepping in front of the bullet. Most of all, she felt a burning, writhing hatred for Alexander Durant.

She threw the mask and train aside, tearing at the laces on the back of her bodice. A sudden need to be free of the blasted thing surged through her. The laces tangled up in knots, and she growled, pulling harder on them.

That sly, manipulative, charismatic snake! He should have worn scales instead of fur. Her ears thrummed as she freed herself from the bodice and threw it on the bed, wrestling with the skirt next.

And to think that she almost loved him! Before she knew his true character, she had let him come too close. She had let her guard down enough for him to worm his way into her emotions. He killed the professor knowing exactly how she would respond, ripped her heart clean apart because it suited his purposes.

And then he was gone. Fled into the night, with every lead they had on him. They had no possible means to track him down. Worst of all, he'd killed her godfather while she stood there and watched.

And was it even necessary? He didn't need to approach her at all. He could have left the masquerade after Boulanger's speech and never crossed paths with her. And yet he had.

She threw her trunk open and rummaged through the contents. Not a scrap of black fabric to be found. A sense of hollowness spread through her at the realization that there couldn't be a funeral until they found the body. Her anger fizzled out.

Mira went through the motions of rinsing her face and

brushing out her hair. She opted for a wrapper, instead of a more complicated dress, and left her hair down, not having the energy for anything more intricate.

She moved down the stairs in a daze and waited at the door of the sitting room. It didn't seem as if anyone was yelling. But she couldn't hear anything at all making it impossible to know how her uncle was handling it. She pushed the door open and stepped inside.

Cyrus was sitting in his armchair, face in his hands. The blood had drained from his features. Byron sat on the sofa, leaning forward. She could tell he needed to sleep by the way he sagged. Mira closed the door behind her and Cyrus looked up at her.

"So, it's true?" his voice wavered.

She nodded.

Cyrus tilted his head back. "Right."

Mira moved over to him, and he stood, pulling her into a tight embrace as if she was the only stable thing in the world. His frame shook under her touch, but when he pulled away after a few moments, his face was dry. The wetness of his eyes betrayed him, though.

She moved to sit on the sofa as close to Byron as she dared. He reached over and took her hand. Her uncle said nothing about their closeness, but moved over to the fireplace. He gripped the mantle as he stared into the flames.

"We'll have to let your brother know. I'm not sure there's . . . I don't think at any rate," Cyrus cleared his throat. "I'll look into any other family we need to inform."

"We need to tell the university," Mira said, voice raw. "He had a lecture this next week."

Cyrus turned back towards her. "Yes. I'll take care of everything. Although we can't hold the funeral until . . ."

Mira winced.

"Spring, at least," Byron said, breaking the silence.

"Couldn't we do something? A memorial?" Mira asked.

Cyrus' voice softened. "Yes. Yes, I think we ought to."

The door opened, and the group turned towards it. Loretta came in.

"Oh, you've made it home. Thank goodness! Your uncle has been worried sick about you."

When no one responded she paused. "Something's happened, hasn't it?"

Cyrus swallowed, blinking a few times. "Lettie, it-it's Edward."

Loretta paled and reached for the back of an armchair to steady herself. "What happened?"

"He was shot," Mira said, voice hollow. It was the first time she'd said it out loud. Somehow it didn't make it seem any more real.

Cyrus moved over to Loretta, guiding her to sit in the chair. He kept hold of her hand. "He's dead."

"Oh." Loretta's gaze grew quite distant. "Oh dear. He—" Her voice cut out.

She looked up at Cyrus and pulled her hand away, standing again. "I-I need to be alone." She left the room.

Cyrus took two steps after her, before sighing and running a hand over his face. After a moment, he said, "I'll be in my room." He paused and looked over at Byron, gesturing to Mira. "Look after her, will you?"

Byron nodded, and Cyrus left the room as well.

"Thank you for telling him," Mira said.

Byron squeezed her hand. "This is difficult enough for you as it is. I just want to help."

Mira managed a shaky smile. "Then thank you. For staying with me."

He tucked some hair behind her ear, his hand settling on her cheek for a moment. "I wouldn't want to be anywhere else. Although I do think that you need to rest."

"I don't think I could sleep. Not with Durant still out there."
The man who had murdered her godfather could be anywhere
in Paris. He could have left France and gone anywhere in the
world. Here they were, stuck with no leads.

"You've been up all night, Mira."

"So have you."

"A fair point, but I do need to take care of some things
before I can sleep."

"Could I help you with them?"

Byron ran a hand over his face. "Alright," he said, reluctance in his voice. "But when we get back, you need to promise
me that you'll sleep."

"I promise. Where are we going?"

"The Trocadéro Palace. Durant had to stash his costume
somewhere, and we need to get to it before it gets thrown out."

"I'll go change."

A GENTLE SHAKE TO HER SHOULDER WOKE Mira up as the carriage arrived in front of Trocadéro Palace. She rubbed the sleep
from her eyes, exhaustion weighing on her. But it was alright.
They needed to find Alexander.

"Are you sure you want to come in? I could have the carriage take you back to the boarding house," Byron said.

Mira folded her arms. "I'm fine."

And she was. Or she would be as soon as Alexander was
behind bars. Byron sighed and helped her down to the pavement.

They walked in silence through the garden paths. It seemed
so different in the daylight. A new, terrible world. Just as cold,
though.

Byron opened the door to the concert hall section of the
Palace and ushered Mira in as the warmth flooded over them

both. Several people mulled about, cleaning things up from the masquerade. The party must have continued until the early hours of the morning. Byron approached the desk where Mira had dropped her coat off the night before. A man stood behind it.

"Excuse me," he said.

The man looked up from what he was doing, a quizzical look on his face. Mira stepped forward and switched to French.

"*Sir, we were here at the masquerade yesterday evening. We were wondering if you had any clothing brought to you that may have been left behind.*"

"*More than you might think,*" the man said. "*What are you looking for?*"

"*A black coat with a blue lining, and a lion's costume.*"

The man held a finger up. "*Just a moment.*"

He stepped into the back.

Byron turned to her. "Do they have it?"

Mira shrugged. "He's going to check."

The man returned a moment later, both items in his arms. "*I just need you to sign for them.*"

Mira nodded and took the pen from him, signing her name and the address of the boarding house. Byron took the costume in one arm, then helped Mira into her coat.

"*Thank you!*" she said as they left the Palace.

Once outside, Byron took a closer look at Durant's costume. "Fascinating."

"What?" Mira asked.

"Well, see here?" he held up the fur cape that made up the mane. "It's covered in a white powder. If we can figure out what the powder is, perhaps we can figure out where he came from."

"And thereby where he is hiding?"

"Exactly. Let's head back to Rue Geoffroy. I brought some of my instruments, so we should be able to test it there."

꧁❦꧂

MIRA LEANED AGAINST THE COUNTER IN THE kitchen as Byron attempted to separate the powder from the costume. He had two glass vials with unknown liquids and another glass container filled with water over a small burner. It was connected to an empty vial via a glass tube. The water had been boiling for close to an hour, and the condensation was trickling into the empty vial.

"Can I help with anything?" Mira asked, stifling a yawn.

"We're just about ready," he said as he scraped what powder he could detach from the lion's mane into an envelope. He used a rag to pull the vial away from the opening and turned off the burner. He took a small spoon and took a bit of the white powder from it, swirling it into the water. He frowned when it didn't dissolve.

"Interesting."

He pulled a bit of purple paper out of a wax sealed packet and dribbled some of the water over it. In the spots where the sediment touched the paper, it turned blue.

Byron smiled. "Excellent."

"What does that mean?" Mira asked, leaning closer.

"It's alkaline. Let me run a few more tests."

He took more of the powder and dropped it into one of the unknown liquids. It bubbled and fizzed before disappearing into nothing. A clear liquid remained.

"What was that?" Mira asked.

"Acid." He put another spoonful of the powder into the last vial.

"This is potassium iodide. Depending on the reaction it makes, I should be able to tell you what the powder is."

This time it bubbled and fizzed, but instead of dissolving to nothing, a new, white substance formed on the bottom of the vial.

"It has calcium carbonate. That much is certain. Based on the construction of the buildings here, my guess would be limestone."

"Can that help us?" Mira asked.

"It's possible. Limestone is not easy to break down into dust like this." He set the vial down and looked at her. "Care for one more trip before I take you home?"

December 11, 1888: Afternoon

*M*IRA WAS SURPRISED WHEN THEY PULLED UP to the police precinct and Byron led her into the building. It was getting harder to keep her yawns at bay, but the chill air kept her awake. Dupont nodded to them as they came in and made their way up the stairs to the front desk.

"May we speak with Prefect Lozé?" Byron asked.

The constable on duty checked a schedule. "I'm afraid he's in an appointment at the moment. If you would care to wait?" He gestured to a bench.

Byron nodded, and the two of them moved over to it. Mira leaned into him as he took her hand.

"This might not come to anything," he said.

"It has to."

"But it might not." He turned to look at her.

"Then we'll find some other way of tracking him."

Byron hummed but said nothing. Constables moved to

and fro. Some leaving to walk the streets. Others moving files between offices. Mira stifled another yawn.

A few more minutes passed, and a man exited Lozé's office. He was shorter than most, with a beard that covered much of his face. He nodded to the constable on duty and then left the police station. Lozé stepped out and, after speaking with the constable, waved the two of them over.

"I must say, Constantine, I am sorry about what happened."

They entered the office, and Lozé closed the door behind them. "I can't help but feel, in part, responsible. If only Inspector Grandpierre hadn't told me that all was resolved."

"He said that?" Byron asked.

Lozé nodded and gestured for them to take a seat. "After you attempted to arrest Durant. He told me that the Scotland Yard group would handle it from there. Seemed rather annoyed about the whole thing. If I had known, we would have sent men to help you at Trocadero."

"I'm not sure it would have made a difference. But I do believe you can help us now," Byron said, leaning forward. "We've found traces of calcium carbonate on the costume that Durant left behind. I believe it's dust from limestone. If we can determine where it came from, we might be able to catch him."

Lozé sighed. "I wish Blanchet had let you through sooner, then. I was just meeting with Keller, our current quarry inspector."

"Quarry inspector?" Mira asked.

"Yes. There is an expanse of tunnels beneath the city leftover from the quarries and mines. It was closed down almost a century ago, but we maintain it on the regular to avoid collapses."

"Limestone quarries?" Byron asked.

Lozé nodded. "Of course, the tunnel system is over two thousand years old, and so large that it hasn't been mapped in full. Even Keller does not know how far it goes. If Durant is hiding in there, then you won't be able to find him."

"You mean, we've lost him?" Mira asked, heart sinking.

"I'm afraid so."

THEY LEFT THE POLICE STATION AND DROVE back to the boarding house in silence. All the while, Mira brooded over all the possibilities. Could they go to Mssr. Keller and ask him to bring them into the quarries? It couldn't be that large, could it? Perhaps he only came from the tunnels, and he escaped somewhere else. That was possible, wasn't it? But if that was the case, how were they ever going to find him with no leads?

Byron paid the driver as she headed up the stairs and into the sitting room. Nervous energy built up inside her as she paced across the room, wringing her hands. Byron came in a moment after.

"This is a minor setback, Mira. We'll catch him."

"How?" She stopped in front of the fire. "We don't have any sense of where he could be. Where do we even start?"

A strange silence came over the room. She paused, turning to face him again. His lips pressed into a thin line, and he avoided her gaze. This wasn't the usual case of him losing his focus to his own thoughts.

"What is it?" she moved back towards him.

"You aren't going to like it. I think," He scratched his neck. "I think it can wait."

"No." She sat next to him again. "Tell me."

He stared at her a moment before letting out a long breath. "I've been mulling this over for some time, but I didn't follow it up because . . . well for one thing, I don't like thinking about it. For the other, it makes things rather difficult."

"What?"

Byron moved back over to the door. He checked outside, then

closed it, returning to sit on the sofa. He spoke in hushed tones. "If what Durant told you back in October is true, Circe wants you alive, Mira. Number Three in particular. The Charger. And one doesn't gain the attention of one of the leaders of Circe by accident."

"What are you saying?"

"Number Three knows you, Mira. And you know them."

Mira's mind went blank. No. That wasn't possible. Or was it?

Byron continued. "Durant worked in close proximity with the Charger. So, if we want to find him, we need to determine who the Charger is, and confront them."

She shook her head, turning away. "You must be mistaken. How could I know them? That would mean . . ."

"I'm sorry, Mira."

"Who do you suspect?" she whispered.

"Are you sure you want to know?"

She looked him in the eyes, shoulders tense. "Who do you suspect?" she repeated.

Byron paused, a sadness in his eyes. But not for himself. No. Mira knew it was for her.

"I'm afraid it might be your uncle."

Mira clenched her fists in her skirts. "No." She laughed. "That's ridiculous. It's not him."

"I don't like it either, Mira. But we need to look at all the evidence, regardless of who it points to."

Her body trembled. This was wrong. Everything about it. How could Byron think that? "What evidence could you possibly have against my uncle?"

Byron stood and paced away, a hand on his brow. "We don't have to talk about this right now. You've just had a rather traumatic shock, and I don't want to make it worse."

"It won't make it worse, because it's not true!" It couldn't be. If it was, then that meant that everything she knew was a lie.

"But it could be!" He raised his voice, throwing a hand out. "I love you, Mira, and I hope that I'm wrong. But I can't just ignore the facts."

"What are they, then?" She crossed her arms over her chest. "Just tell me!" She burst out. It was worse not knowing, sitting in suspense, waiting for the possibility of a condemning truth to come tumbling out.

"Alright." Byron deflated and grabbed his journal from where he'd left it and flipped it open.

"You've written it down?" she said, mouth agape. Had Byron considered this long enough that he had a full list? She squeezed down her anger, digging her nails into her arms.

He ignored her comment in favor of reading off his evidence. "I started by writing down what we knew about the Charger. It needed to be someone older. We know that they were involved in the deaths of your parents, so it can't be anyone close to your age."

"They could have stepped up to the position afterwards," Mira said.

Byron sucked in a breath. "That is a possibility. But it still seems to me that they would have more experience."

Mira conceded the point and kept quiet as Byron continued.

"We also know that the Charger is the head of the smuggling section of Circe. So, they needed connections to shipping and commerce in one regard or another."

"But there are any number of people that could fall under scrutiny for that."

"We can narrow it down to quite a small circle when we add in their connection to you."

Mira swallowed. If Byron was right about it being someone close to her, there were a handful of suspects, if that. "What evidence makes you think it's my uncle?"

"He owns a shipping company. That in of itself gives him access to things that the smugglers would need. He merged said company with Sutherland's, effectively increasing the breadth of his influence. Not only that, but he actively pushed Walker towards an apprenticeship with Alexander Durant. He's attempted to dissuade you from working with me, time and time again."

Mira frowned. Something wasn't lining up. A spark of hope fluttered in her chest. "Hold on a moment. If he and Sutherland were merging companies anyway, then why on earth would he have wanted Sutherland dead? And even if it would be advantageous to have Sutherland out of the way, why would my uncle put himself in such a place to be suspected of murdering him? If he had known about Sutherland's murder beforehand, he would have arranged for an alibi, wouldn't he?"

Byron opened his mouth a moment as if to speak, then closed it, brow furrowing.

"And I know that if my uncle were the Charger, he would have pushed me to court Alexander. As it was, he didn't really try to inform my decision whatsoever. In fact, he has been nothing but approving of my relationship with you since we've started courting." She stood, drumming her fingers on her arm as she walked up and down the room. "And that isn't even taking into account the fact that I know beyond a shadow of a doubt that he would *never* consider murdering my mother. My father, maybe. But not mum. And certainly not Professor Burke."

"We don't know for certain if Durant intended on killing Burke. It could have just been the circumstance."

"But if it was Cyrus, he would have made it clear that Burke wouldn't be harmed. I know my uncle well enough to know that. And there's one other thing you haven't taken into account."

"What's that?"

"Whoever it is, they need to be able to move freely enough

that they can oversee things in England and in France. My uncle hasn't traveled for his business since I was little."

"Hm." Byron closed his journal, pursing his lips in thought. "Alright. It's not your uncle."

Mira narrowed her eyes. It wasn't like Byron to give up on a theory so soon after offering it. Was he just agreeing because it was such a touchy subject? But regardless of his true feelings on the matter, she didn't have the energy to confront him about it, one way or the other.

"Thank you." Mira slumped into the armchair, exhaustion weighing down on her. "But that still leaves the problem of who the real culprit is."

He let out a breath and threw his journal onto the sofa. "We're back to the beginning, aren't we?"

"I'm afraid so."

Footsteps sounded in the hall, and Mira sat up. The door opened and Emilie poked her head in.

"Oh, I'm sorry! I was just looking for my mother. I left something here the other evening."

She paused, looking closer at the two of them. "Are the two of you alright? You look positively exhausted."

Mira slumped further into her seat. "We're fine."

Byron shot her a look. "You've been up for over twenty-four hours."

"As if you haven't."

Emilie cleared her throat. "Then both of you need some rest. Have you eaten?"

Mira and Byron both fell silent. Emilie muttered something in French.

"We'll get you some food and then off to bed, both of you. It's a wonder my mother hasn't sent you off already."

"I don't want to intrude," Byron said. "I can head back to my lodgings."

"You won't be intruding," Emilie said. "There's an empty

room on the second floor you can use. I'm sure Maman won't mind."

"You're certain?" Byron asked.

"Positive. Now, let's get you to the kitchens."

December 12, 1888

AFTER EATING A LITTLE AND GETTING HERDED off to bed by an insistent Emile, Mira tried to sleep. She really did. But whenever she started to doze off, a new thought would come to her. About the way the professor died. About Alexander and the masquerade. When she pushed those thoughts from her mind new ones replaced them. Was Walker safe? And Liza? And Landon?

If they discovered the identity of the Charger, would they be able to use them to track down Alexander? She slumped onto the bed and flinched as her loose corset bone jabbed her again. She pushed it back into place.

Byron may have not admitted it, but Mira doubted that he had abandoned his suspicions about her uncle. And Byron was seldom wrong.

Could it be her uncle? It pained her to even think of it, but she needed to look at every possibility. Perhaps he was able to handle things well enough from London that he didn't need to travel. And though he wouldn't have been involved in her parents' accident, he could have been a member of Circe at that time and later came into a position of power. But it still came down to the fact that he was arrested. If he were the Charger, wouldn't he have known that Sutherland was going to be murdered? Why didn't he have an alibi?

She frowned. A strange, unfortunate idea popped into her head. What if it was Fred? Selene had mentioned that Alexander had somehow had access to the cells. If Circe had someone inside of Scotland Yard, it would be much easier to know when to commit crimes and how to throw off the police. And had Fred actually been knocked out at the masquerade? Or had he given Alexander his costume and stepped aside? Then again, Fred did have quite the hefty bruise on his forehead from falling. That couldn't be faked. And he was much too young.

For the sake of covering every possibility, she allowed herself to consider Landon as a suspect, if only for a moment. Even if Cyrus had been the one to take her and Walker in, Landon had been the one who raised her. And he'd been in service with her parents since before she was born.

But people didn't often pay attention to the staff, did they? And he did go on holiday twice a year. He would have had plenty of opportunities to slip away to France or Prussia, or anywhere he needed to go. But did he have the necessary connections to be in charge of a smuggling ring?

Perhaps they were looking at this the wrong way. It could be that the Charger wasn't in direct relation to her. They only needed some reason needed to keep her alive. Why, Byron's brother, Castel could be involved in Circe for all they knew! That would explain why he was so against Byron's detective work. And he had access to parliament. If he were the Charger, he'd have reason to want to keep her alive, even if it were just for his brother's sake.

Except that she hadn't met Castel until mid-October, and if the Shadow was to be trusted, Number Three had already known about her before the end of September. Who else could it be?

Her eyes drooped closed. All she wanted to do was sleep, but her mind wouldn't stop turning in circles and coming back with nothing. She yawned and stood to light the gas lamps. Maybe if she wrote everything out, it would help.

She pulled out a sheet of paper and a pen and wrote, *"Things we know about the Charger,"* at the top of the page.

1. *They have a reason to keep me alive.*

Of course, Alexander had told her that. What if he lied to throw them off? It didn't seem like he was lying at the time. She added onto the end of the line.

1. *They have a reason to keep me alive. If Durant can be believed.*

There. That was more accurate. Granted, if Durant had been lying, it wouldn't do much good to track down the Charger. Then again, the Shadow had also mentioned Number Three wanting to keep Mira unharmed. It was unlikely that both of them would lie about that. Chewing on her lip, she moved onto the next item.

2. *They have access to commerce, shipping, routes of travel, politics, etc.*

That brought things back to her uncle and Castel. But that answer just didn't feel right. She didn't have enough evidence.

3. *They travel to France frequently.*

But was that true? Could one manage a crime empire through correspondence? It seemed a silly thought, but it was possible. Although, it would be difficult with the amount of time it took for letters to be delivered. She crossed that line off and instead wrote:

3. *They have contacts in France.*

That seemed more reasonable. She tapped her pen against her cheek. Did they know anything else about them? Not really. Was this even helping? She placed the pen aside and put the paper on the side table.

She was just so tired. Maybe if she closed her eyes for a while it would help.

The winter sun shone through the windows and Mira blinked against the light. Her eyes were sticky with sleep. Morning had come again, and she felt dreadful. With a groan, she moved over to the window and pulled the curtains closed. The room flooded with shadows. Somehow that was worse, so she opened them again.

It didn't feel like she had slept at all. But she didn't want to go back to bed. Not with nightmares and reality melding together in her mind.

She started to get dressed. Once again, she opted not to bother with her hair, but she chose a more reasonable dress for the day. That way, she wouldn't have to change should she and Byron need to go out. She grabbed the paper from the side table and put it in her pocket.

Her eyes landed on the peacock train and mask sitting on the dressing table. The masquerade seemed eons away. The professor—

She cut that thought off. She couldn't think about him. Not now.

Instead, she picked up the mask, dress, and train and left

her room. She headed down to Klasha's room and knocked on the door.

A moment later, it opened and Klasha smiled at her.

"So, you have returned!" She cocked her head. "And the dress has returned too."

"Yes, I'm sorry. The hem is a bit of a mess."

"We'll see about that. Come in, come in."

The older woman ushered her into the room and directed Mira to place the dress on the bed. She tutted as she examined the hem and looked over the feathers in the train.

"Nothing that cannot be fixed," Klasha said. "Can you get me my sewing kit? It is in the second drawer of the vanity."

Mira nodded and moved to retrieve it. As she opened the drawer, a glimmer of gold caught the light. A necklace. It was a triangle enclosed in a circle, with three small gems at each point. The symbol of Circe. Mira gasped.

Klasha looked up at her. "Is something wrong?"

Mira shook her head, swallowing. How could Klasha be a member of Circe? Is that how Durant knew she was in Paris?

Klasha followed her line of sight and frowned. "Why are you looking like a cat has eaten your dinner?" The Russian moved over and chuckled when she saw the necklace. "If you wanted to see it, you only needed to ask." She pulled it from the drawer and held the pendant out to Mira.

Hesitating, Mira plucked it from the air. It was cold in her hand as she traced the outline of it.

"It is very pretty, yes?" Klasha said. "I wish I knew where it came from."

Mira whipped her head up. "You don't know?" Was this a trick? Or did Klasha not know what the symbol meant?

Klasha pursed her lips and shrugged. "No. It just showed up one day." Her eyes narrowed. "Although perhaps I know the culprit."

Klasha grabbed the necklace from Mira and left the room,

turning in the direction of the children's rooms. Mira stood in shock. Should she follow? Was it a trap? With a sigh, she hurried after, hoping she wasn't making a mistake. They came to Clarisse's room and Klasha rapped on the door. Small footsteps came running towards them and the door creaked open.

"Hello! How-how can I help you?" the little girl greeted them, stumbling over her English phrases.

Klasha held the necklace out and it swayed beneath her hand. "Explain."

Clarisse's eyes widened to saucers, and she switched back to French. "*Oh no! I forgot to put it back!*"

"*Put it back where?*" Mira asked matching the language.

"*In Maman's special box. I took it to wear with one of the dresses in the trunk.*"

Mira's stomach dropped, and she gave a slow nod as she realized what that meant. The necklace belonged to Loretta. And *Loretta* belonged to Circe. This changed everything.

Forcing a smile on her face she crouched to Clarisse's eye level. "*I need to return something of your mother's as well. Do you want me to take it back to her?*"

Clarisse grinned. "*Would you?*"

"*Of course.*"

MIRA WAS NOTHING BUT A LIAR, BECAUSE once Clarisse had closed the door and Klasha had returned to her own room, she headed straight to where Byron was resting.

It was a room on the second floor, clear at the end of the hall. Steeling a breath, she knocked on the door. When no answer came, she knocked again. Was he still asleep? Or was he somewhere else in the house?

The door opened, and Byron rubbed a hand over his face. His shirt was half done up with the buttons in the wrong places.

She almost felt bad for waking him. He blinked a couple times upon seeing her, and a new sense of alertness came over him.

"Is something wrong?"

Mira glanced down the hall. No one was there, but anyone could be listening in on the staircase.

"May I come in?"

He paused a moment, frowning, then opened the door wider so she could enter. After they were both inside, he closed the door and went about turning on the lamps and opening the curtains for more light.

The room was green with gold detailing. The bed was a tangled mess of sheets. He must have been tossing and turning as much as she had been. Another wave of guilt washed over her. Maybe she should have let him sleep. But could it have waited?

As he turned back to her from the window, he fiddled with his buttons. "Did something happen?"

"I-I found something."

He cocked his head to the side, curiosity piqued. "What is it?"

Mira held the necklace out to him, and with a gentle touch, he took it from her grasp. His eyes widened as he ran his hand over it. "Where did you find this?"

"Klasha had it. But it belongs to Loretta."

Byron's eyes narrowed, and he passed the necklace back to her. "You know what this means?"

"Of course I do!" She turned away from him, hugging her arms close to her chest. "If Loretta is part of Circe, then Cyrus must be too."

"Why?" Byron asked as he slipped on his waistcoat. "What does Loretta have to do with your uncle?"

"They met in India. They were in love, but she—" Mira stopped short. "She said she loved someone else. She sent him away."

Mira came to face Byron again. "Loretta is the Charger."

"What?" His brow furrowed. "Are you certain?"

"I wish I wasn't. But it all makes sense."

"Start at the beginning." Byron pulled his tie from the back of a chair, before gesturing for her to sit in it. He settled on the bed himself.

Mira lowered herself into her seat. "My uncle traveled to India several times with my grandfather when he was younger. While he was there, he and Loretta met, and they fell in love. I know they both loved each other because I talked to Loretta about it. She said she hated to break his heart. She didn't tell me why it was necessary."

She took a deep breath. "A few days ago, I overheard a conversation between her and the professor. He said something about how he hated all the secrets. At the time, I thought he could have been the other man. The one she said she was in love with. But I think it was something else."

The light from the window hit the necklace, and it gleamed in her hands. "I think she was already part of Circe when she met my uncle. Perhaps she pushed him away so that he wouldn't get involved. So he wouldn't get hurt. She loved him enough that she let him go and thought that would be that." Her voice caught in her throat. "And I think Professor Burke knew something about it. I don't know what, or how. But that's why he was killed. Not only would it help Durant escape, but it would ensure her secret was safe."

Byron steepled his fingers, leaning forward. He let out a slow breath. "Alright. I'm following you so far, but why do you think she's the Charger?"

She pulled her list out of her pocket and handed it over. "These are the three things we know about the Charger, yes?"

"The three things we know for certain," Byron agreed.

"Let's go over them. She lives in France, and I'm sure if she needed to, she could travel. Otherwise, everything else can be handled by those working under her. No one would question why a random person would come to a boarding house, even staying the night. There are plenty of rooms here where Circe could meet if necessary."

Byron nodded as he settled his tie around his neck. Mira continued.

"Then the matter of having connections. I don't know much about her late husband, but when one marries, often you marry a person for their connections, if not for love. We'd have to look into it further. I do know her father worked with the British government in India. Perhaps even with the East India Trading Company before it disbanded. Between those two, she would have enough knowledge that if she was a member of Circe, she could rise up the ranks and be able to manage the smugglers."

"I'm following so far, but you've completely disregarded point number one." He undid the knot he was tying and started again. "They need to have a reason to want to keep you alive."

"I've been thinking about that. And she does have one. She loves my uncle. I'm sure she didn't know that Octavian Blayse was married to Rose Griffon when she ordered his death. But I doubt she would have forgotten about my uncle entirely. And being in Circe, she would have had the means to check in on him from time to time. It would have been hard to miss that all of a sudden he had custody of twins, and it would take little effort to find the connection." She paused to take a breath. "I'm sure she was heartbroken when she realized what had happened. And so, she ensured that she could save him further pain by ordering Circe to keep me and Walker safe. It just became more difficult when I began investigating things with you."

Byron sat there for a moment. "That is an interesting theory."

"It makes sense, doesn't it? And we have the necklace as proof."

"Hm." He sat back, adjusting the knot on his tie. "I think we won't know for certain until we ask her."

"Ask her?" Mira sat there dumbfounded. He wasn't about to approach Loretta and ask her outright if she was a leader of Circe, was he?

He nodded and stood, grabbing his jacket from where he left it on the dressing table. "That is the most direct approach."

Mira moved over to him, placing a hand on his arm. "But if she's the Charger, then she's dangerous!"

"You've been living under her roof for several days, Mira. If she was going to do something to either of us, don't you think she would have done it already?"

Her mouth fell open. He did have a point, didn't he?

He pulled out of her grasp and smoothed down his jacket. "Besides, if you are right, then she won't want to hurt you in fear of hurting Cyrus. I doubt she will change her mind simply because we know who she is."

"But Professor Burke knew who she was. And, well . . ."

Byron considered the statement, frowning for a moment before shaking his head. "I don't think that's why he died. He may have known her secret, but she seemed genuinely shocked at the news of his death." He opened the door. "There's only one way of knowing for certain."

Mira held the necklace tight in her hand as they made their way down the stairs. She tried to keep her breaths even, but she could feel her heart in her throat. Why was it that Circe was so inexplicably linked with her family? Her parents, herself, and now her uncle were all caught up in its threads. And she dreaded the conversation that she would need to have with Cyrus. Poor man. Not only had he lost his sister and his best friend to Circe, but it was the woman he loved that was behind it all.

When they reached the entry hall, Georges was there, slipping into his coat.

"Do you know where your mother is?" Mira asked, in French.

"She and your uncle are in the library. At least, they were a little while ago."

Mira swallowed. If they were together, then that would make this confrontation all the more difficult. *"Thank you,"* Mira said. *"Don't let us keep you."*

Georges nodded to both of them and opened the door, disappearing into the cold afternoon. Mira's anxiety returned. Loretta's poor children. Did they know that their mother was leading a criminal organization? Or had she kept them in the dark? Mira couldn't imagine that Emilie knew, or little Clarisse. Were the boys working for Circe as well? It made her quite ill to think about it.

They approached the library, and Mira froze. If her uncle was in there too, would they be able to convince him to leave? She didn't want to hurt him more, so soon after learning of Burke's death. Byron reached over, taking her hand in his. He gently turned it over and opened her fingers so he could take the necklace. A harsh indent was left on her palm from where she had been clutching it.

"It's going to be alright," Byron said, catching her gaze.

She took a deep breath and nodded. He pushed the door open.

It was a nice little room. The walls were lined with shelves and full of books. The fireplace roared, and Cyrus and Lettie sat on the sofa nearest to it. Both of them looked up as they came through the door. Loretta's eyes were red and puffy, and she held a handkerchief in her hand. Cyrus had an arm around Loretta's shoulders, and made no effort to move it, despite having company. They seemed much closer than they ever had been before, and had Mira not known what she did about Loretta, she would have been thrilled. As it was, she only felt more nauseated.

"Sorry, are we interrupting something?" Byron asked.

Loretta dabbed at her eyes. "No, it's alright. Please come in."

"We can come back," Mira said, already inching towards the door.

"No," Cyrus said. "We were just about finished. Did you need something?"

"We just had a question. May we sit down?" Byron asked.

"Of course." Loretta gestured to the vacant armchairs and Byron moved over to them. Mira took a moment to close the door before joining the group.

Byron lifted his hand and let the necklace hang off from it. "We found this upstairs. Does it belong to either of you?"

Loretta's mouth quirked up in surprise, and she leaned over to take it. "I thought I'd lost it!"

Byron smiled and handed it over. "Where did you get such a pretty thing? I'm sure I've seen one like it before, but I can't remember where."

"It's a family heirloom, actually." She settled back next to Cyrus. "My father gave it to me when I was married to Charles."

Mira frowned. If Loretta was the Charger, then surely she wouldn't have admitted to owning the necklace, would she? Or was she just playing a game?

"Do you know what the symbol means?" Byron asked.

Loretta shook her head, fondling the necklace. "Is it meant to be something in particular?"

"It represents a group known as Circe," Byron said.

Cyrus tensed. "Are you certain?"

"Positive," Byron said.

"Circe?" Loretta's brow furrowed. "My father mentioned it before. That's what they called the shipping system under the East India Company, isn't it?"

Cyrus turned to her. "Did your father tell you that?"

Loretta nodded. "I overheard him talking with one of his merchants about it, and he explained it to me afterwards. It stands for something." She chewed on her lip. "Central Indian Routes . . . I can't remember the rest. It's been so long."

Mira narrowed her gaze. Was she telling the truth or was she trying to throw them off?

Byron continued. "What exactly did your father do?"

Loretta gave a slight shrug. "I'm not sure that I know for certain. I know he was in charge of that branch and that things got rather complicated after the company was taken over by the government. We didn't really speak of it." She frowned looking around at them. "Why are you all acting so strange?"

"I'll explain in a moment, Mrs. Lavigne. But I need you to answer a few more questions for me."

She wrung her handkerchief. "Alright. I'll do my best."

"How did your father seal his letters?"

She blinked. "His letters?"

"Yes." Byron leaned forward.

"Why do you care about my father's letters? He died decades ago."

"I promise you it is relevant. Crucial, even. Were there any symbols that he used?"

Loretta's eyes grew distant. "If I remember right, he had two. One was our family crest. That one was a wax stamp. The other he only used on occasion. It was his ring, and it had a small picture of a horse's head on it, with the mane all wild behind it." She smiled. "When I was little, I used to ask to look at it." Her smile faltered a fraction. "I'm not sure where it ended up. I know it wasn't with his things after he died."

Mira's mouth fell open. "A horse." She turned to Byron. "Could he have been the Charger?"

Her theory was falling neatly into place. Except, Loretta didn't seem guilty, did she? Either this was an elaborate act, and they were all falling for it, or she was truly innocent.

"It seems likely," Byron said.

Loretta looked between the two of them. "What is this all about?"

Byron took a breath. "I'm afraid that Circe is not a shipping system, nor is it directly related to the East India Company."

"Then what is it?"

"Circe is a criminal organization, one that I believe your father worked for."

Loretta's eyes widened, and her face turned white. "What?"

Byron continued. "In fact, if I'm correct, he was the leader of a rather large smuggling operation."

Loretta sat back in her seat. "Oh." She turned towards Cyrus, searching his face. "That's why."

Cyrus' eyes were shining with unshed tears, but he was smiling at her. "That's why."

"Why what?" Mira asked.

Cyrus reached over and took Loretta's hand in his. "I think I can tell this part of the story."

Loretta nodded and Cyrus took a deep breath.

"When I was twenty, I went on my first solo trip to India. My father," he looked at Mira, "your grandfather, had decided that he was done with his travels, and since I was taking up his company, it fell to me. I'd been there plenty of times before, mind you. But this was my first trip on my own. That being said, I was a bit nervous, and so when Edward approached me and asked to sit with me in my train car, I was quite relieved."

As he mentioned Professor Burke, he grew a bit more somber and nostalgic in his tone and Mira's heart broke.

"We became good friends on the journey. He was going to be joining the civil service down there, and was quite excited about the whole thing. Once we got to India, we went our separate ways. Him to Madras and me to Waltair. However, we kept in contact through letters."

He turned to Loretta. "Am I rambling too much?"

She smiled. "You're telling it splendidly."

"Right. Well. When I came the next year, I happened to be in Madras on business and ran into him. He invited me to a gathering at the Elliot home. And that's where I met Loretta."

"Elliot is my maiden name," Loretta clarified.

Cyrus smiled at her, eyes not wavering from her for a moment. "I stayed in Madras for a few months, and every spare moment, I came to visit her. And we fell in love."

Mira glanced at Byron and blushed when she realized he was looking at her.

"That's where things get complicated." Loretta sighed. "My father didn't approve of the match. He never said why, just that it wouldn't be a good fit."

Cyrus swallowed, looking down at where his hand met Loretta's. "And so, we got married in secret."

Mira choked on some air. "You did what?"

Loretta nodded. "I arranged for a holiday down the coast for me and a few close friends. Cyrus and Edward met us there. It was easy to find a minister to do it. And Edward was our witness."

"I can't believe this." Mira gaped at her uncle. He was so strict about propriety and yet he had eloped himself?

"It seemed to be the best thing to do at the time," he explained, a tinge of red on his cheeks. "And it was. For two weeks, we were blissfully happy."

"But then I had to return home. And I must have not hidden the ring well enough, because my father found out. He was livid." Loretta took a shaky breath. "He threatened me, he threatened Cyrus. He told me that he had connections, and that if I didn't break it off with Cyrus, that he would have him killed." She looked down at her hands. "My father was not always the kindest man, but I had never seen him like that before. There was a threat behind his words. I knew that he wasn't bluffing. And so, I went to Cyrus and told him that I didn't love him anymore."

Cyrus tipped his head back. "The marriage didn't even have to be annulled. Since we were married before she was twenty-one, and without her parents' permission, the law stated that our union was void. I left India and never came back."

Loretta's lower lip wobbled. "If Circe really is a criminal organization, he could have killed you!"

Cyrus moved to wrap an arm around her again, holding her tight. "I'm right here, Lettie. Safe and sound." He pressed a kiss into her hairline, and she choked on a sob.

Immense guilt flooded through Mira. How could she have assumed that Loretta was the Charger? Or even part of Circe? A thought occurred to her, pushing the guilt away as laughter bubbled up.

"To think that you told me she never even loved you, when all the time the two of you eloped!" she said.

Cyrus flushed. "I didn't like to think about it. I'm sorry I lied to you, Mira."

"There's something else though, isn't there?" Byron asked. "One other secret?"

Loretta pulled back, tears stopping for a moment as she stared wide-eyed at Byron.

"Is there?" Cyrus asked.

Her gaze came back to his, and a new stream of tears came. "Yes," she wailed, crying into his chest.

Byron pulled a handkerchief from his pocket and handed it over to Cyrus, who nodded his thanks and replaced the one Loretta had already ruined. After a minute or so, Loretta had calmed down enough to speak.

"After you left, I planned to escape and come to England to find you. Edward was still in Madras, and he was going to help me. But it was difficult getting the money to travel without my father realizing. And then I fell incredibly ill. For days I felt nauseous and light-headed. They called for a doctor and" — she took a deep breath— "I was pregnant."

Mira's jaw dropped. Her uncle was in a similar state of surprise. His mouth trembled up and down a few times before he said, "Emilie?"

Loretta looked down and nodded. "Emilie."

"But if I had known," Cyrus trailed off.

"I know. But you didn't. To avoid the scandal, my father married me off as soon as he could. And Charles was there on business at the time. He never knew that she wasn't his." She reached up and cupped Cyrus' face. "But she has your green eyes."

Mira took a few deep breaths. She had a cousin. And her uncle was married. She had an aunt? And while these were incredible revelations, and much better than discovering that Loretta was a criminal, she couldn't help but feel like she was intruding on an intimate and personal scene.

After a moment, Loretta turned to look at Byron. "Who told you?"

"No one."

"There had to be someone," Loretta insisted. "How could you have known?"

Byron smiled. "Mira mentioned that she overheard you and the professor talking about a secret. Since you didn't know about Circe, it must have been something else."

Cyrus' gaze softened. "Edward knew?"

Loretta nodded. "He wanted me to tell you. But I was scared. It's been so long, Cy, and I thought you would hate me."

"No, Lettie. I could never hate you," he said, voice soft as he reassured her.

Byron stood and offered a hand to Mira, helping her up. "I think we'll leave the two of you alone. You have quite a bit to talk about."

"Yes. We do," Cyrus said.

~੦❧੦~

AFTER LEADING HER TO THE SITTING ROOM, Byron closed the
door and turned to Mira. "I'm sure you have questions."

Mira walked the length of the room, shaking out her hands.
"You knew."

"Knew what?" He hid his smile as he sat in the closest armchair.

"That she wasn't the Charger. You knew before we even
came down the stairs, didn't you?"

He shrugged. "I had a hunch."

"How?" She stopped and crossed her arms over her chest.

"If she was a member of Circe, that necklace would never
have been lost in the first place. She would always be wearing it,
just under her dress. And if she were the Charger, she wouldn't
have a necklace like that. She'd have her own symbol."

"What?" Mira sat on the sofa, baffled.

Byron leaned forward. "The purpose of the symbol is not
to make a fashion statement. It is a way of communicating
with other members of the Order. Necklace, tattoo, bracelet. It
wouldn't do to have it out in the open all the time. Remember
when we first met the Shadow? We could see the chain, but not
the pendant. But in the Pit, surrounded by other criminals, it
was an open threat."

"Then why did you let me go on like that?"

"Because you were so certain, and I didn't want to ruin it
for you." His eyes twinkled. "And aside from that, she did need
to get that necklace from somewhere."

"From her father," Mira hummed. "Who was the Charger,
and died before I was even born, leaving us with no leads or
suspects whatsoever. At this point, we're shooting in the dark."
She slumped back in her chair, blowing a strand of hair from
her face. "Maybe we need to go back to searching for Durant
without the help of the ignoble steed."

"Maybe." Byron's gaze narrowed for a moment before it trailed back to her. "How are you feeling?"

"What?"

"It's been a rather trying few days for you. I just wanted to know if you were alright."

"To be honest, I'm exhausted. I didn't sleep well last night."

"I can tell. It's not normal for you to jump to conclusions like that," he teased.

A small laugh escaped her. "No. It isn't."

Byron hesitated. "And how are you feeling about what happened at the masquerade?"

Mira swallowed. "I've been trying not to think about it, to be honest. Finding that necklace kind of made me forget."

"Forgetting can be a wonderful thing," Byron said. "But the pain doesn't disappear when we don't remember the cause. It only stays longer."

She wiped a tear away from under her eye with a short laugh. "You'd know that, wouldn't you?"

"All too well." He moved to sit next to her, setting a hand on top of hers.

The light outside was dwindling, and the fire popped in the grate.

"Is it alright if I want to forget for just a little longer?" Mira whispered, searching his face.

He squeezed her hand. "Of course it is."

She acted before she could think and captured his lips with hers. He hesitated before bringing his hand up to cup her cheek, kissing her back. Warmth spread outwards from his touch, and she leaned closer. After a moment he pulled back, tipping their foreheads together.

"I think it's time for you to sleep, my love."

She nodded, eyes drooping. "Will you stay?"

He released her and reluctantly pulled away. "No, I have some things I need to look into. But I'll be back, I promise."

"I'll be here."

"I know. Goodnight, Miss Blayse."

"Goodnight, Mr. Constantine."

Byron pressed one last kiss onto her forehead and left the room.

December 13, 1888:
The Witching Hour

A HARSH KNOCKING AT THE FRONT DOOR OF the boarding house woke Mira from her sleep and just about
had her tumbling to the floor. Wincing as the loose bone in her
corset jabbed her again, she sat up and rubbed the grogginess
from her eyes. How long had she been asleep? The fire had died
down to its coals and the sun must have set hours before. She
glanced at the clock on the mantle and was surprised to find
that it was just after midnight. She was still in the sitting room,
having fallen asleep on the sofa after Byron had left around six
the day before.

The knocking started up again and Mira stood, moving to
the door. She was met in the entry by an exhausted Loretta, who
was in the process of tying a dressing gown round her waist.

"They'll wake the whole house with that racket," Loretta
mumbled as she opened the door. *"Can I help you?"* She said
in French.

Selene Vermielle stood on the step. "*Sorry to disturb you. Is Mira Blayse here?*"

Mira's fatigue melted away, replaced with anxiety. She stepped into the doorframe. "Selene? What are you doing here?"

"Oh," the thief gave a sigh of relief. "Thank goodness you're here. May I come in?"

Mira pulled the door open more and Loretta moved to the side. "Of course. Is something wrong?"

"I'm not sure," Selene hedged, stepping in. "But I thought you should know something."

Mira ushered her into the sitting room and lit the lamps. Loretta paused at the door. "Shall I make some tea?"

"That would be wonderful." Mira nodded at her, and Loretta left the room.

Mira stoked the fire up. "Start from the beginning."

"Well," Selene took a seat in an armchair, fidgeting with her hands. "When did you last see Byron?"

Mira frowned. "It was a few hours ago. Why?"

"He came to my gallery earlier this evening and asked me about the tunnels beneath the city. It didn't occur to me until after he left that he might try to enter them himself."

"You mean the quarries?" Mira asked. Byron had been in a hurry when he had left the boarding house. If Selene knew anything about the tunnels, that information could help them find Durant.

Selene smiled. "There is much you don't know about Paris. Yes, there are quarries beneath the city. But there's much more than that. Wells, fountains, catacombs. Chambers long left forgotten. Centuries of history and detritus. It is known as the Empire of the Dead."

"And Durant is down there?"

Selene glanced away. "That I do not know. But I know that Constantine was looking for an entrance and hoping to find Circe's base of operation."

Mira gripped the mantle. "Did you tell Byron where it was?"

"I couldn't." Selene fidgeted with her hands. "While I know of several entrances to the catacombs, I do not know where Circe's chamber is. They keep it secret, and most members in Paris are not aware of its location. However, there are rumors, and the rumors lead to Montparnasse cemetery. I told him as much."

Mira paused. "Why are you telling me this?"

Selene grew quiet for a moment, staring into the flames. "He owes me a favor. If he dies, I won't receive it."

Mira's heart jolted. "You think he's in danger then?"

The thief brought her head up, gaze heavy. "I would be surprised if he was not."

MIRA TUGGED ON HER COAT AS SHE sprinted down the street, her cheeks stinging from the icy wind. Selene was at her side. They waved down the first carriage that passed them and Mira paid the driver in advance to take them to the cemetery. All the while, terrible things played out in her mind. Why the cemetery? What if Circe had him? Would they kill him? Was he already dead?

Selene placed a hand on her arm.

"It's alright. He probably hasn't found the entrance yet."

That calmed Mira a fraction as the carriage stopped in front of the cemetery and they stepped out onto the pavement. The moon was closer to full than it was the night before, and the moonlight bled onto the stones, highlighting the writing on each. Bodies moldered beneath their feet. Mira shivered at the thought. It had been only one day since the professor had been shot. If they managed to find the body, would they bury him in Paris, or bring him back to London?

She pulled the collar of her coat tighter around her shoulders. *Not now, Mira*, she thought. She had more important things at hand. Such as, where was Byron? The cemetery was enormous, and the shadows seemed to lengthen as she walked. Every inch of her was on edge. Weren't there usually watchmen in a cemetery? Were they trespassing?

"You're sure he's here?" Mira asked.

Selene nodded. "We can search by sections," she said. "Stay within sight."

Mira nodded, a cold anxiety in her stomach. Did she trust the thief? After all, she only had Selene's word that Byron had even come to the cemetery. Even if the thief had left the world of Circe behind, she was still a thief. But if Byron was in trouble, could she afford to ignore the warning?

Mira's breath clung to the air as she moved down another row of gravestones. Part of her wanted to call out for him, but what if he needed to remain unseen? Was she ruining everything by walking straight through the cemetery?

Mira took a long deep breath, the cold filling her lungs. She just hoped that Byron hadn't decided to go in alone. Maybe Fred was with him. They wouldn't have entered the catacombs without a map, would they?

"What does the entrance look like?" Mira said.

"You want to go down?" Selene looked up at her in surprise.

"If he was looking for the entrance, that's where we'll find him."

Selene relented. "The ones I know about are obvious, although the city has tried to cover most of them up. After the Revolution in 1848, they thought that those opposed to the republic may try to meet there. They weren't wrong. Circe, and other groups, had to hide their entrances to avoid discovery. But they are hidden in plain sight."

They split ways at the far wall, keeping within sight of one another, but covering more ground. Selene kept ensuring her that she would know it when she found it, but what if she had missed something?

She knelt next to an ancient marker and rubbed the frozen lichen from it, trying to read what was carved there.

"I've found it!" Selene called from down the wall.

Mira picked up her skirts and ran over. Selene stood in front of a gothic style crypt. It had carvings on either side of a pointed arch. Inside was a statue of three women, standing back-to-back. Each held a single object in their hand. The first held a dagger, the second a key, and the last a torch. The inscription read: "Hecate." And then the Latin phrase, "Nitimur in vetitum." She noted the lack of birth or death dates. Just the single inscription.

Byron was nowhere to be seen.

"Are you sure?" Mira asked, running a hand over the inscription. If only she knew Latin.

"Do you know much of Greek mythology?"

"A little," Mira said.

Selene stepped closer to the statue. "Hecate is the mother of Circe."

Mira swallowed, her blood running cold. "So, then this would be . . ."

"Yes." Selene nodded. "There must be a way to open a door."

Mira stepped back, examining the crypt in full. If Byron had been there before and found the entrance, there must be some evidence of that. What would he have seen? Her eyes flicked over the objects in each of the hands and then up the arms. Meanwhile Selene pushed and pulled on the different bits of tracery covering the statue. Nothing happened. Mira looked at each piece in turn. The arm that held the dagger had a harsher indent where it met the body of the statue. A strange groove extended above it. She cocked her head, then placed a hand below the arm. With a gentle nudge, she pushed it towards the ceiling. The arm moved along the groove, almost like a track, and then slotted into place.

The piece of the wall next to the statue swung open a crack. Mira stepped towards it, pulling it all the way open. The arm was attached to a latch in the frame of the door. If they closed the door behind them, gravity would pull the arm down until it locked the door again. On the other side, she found a lever that would open the entrance from the inside. Up ahead, a staircase led down, presumably into the tunnels.

"You opened it," Selene said, surprise evident on her face.

"Yes." Mira took a shaky breath and stepped back. "But I'm not sure Byron has been here."

Selene moved over to examine the mechanism. "How could we tell if . . ." She paused. "What's that?" she pointed to a patch of white on the ground.

Mira crouched. A handkerchief. Something crinkled inside as she picked it up. She frowned and unfolded it. There, in the center, was a letter with her own wax seal. Nestled between the pages was a lock of her hair. The same small braid that she had sent Byron over a week before.

She stared into the darkness, her insides going numb. "He's already gone down."

"Are you sure?" Selene asked.

Mira folded the letter around the lock of hair again and placed it in her pocket. She tucked Byron's handkerchief into her bodice just above her heart. Her hands shook as she did so. "There's no question."

Near the top of the stairs was a shelf with candles and matches. Mira took a box of matches and lit a candle. It didn't provide much light, but it was better than nothing. Holding it out, she found that the stone steps were steep and curved, and she couldn't see the end of them. The walls were hewn from the stone with no patterns or carvings. A glint of silver caught her eye, and she turned towards it. A lantern. She placed the candle inside, and the reflective walls amplified the light, sending it farther into the darkness.

Selene closed the entrance behind them. "It looks like we'll need to go one at a time," she said as she came up next to Mira.

Mira nodded, hesitating at the top of the steps. It was so dark below them. But Byron needed her help. With a breath, she took the first step. "Let me know if you hear anything behind us."

"Of course," Selene said.

It was warmer in the catacombs, for which Mira was grateful. She couldn't see her breath anymore, but perhaps that was because of the warmth radiating from the lantern in her hand. In any case, she was glad to be out of the cemetery. Although she felt more unease as she traversed the spiral stairs to the beginning of the labyrinth. Was it because it was darker? Or that they, like the dead, were stuck underground?

They came to a place where they could exit the staircase into a tunnel, or continue down into the darkness. She poked the lantern out of the stairwell. The tunnel forked into two paths, with no curves.

"Do we search here or keep going down?" Mira asked Selene.

"Down, I'd say," Selene said. "We'll want to be quiet and listen for any echoes. We might be able to hear them before we get there."

Mira nodded and continued down the stairs. It was getting colder as they went, and the marks in the stone were rougher. They came to another place where they could continue down or exit into a tunnel. Mira paused as the ambient reflections of other lights came into view at the end of the tunnel, just before it curved. She placed a finger to her lips, then pointed toward the light.

Selene nodded and gestured for her to continue. Mira extinguished the candle in her lantern to avoid being seen as they moved along the tunnel. Voices echoed from further along, and the two women stopped, pressed flat against the wall.

"It's close to time, wouldn't you say?" a man said. Mira didn't recognize the voice, but she was surprised to hear him speak in English, and with a Scottish accent, no less.

"The boss ain't here yet, so it can't be time yet," another man, gruffer in his tone, said.

"Can't stay here forever, though," the first said. "We've been waiting all night."

A pair of footsteps sounded from further down the corridor, and a new voice broke the silence. "And I've been waiting years for this moment, Duncan. I suppose, we'll just have to wait a little longer."

Mira's body stiffened at the sound of it. Once it held such warmth and affection, but now it was only cold and harsh. Alexander Durant stood around that corner, mere steps away. But it didn't seem as if Byron was there as well. Did he take a different path? Perhaps they should turn back. She turned to communicate this to Selene and found a knife unsheathed between them.

"For what it is worth, I am sorry," Selene whispered.

The anxiety that had been with Mira since Selene showed up on her doorstep twisted within her gut. She took a step back, mouth open as she realized just how stupid she'd been. The thief had led her straight to Alexander. But how had they gotten her letter? Her fingers ghosted over where the handkerchief lay, just over her heart. She had been so certain.

"Byron?" she asked, voice shaking.

"Safe." Selene nodded. "For now."

A small comfort considering that Mira was about to be handed over to the lions herself. She'd been in Circe's custody once before, and once was more than enough. Just as she was considering the possibility of running past Selene and escaping, the thief yelled, "Patience is always rewarded," and pushed Mira so she was facing towards the ambient light.

With a few steps, they turned the corner and found four men waiting for them. Alexander stood at the front, smirking. The light of two kerosene lanterns illuminated the space.

"Why, Mira! I was beginning to think you wouldn't make it," he said, as if she had appeared on his doorstep for afternoon tea.

She straightened her shoulders. "It seems I missed your invitation."

"And yet you came, anyway. I'm glad to know that you're capable of being trained."

Mira tightened her hands around the handle of the lantern. It was a flimsy weapon, but better than nothing.

"Why did you bring me here?" she asked between clenched teeth.

Durant let out a huff of breath. "So impatient. Why don't you come closer?"

"I can hear fine from where I am."

He extended a hand, and Selene pushed her from behind. Mira stumbled, but didn't fall. Three feet stood between her and her new captor.

"Yes, but the light is much better over here." His gaze slipped down her body. "Lovely as always, beloved."

He moved to grab her, and she raised the lantern, attempting to bring it down on him. He dodged out of the way, latching onto her arm and twisting it behind her back. His breath was hot in her ear as he pulled her close to him. "Your persistence is remarkable." His hand squeezed, and she hissed at the pain, dropping the lantern. He kicked it out of reach with a soft clang. She tried to pull away, but he kept a firm grasp on her arm. Even if she could escape, it would be impossible for her to outrun four men.

Selene rolled her eyes and stepped back. "Enough of this. I've done as you've asked. Does your promise stand?"

Durant glanced up at her. "Remind me of the agreement?"

The thief glared. "My freedom in exchange for hers."

Mira's breathing stilled a moment as she realized the implication.

"Oh yes," Durant said, releasing Mira. The other men stepped forward, pinning her in. "Consider yourself free of your obligations to Circe," Durant continued. "You may leave."

Selene took a long deep breath, considered Mira a moment longer, then turned towards the entrance of the catacombs. Alexander shifted in his stance, and Mira caught a glint of silver before the shot rang out. She screamed.

Selene made no noise as she brought one hand to her gut and crumpled to her knees. Mira rushed to her side, kneeling beside her as she searched for something to stanch the blood. She pulled the handkerchief from her bodice and pressed it into the wound. Selene groaned, shifting her weight. She pushed herself up, eyes wide with panic and confusion, mouth opening but no sound coming out. The thief's knife shone from where it fell beneath her, out of view of the men. A ringing came to Mira's ears, and she realized the gunshot had deafened her. Bit by bit, her hearing came back to her.

"I-I'm sorry," Selene coughed out. "He gave me no choice."

"I forgive you," Mira whispered, slipping the knife into her inside coat pocket with her free hand. "Just take deep breaths."

A shadow fell over both of them and Mira gasped as one of the guards pulled her away. He released her as Alexander descended on his prey.

Selene twisted towards them, but slipped and fell to the ground again. Her gaze lifted and latched onto her murderer.

"Y-you promised . . ." she gasped out, her blood pooling on the stone beneath her.

Alexander stood over her, voice soft even as his words cut through the air. "What is death, but freedom from the burdens of this world?"

He turned away from her, blood on his boots. His smile landed on Mira. "Shall we?"

December 13, 1888: Early Morning

MIRA STARED AT THE COOLING CORPSE OF Selene Vermielle, shaking all over. One guard stood next to her. Two others stood behind her holding the lanterns. Alexander Durant stayed between her and the exit. The catacombs whistled with an unknown wind.

"She didn't have to die." Mira's hoarse voice echoed in the chamber, fists clenching at her sides. "She did as you asked."

"Yes." Alexander slipped the revolver back into his suit jacket. As he straightened his lapels, it became impossible to tell he had a gun in the first place. "She did what I needed her to do."

"Then why kill her?" Mira brought her gaze up to his face. He only smiled.

"She's proven that her loyalty does not belong to us. It didn't take much convincing for her to agree to lead you to the Pit, did it? She wanted to cut ties with Circe almost from the beginning. What I did was a mercy." He adjusted the cuffs of his jacket. The action seemed so mundane for the setting. Mira's jaw tightened.

"Mercy? You murdered her."

He stepped closer, golden eyes glinting in the light. "I think you should be more concerned about what's going to happen to you."

Mira's eyes widened, and she swallowed, gaze flicking behind him to the stairs. Could she make it? But as she stepped forward to break into a run, Alexander caught her arm again, faster than she anticipated.

"I don't think I need to tell you how foolish of an idea that was," he said, pulling her to face away from the stairs. "And not because it was futile." He raised a hand, gesturing to his men. "Lads, why don't you show her what the catacombs really look like?"

The two lanterns dimmed in quick succession and shadows consumed the tunnel. Mira couldn't see anything. She couldn't hear anything aside from the soft breaths of the men and her heart in her ears. The darkness was so complete that though she had just seen the way out, she didn't know which direction it was. In fact, the only true sense of direction she had was Alexander's hand on her arm. It was like a tether, letting her know that the world hadn't stopped existing just because the light was gone.

A voice spoke in her ear, "I'd suggest you don't try to run, Mira. Even with a map, these tunnels are difficult to navigate, and starvation is such a cruel way to die."

Alexander snapped his fingers and two small flames burst in her periphery, followed by the hiss and crackle of the lantern wicks coming to life. She blinked a few times to take in her surroundings.

"Let's go," Alexander said.

Two of the guards moved behind them, further blocking the way to freedom. The last cocked his head.

"Section A, B, or C?" the man said, his English thick with a French accent.

"B," Durant said, glancing at Mira. "I'd like to keep this little development secret for the time being."

Mira glared at him. "Keeping secrets from Circe, Alexander? Isn't that a dangerous game?"

He adjusted his grip so that her arm was resting on his, then moved down the corridor. "Circe thrives on secrets. I think I'll be forgiven for putting a new pawn into play."

THE WALLS SEEMED TO CLOSE IN ON them as they walked further into the catacombs. Lamplight flickered off the stone with a warm glow despite the cold that seeped into Mira's skin. The tunnels curved and twisted. Each time they came to a turn, Alexander would pause, consult a map, and point them in another direction. Side-paths they didn't take seemed to ooze with shadows, making it impossible to see past where the light touched. The walls were lined with debris and rubble from years past. Discarded torches, candle stubs, and the like.

The ceiling height changed drastically as they moved down the stone paths, in some places tall enough that Mira wouldn't be able to touch the ceiling if she jumped, and in others she needed to crouch to avoid hitting her head against the rough surface. The tunnel became narrower as they continued, forcing them to file one by one. And the farther they moved away from the entrance, the warmer it became. She soon shed her coat, carrying it instead, careful to keep the knife concealed.

After a few minutes of walking, they came to a place where the path veered off to the side, avoiding a gaping chasm in the ground. Alexander traversed the path with ease, extending a hand to help her across. She glared at him and took small steps along the side, ignoring his hand. As she came to the center, she peered down. The lamplight flickered, but it was easy to see that the hole was filled with bones. She stumbled, and Alexander caught her around the waist, pulling her to safety.

"Careful, my dear. You wouldn't want to fall in."

An undertone of malice threaded his voice, her skin prickling beneath his touch. She hated not knowing Alexander's plans. Her pulse raced as she looked back at the well of bones and decay. The other guards came across without flinching.

Soon enough, they took a staircase down to a lower level of the catacombs, further disorienting her. She had tried to keep track of how many turns they were taking in her head, but with each corner it became harder to remember which direction they had come from.

The strange thing was, there didn't seem to be any sort of life around them. It was easy to imagine a rat skittering across their path or a spider keeping a web in the unnatural warmth. And yet, as they turned within the labyrinth of tunnels, they never encountered another living thing. Just dust and looming darkness accompanied by their own breaths and footfalls.

They came to a straight corridor, almost perfect in its construction, and followed it for a few minutes. At the end, they came to a circular path with branches of tunnels going off in several directions, a central column keeping the ceiling up. As they came around the bend, something crunched beneath Mira's foot. She stepped back and gasped, bile creeping up her throat. They were walking amidst human remains, and beneath her shoe was a splintered bone. The broken pieces revealed the spongy, yellowed interior. She turned in a slow circle as her breaths became ragged. Several of the tunnel offshoots were piled high with bones, hundreds of incomplete skeletons gleaming in the dim light. She wanted to scream, but the silence around her felt impenetrable. She had no way out, and no way of knowing what fell beyond the darkness.

Alexander placed a hand on her back, and she hated how

calming it was. He guided her away from the long-abandoned remains.

"Just a little further," he soothed.

He kept his arm around her and forced her towards one of the empty tunnels. Piles of bones lay scattered along the walls with other debris, but none fell into their direct path.

Eventually, the bones dwindled down to nothing and Alexander forced her to pick up the pace. The ground became softer, as the stone gradually gave way to loose dirt. Her skirts were covered in a white powder, and she hoped it was limestone and not the dust of the dead.

She forced herself to keep her breaths even. It wouldn't do to panic, not here. She'd had her moment of terror, but if she was going to escape, she needed to keep her wits about her. And she was going to escape. The alternative was worse, especially when she didn't know why Alexander lured her there.

He had managed to elude capture and left no trace behind. He could have very well escaped to another part of France, or any country in Europe, without their noticing. Or stayed in Paris and continued to do the bidding of Circe from the shadows. And yet, not two days after his last confrontation with the authorities, he chose to kidnap her.

It didn't make sense.

They turned again, and the floor ebbed and flowed ahead of them, reflecting the light from the lanterns. Water spread out in the chamber, clear enough that you could see to the bottom. The group paused at the edge, and the dust that they kicked up muddled the surface.

The guard at the front said, "Is this the right way?"

Alexander consulted his map again. "One of the right ways. Seems to have flooded since last week." He folded it up and tucked it back into his pocket. Mira tracked his movements, memorizing which pocket he placed it into. She needed that map. But how could she manage to get it?

"It's still the fastest route," Alexander said.

The guard that had led the way thus far nodded and sloshed across, careful to keep his lantern away from any moisture.

Alexander took Mira's coat from her arms before she could protest. "I'd carry you across, love, but there isn't enough room."

Her breath caught in her throat, and she prayed that he wouldn't find the knife. Alexander moved across the flooded area. Two guards still stood behind her. The water clouded from Alexander's movements. She grimaced and picked up her skirts, keeping them above the surface. The tepid water seeped into her boots and reached to her mid-calf. Alexander handed the coat back when she reached the other side, and she tried to keep the relief she felt from showing on her face as they continued down the corridor.

A pile of debris cropped up on the side of the path and Mira held her breath, hoping it wasn't another body. Instead of bones, she found abandoned mining supplies, tools, and bits of decaying, moldy canvas—evidence of the quarry's long history.

The path inclined, moving closer to the surface. It was getting colder, too. She slipped her coat back on. They came around another corner, and a pinprick of light shone out from ahead of them. Was that another person with a lantern? Or was it light from the outside? As they approached, she slowed her gait. A small hole, no larger than a slot for a key, allowed a glimmer of light to slip through. She stopped and looked through it. Somehow, they were at street level again, and the light of the moon shone down on everything. It was blinding in comparison to the dim lamplight.

She caught the moonlight in her hands. Was this her last look at freedom? A tiny perforation in the immense darkness of the underground labyrinth? If only she could get a message to someone on the outside. If only Byron knew where she was.

The guards behind her forced her forward, and they continued on descending back into the depths of the catacombs. With a few more turns, the tunnel opened up into a much larger chamber. Kerosene lamps hung from the walls, lighting the place more with flickering oranges and yellows. The walls were black with soot from the burning lamps, and the air held an oily smoke that assaulted her senses. A few torch brackets dotted the walls, but most were empty, and none of them were lit. More relics from the times past. It was an odd-shaped room, with columns here and there for structural stability. Crates were stacked against the walls, and several other men moved supplies farther back.

Alexander led the group past them and into another small corridor which led to a large, irregular chamber. Alexander motioned for the group to stop. Unlike the room before, no crates sat along the walls. Instead, bookshelves and insulating curtains lined the space.

A table stood at the center of the room with a map covering it. Mira couldn't tell what it was meant to be a map of from where she stood. Behind the table were two armchairs, facing a fireplace carved into the rock. There had to be a chimney leading to the surface, given the absence of visible smoke from the crackling fire. The chamber extended around a curve in the wall, and Mira couldn't see what was past it.

"Welcome to the heart of Circe, darling." Alexander moved over to the armchairs and gestured for her to take a seat. "Would you like some tea?"

Something about the way he said it made her chest burst with fury. It was nonchalant, as if he hadn't kidnapped her and dragged her against her will through the Empire of the Dead. She stayed where she was, pinning him with a glare. "You needn't pretend to be a gentleman on my account. We both know that you are not."

His expression darkened and his gaze flicked to his men. "Leave us."

Their footsteps echoed down the corridor. Mira crossed her arms, holding her ground. She kept her gaze on him as he moved towards her.

"I am a gentleman, Mira." He reached out and laid a hand on her loose hair. "But you make it so," His fingers caught on a tangle. "Difficult." His golden eyes met hers and flashed with desire.

Mira's anger faded back into fear. And uncertainty. She was entirely in Alexander's power, and she still didn't know why he had brought her there. A shiver ran through her. Why was she testing his patience when she was so fully under his control? She moved her hand into the folds of her coat, feeling for the knife. But before she found it, his fingers stilled in her hair, and he pulled back with a chuckle, moving back to the fireplace.

"You truly think ill of me, don't you?" He grabbed a metal poker from the rack and stoked the flames with it. "I don't know if I'll ever shake your first impression of me."

"It wasn't the first impression that condemned you, Alexander."

"It tainted it though, didn't it? A strange man coming from the mists, offering cryptic warnings from Circe." He leaned the poker up against the wall and stood, moving to a side table to pick up a kettle. "Not exactly the kind of man you'd fall in love with."

Mira stayed silent.

"No, you're much more interested in that detective of yours." He filled the kettle with water from a pitcher and placed it on the chimney crane before pushing it into the fire. "Your letters to each other were quite fascinating."

The blood drained from her face. He'd read their letters! Their private words to each other. She couldn't even remember everything she had written. Did Circe have access to the post? Or did thieves come into their rooms? She didn't know which would be worse. Her jaw tightened. "How dare you?"

"Oh, don't worry." He straightened and brushed his hands off. "I sent them along after I read them. Didn't you wonder why it took so long for his letters to reach you?"

It had taken a little longer, hadn't it? It only took a few days when she wrote to Walker during his studies, and yet it had been almost two weeks for Byron's correspondence to reach London. She hadn't even considered that it could have been tampered with.

"Although, I did keep one of the letters, as I believe you know." She clenched and unclenched her fists.

He continued. "It was rather decent of you to send that lock of your hair. Made it much easier to convince you to come. After all, Selene isn't the most trustworthy person. I figured you would need a little extra encouragement."

Mira swallowed. Alexander knew her too well, and the letter was the perfect bait. She'd been a fool, letting her guard down to walk into Durant's clutches. Why hadn't she questioned it? After all, she knew Durant would stop at nothing to succeed in his plan. But why did he need her? It would be impossible for her to escape from the catacombs on her own. He had her well and truly trapped. But if he was going to kill her, wouldn't he have done that already? She clutched her arms closer to herself, gooseflesh prickling on her skin.

"Why am I here, Alexander?" Her voice sounded hollow to her ears.

"I mentioned earlier that you were a pawn in this game. That was a lie." He strode over to her. "You, my darling, are the queen."

"What?" Her chest tightened.

He leaned closer to her. "Mira Blayse, you may not know it, but you are the key to toppling the Charger once and for all."

December 13, 1888: Morning

MIRA TOOK A STEP BACK. "THE CHARGER?"
"I know you've heard that name before." He placed a gentle hand on her back and pushed her towards the armchairs.

This time she followed, if only to satisfy her curiosity. "They're the leader of the Crossroads. Number Three."

"Exactly," he moved back over to the fire, pulling the kettle out of the flames.

She frowned. "I don't understand. Don't you work for them?"

"I do. Have done for over a year." He grabbed a teapot from the side table and poured the water into it, adding the tea leaves.

"Then why would you want to . . . "

"Stage a coup?" He sat across from her. "Well, I believe that the Guild of the Crossroads has been stifled, as of late. I'd like to bring some new life into it."

"You mean, you wish to take over?"

He settled back in his seat, a small smile tugging at the corner of his lips. "I can think of no one better for the position."

Mira's brow furrowed even more. "But if you work for the Charger—"

Alexander held up a finger. "I work for someone much more important." He slipped a hand into his pocket and pulled out a small coin. He leaned over and handed it to her. She turned it over in her palm. A small image of a three-headed dog was printed on one side. The symbol of Circe was on the opposite.

"The Hound," Mira said, looking up at him. "You work for Number One."

He reached over, and she set the coin back in his hand. "One was not particularly enthused with Three's recent decisions about the Crossroads. He'd been acting out of character, you see." He rolled the coin over his knuckles. "Displaying restraint where cunning and ruthlessness was required. One sent me, essentially, as a scout, to figure out what was really going on. Imagine my surprise when I discovered that the reason for the Charger's change in attitude was you, of all people."

"So, it's true then. The Charger is related to me."

"You mean you don't know?" He laughed. "I suppose he's better at playing the fool than I thought," he muttered as he tucked the coin back into his pocket. "I think this all started when you became Constantine's secretary. Being in such close proximity with everything, I think it spooked the Charger into acting in an irrational manner. He made specific rules when it came to you. I informed the Hound of this and waited for instructions. In the meantime, I needed to play the perfect loyal follower for the Charger. That bit wasn't so hard, especially when he sent me to warn you about interfering with Circe. But you don't listen all that well, do you?"

He moved back to the side table and poured the tea into two cups. "Milk or sugar?"

Mira stayed silent.

"I'm not going to poison you, dear one." He plopped some sugar and milk into the cup and stirred it up. "Not yet, anyway."

He handed it to her. She held it in her lap, but didn't sip at it.

"Suit yourself," he said with a shrug as he took his cup back to his armchair. "Now where was I?"

"The threats."

"Ah. Yes." He took a sip of his tea. "My next assignment was to take care of Sutherland, as you know. And all the while, I was watching the Charger. Unlike the other members of the Trio, he had a problem with cutting ties to his former life. At first glance, one might even think that those ties were advantageous, as it placed him in the optimal position for furthering our interests. I tried to help maintain that connection, of course, by courting you." A sigh escaped him. "But it's obvious now that his ridiculous loyalty to you and your family has become more of a hindrance rather than a help. It's too bad, really. I quite like him."

Mira bit her lip. "Who is he?"

Alexander's lips quirked up in a smile. "You'll find out soon enough. I'd rather not spoil the surprise."

"I wouldn't mind," Mira said, much too fast.

"No, my dear. If you don't know, then I won't tell you."

They sat in silence for a few moments, Alexander sipping his tea, the fire crackling, and Mira keeping a hand over where the knife was in her coat pocket. She didn't know if she'd be able to use it, even if she had to, but knowing it was there comforted her in any case.

Alexander broke the silence. "I assumed you'd have more questions."

"What's the sense of asking questions that won't be answered?"

He tapped the side of his teacup. "What question haven't I answered? Other than the identity of the Charger, of course."

"You never explained why you brought me here," she said, setting the teacup aside.

"Ah, that. Lovely though your company may be, you are here for two purposes. The first," he sucked in a breath through his teeth. "Well, it is rather difficult to explain without your knowing the Charger's identity. But rest assured that your being here is the key to him stepping down. The second is much simpler. I needed bait."

"Bait?"

"For Byron, you see."

Mira froze. Alexander could only want Byron to come for one purpose. Icy tendrils curled up her spine as she voiced it.

"You mean to kill him."

"He is the main obstacle that the Crossroads has encountered as of late. Granted, that is entirely because of your influence, but we can deal with you later. We would have had him out of the way already, but the Charger has this erroneous notion that it is better to have a known adversary rather than eliminate the current one and wait for a new enemy to step into play." He sucked in a breath, tutting. "I still don't understand his reasoning."

"The Shadow tried to kill Byron before. She failed."

"Yes, but she didn't account for your interference. I have." He sipped his tea. "In fact, I'm using you to my advantage. Once Constantine learns that you are missing, he'll be off to that cemetery to find you, and I can't imagine it will take him long to find the secret entrance."

"The cemetery?"

"Yes." He glanced up at her. "You did tell someone where you were going, didn't you?"

Mira froze, a dizziness coming over her. She had been so certain that Byron was in trouble that she hadn't even considered telling anyone. And she'd left before Loretta had returned with the tea.

He set his teacup to the side. "You didn't tell anyone?"

Should she lie? Tell him that Byron was on his way? That would keep him safe for longer, wouldn't it? But before she could figure out what to say, her expression gave her away.

Alexander let out a long breath. "Well. That does change things, doesn't it?" He ran a hand through his hair and paced in front of the fireplace. "He was supposed to come first. If he doesn't know . . ." He whirled on her. "Why on earth didn't you tell anyone?"

"It didn't occur to me. Selene and I left straightaway."

Alexander pinched the bridge of his nose. "Of course you did."

She couldn't help the small smile that formed on her face. Here he had thought that he'd examined every possibility, and yet she still managed to ruin things for him, even if it was by accident. "Is that a problem?"

His posture tightened in anger, before he relaxed, composing himself with a forced smile. "Not at all." He picked up both of their teacups and set them on the side table. "Any other questions?"

Mira paused a moment. "Does the Hound know what you're up to?"

Alexander paused, his gaze narrowing. "I'm sure if the Hound did know, that they would agree with me. Constantine continues to be a nuisance, and the Charger's loyalty is obviously split. Emotional attachments are never a good idea in this line of work."

She stood and moved away towards the wall. "I knew you were a scoundrel and a coward, but I did not think you were a hypocrite."

"What makes you say that?" he said, a darkness in his tone.

"The Charger, whoever he may be, has some sentimentality

that gives him reason to keep me alive and you deride him for it." She turned towards him. "And yet, had I not discovered your true nature, you would have married me without a second thought."

"Of course." He stepped closer. "You would have made the perfect wife. Devoted, loving, beautiful, oblivious."

She clenched her fists, holding her ground. "And what then? Would you have lived in sanctimonious bliss? Pretending to love me, whilst maintaining your distance for Circe?"

"I wouldn't have had to pretend."

His gaze softened. She glared.

"And this is why you are a hypocrite, even if you refuse to see it."

"It would be different. If we were married, you would be under my complete control, and thereby your threat to Circe would be resolved."

"That's where you are wrong. You think that if I didn't know about your true nature and relation to Circe that I would have been mindless in my undying devotion to you. But what you don't realize, Alexander, is that devotion cannot come without trust." She moved towards the fire, staring into the flames. "And how could I trust a man who kept such secrets? I have no doubt that I would have learned the truth in time."

"Well," he said, moving behind her. "I suppose we don't need to worry about that, do we? As it stands, we are practically strangers."

She jolted as his arms came around her waist. The loose bone in her corset pushed into her, and she hissed in pain, trying to pull away. He only held her tighter, his breath on her neck. "Which makes what happens next much easier for me."

"Take your hands off me," she said through clenched teeth.

"There's no one to stop me, is there? Even your precious detective doesn't know where you are."

Mira swallowed, pulse racing. He was right. They were alone.

He could kill her or worse if she didn't get away. In a last-ditch effort, she lifted her heel and brought it down as hard as she could on top of his foot. In an instant, he recoiled with a shout of pain, pushing her away. She twisted to face him, slipping her hand into her pocket. Her fingers brushed the handle of the knife. She pulled it out, grip tight as she pointed it towards him.

He recovered too fast, his mouth pressed into a thin line. His fingers flexed at his sides as a glint came to his eyes.

"Is this the game you'd like to play, dearest?"

"This isn't a game, Alexander."

He laughed. "Now, what?"

Her gaze flickered to the door. "You'll give me the map and let me go."

"Just like that?" He stepped closer. "And if I don't?"

She fought to keep her voice level as she stepped back. "I'll be forced to use this."

"You mean, you'd kill me?" He tutted. "And here I thought you didn't approve of murder."

"I don't. But I won't let you use me for your own gain."

"You don't have a choice in the matter, dearest."

In one swift motion, Alexander lunged forward, twisting the knife out of her grip and throwing her to the ground. The knife skittered off under the armchair.

Mira pushed herself back, struggling to get up because of her skirts. He strode to her in two steps and pulled her to standing. His nails dug into her skin as he dragged her farther into the chamber.

"Let me go!" she struggled with him, trying to break away. She tore at his clothes with her free hand.

They turned a corner and found a long conference table with various papers on it. Alexander pulled her past it and into a smaller corridor. He kept his grip firm as they approached a cell. With his free hand, he pushed the door open, and he threw her inside.

She landed hard on the stone floor, breaths heavy. She pushed herself up, pain shooting through her arm. He leaned over her, face dark as the light of the lamps flickered behind him.

"I had considered the thought of keeping you here whilst I took care of Constantine. But with that little outburst, I think I will take great pleasure in making you watch."

The cell bars swung closed with a clang, and Alexander set a heavy lock on the door. *Click*. His footsteps echoed as he walked away.

She took several shaky breaths and waited for the sound to stop. When she was certain he was gone, she lifted herself up and pulled a folded paper out from where she had fallen. The map. She'd managed to grab it as she had struggled to get away.

Wincing as she stood, she moved closer to the bars and lamplight. She unfolded the map and studied it. The catacombs were larger than she anticipated, and it took her several minutes to even find where she was. Section B, that's what they had called it. There had to be an entrance closer than the one they had taken.

She folded it up and placed it in her pocket, choosing instead to focus on the bars. They were thick and close together. She could get her arm through, but nothing else. The lock was out of reach, and even if it wasn't, she didn't have anything to pick it with. The only other things she had on her person were a box of matches, a letter written in her own hand, and a braided lock of her hair. Completely useless.

So much for getting the map.

But there had to be a way to escape! She needed to warn Byron. Part of her wished that he still didn't remember her. If he didn't, then he'd be safe. There would be no reason for him to come looking for her if he didn't know she existed.

She had no doubt that Byron would find his way to the catacombs. It didn't matter that no one knew where she went.

He already had his suspicions about the quarries. Surely, he'd find his way down to the catacombs. He would find her, and then . . .

Then Alexander would kill him.

Wasn't there anything she could do?

The cell was quite small, and rather damp. A cot rested against one of the walls. She pressed down on the surface of it to see if it would hold her weight. It was covered in the white powder that seemed to be everywhere in the catacombs. Limestone.

She sat down on the cot with a sigh. Somehow no tears came. Was she still in shock?

A yawn escaped her. Her thoughts were muddled. Perhaps sleep was the answer. This all could just be a nightmare. She just needed to wake up.

December 14, 1888:
Morning

*D*RIP. *D*RIP. *D*RIP.

MIRA WINCED AS WATER droplets hit her. Blinking, she sat up. How long had she been asleep? She rubbed at her eyes. It was impossible to tell what time it was. Had she slept through the day? What day was it last?

She'd left the boarding house just after midnight. So it was the thirteenth. Except so much had happened since she had entered the catacombs. Could it be the fourteenth already?

The lamplight continued to flicker against the wall. It was silent aside from a tapping coming from far above her. She looked up and found a chute, about five feet in diameter, stretching upwards. It was dark enough that she couldn't quite tell where it ended. But she could make out bits of metal, bent into rungs, coming out of the wall. A ladder of sorts. It was too far up for her to reach, but looking closer, she found several equidistant holes at her eye level, leading upwards. That meant the ladder used to come all the way down. An access tunnel, perhaps?

Whatever it was, it seemed to be blocked off from above, other than the water dripping down through the cracks. Was it raining?

She ran her fingers over the holes. Could she use them to climb up and reach the ladder? It seemed rather high up. While she could try, she didn't want to risk falling and hurting herself. Not yet, anyway.

Turning towards the front of the cell, she examined the bars. Could there be a fault that she could use to escape? She pulled and pushed on each of them in turn, but they were fixed fast in concrete.

She moved on to the door. Horizontal and vertical slats barred her view. If the padlock wasn't holding it in place, it would swing inwards towards her. She couldn't reach the lock, but the hinges were on her side. The wind whistled through the access tunnel. She frowned. This wasn't meant to be a cell at all. The bars reinforced the passage between the quarries and the exit.

Could the hinges be her key to escaping? Two twisted bits of metal between her and freedom? Crouching, she examined the one at the base of the door. It held five barrels, three on one side, two on the other. A pin in the center kept them in place with a small gap between the head of the pin and the top barrel. She gripped the pin as best she could and pulled. Her fingers slipped off, and the pin stayed in place.

Perhaps if she was able to get something into that little gap, she could wedge it up. A cursory glance over the cell came up with nothing but rocks. She needed something thin and strong. As she bent over to examine the cot, something jabbed her beneath her arm. Her eyes widened, and a small smile broke out as an idea formed. Would it work?

Ensuring that her back was to the door, she undid her bodice and snuck her hand underneath her corset cover. She slid the bone out of the channel and fastened her bodice again. The bone was warm in her hands, quickly cooling in the damp air. But it was thin enough, and strong.

She found a larger rock and set it beneath the door. It wouldn't do for her to get the hinges off and have the door come crashing down on her. Then, she wedged the center of the bone into the gap beneath the pin on the bottom hinge. It stayed in place, leaving either side of the bone open to be handles.

Grabbing either end, she pushed upwards. The metal dug into her palms, and she stopped. She needed something to wrap around the metal, otherwise she wouldn't be able to push hard enough. Alexander's decoy handkerchief was still in the tunnels near Selene, covered with blood. But she did have another.

She pulled her own handkerchief from her pocket and folded it over the two ends of the corset bone. She gripped either side of the bone with her hands, placing her thumbs beneath the center point. Then, with a huff, she pushed upwards as hard as she could.

At first, nothing happened. Then the pin shuddered a bit, lifting upwards by a fraction. A second later, it came out much too fast and clattered to the ground. The metal of the door groaned as it shifted its weight onto the rock beneath it. Mira stood and reached for the next hinge, treating it in a similar fashion. The top one took more effort. She moved the cot over so she could stand on it to get more leverage. After repositioning herself, she was able to pop the second pin free, the metal ringing out as it hit the ground.

She held the door in place until she could get down from the cot and then pulled it open. The lock protested, but she was able to slip outside the bars and set the door down with a soft thump. Adrenaline coursed through her. She was free, but if she wasn't careful, that freedom would be short-lived.

First, she needed to get out of Section B and away from Circe.

Second, she needed to get to the surface.

Third, find Byron.

She could do this.

No voices or shuffling papers caught her ear, which would suggest she was alone in this part of the chamber. She moved to the end of the short corridor, listening at the corner before peeking around it.

The long table still stood at the center of the room, covered with papers and maps. But not a person in sight. She moved close enough to make out the documents. The largest map depicted the entirety of Europe. It had trade routes written on it. It was difficult to tell if they were for usual merchant use or if they were smuggling routes. Perhaps she could find some notes about it somewhere? If Byron was with her, he'd know what to make of everything.

Another document had a list of countries on it.

Allied
Austria-Hungary, Italy, Prussia

Neutral
Russia

Hostile
Prussia—France
Austria-Hungary—Bosnia, The Ottoman Empire

Unknown
United States, United Kingdom

Next to it was a list of the various leaders of countries in Europe and their relationships to each other. A line connected Queen Victoria of England and Empress Victoria of Prussia. Mother and daughter. A small note in the margin read, "*War possible, but unlikely.*" Further down were notes on Boulanger, his revanchists, and their coup on the French government. Alexander had mentioned Circe's plans for war back in October, but she didn't realize it was on such a grand scale.

She forced herself to tear her gaze away from the documents. They wouldn't help her escape. Instead, she moved back to the wall, pausing at the corner again. When she didn't hear anything, she poked her head out.

No one.

Good.

The fire still blazed in the hearth, and their teacups hadn't been cleaned up. Alexander must have left to make arrangements for Byron. The notion made her shiver.

The gleam of the knife caught her eye. It was still underneath the armchair. She grabbed it and put it back in her pocket—a comfortable weight against her side.

She pulled the map out and unfolded it, checking over a possible route. If the map was correct, she could find an exit at the back of the next chamber, but that would mean sneaking through the men that worked with the crates. The next closest exit was on the other side of Section A. Circe would have people there too. Should she risk it? Or go the safer, but darker path, that would take her the long way round, deeper into the quarries?

She could make it if she had a candle or a lamp. But the kerosene lamps on the walls were attached in such a way that she couldn't free them without burning herself. And it didn't seem like they would keep a store of candles or lanterns available for anyone to find. If only she had taken an extra candle at the entrance of the catacombs. Or maybe she could light one of the old torches?

With a deep breath, she entered the corridor that would take her back to the storage chamber. She kept against the wall, taking soft steps to not alert anyone to her presence. Voices echoed down the hall.

"Think it'll work?" the first voice asked in French, gruff and pained, as if he were moving something.

"I'll bet you twenty francs that it won't. There's a reason the Trio is in charge," another voice said, equally pained. A rush of breath followed a loud thump, presumably as the two men dropped the crate.

They were talking about Alexander's plan, weren't they? Part of her didn't want to know. If she just left, it wouldn't matter what his plan was. But her curiosity was too strong. She moved closer, straining to hear.

"But he's right about the Charger. He's getting old and soft."

"I'd be careful what you say, Marc. The Charger is back, just this morning. Think of what'll happen if he hears you."

Footsteps sounded in the hall. Alexander's voice joined the others, still speaking in French. *"We need to move the girl. Three will be inspecting the chambers, and we don't want him to see her until after we've dealt with the detective."*

Mira darted into an alcove, pushing herself deeper into the shadows and prayed that they wouldn't see her.

"Yes, sir. Where are we taking her?"

"Section C. Get to it." Alexander's steps moved off.

The men moved down the corridor towards her, and she held her breath. They passed by, and she stepped out, hurrying into the next chamber. It wouldn't take long for them to realize she was missing, and she needed to take advantage of the time that she had.

When she came to the end of the corridor that led to the room with the crates, she paused, listening. Alexander was towards the back of the chamber talking to one of the workers. That meant she wouldn't be able to take the closest exit. No. She'd need to find another way.

Sneaking along the outer wall, she slipped into the smaller corridor that would lead her back into the main catacomb tunnels. The lamps dwindled as she moved away from Section

B. She stopped at one of the ancient torch brackets and pried the old torch free. It made a terrible wrenching noise as she did so, and her heart raced as she tried to light it with the matches. But it just wouldn't light. The fuel source had either already been used or had dried up.

She heard voices again and abandoned the torch. She'd have to brave section A after all, or risk being caught. Once she reached the end of the tunnel she was in, she found that it branched off to the left and the right. If she remembered, Section A would be to the left, and when she looked down that way, she found a faint glow. She couldn't see the path between her and the glow, but she didn't have time to dither.

She kept a hand on the cold stone wall and started down the corridor. Shadows loomed over her as she pressed into the darkness. She tried not to think of what might be underfoot and hoped that she wouldn't trip on anything.

Shouts echoed from behind her, and she picked up the pace. The hallway seemed to stretch longer and longer, the glow getting further away. The shouts were getting closer. She took her hand off of the wall and sprinted as fast as she could. After a few moments, the glow hit the ground in front of her, and she turned towards the light.

She slowed her pace and ducked into another alcove. From here she didn't quite know where to go. Unfolding the map, she traced her steps from Section B and looked at the surrounding chamber. The map showed a well near the entrance, and sure enough, a well sat against the chamber wall just under another old bracket and torch. She still had quite a way to go to get to the exit, but at least she was going in the right direction.

Keeping close to the wall, she made her way towards the entrance, listening for any signs of movement. She couldn't hear the shouting anymore. Hopefully, they had gone the wrong way. She followed the corridor around and into a rather small chamber. This continued on into a smaller tunnel, snaking its way through. Her heartbeat was in her throat. Only a few more turns and she'd be free.

But wait. That tunnel wasn't on the map, was it? She consulted it again, brows knit together when the map didn't match. Was she going the right way? Was the map false?

She forced herself to take slow, calm, deep breaths. Hyperventilation would get her nowhere, least of all to freedom. Durant had used the map with no problem. So could she.

The yelling started up again, closer still, and so she picked up her skirts and hurried further on, following the path she hoped was right.

However, in the next turn, she stopped. A distinct smell wafted down the tunnel despite the stagnant air. A familiar smell. Citrus. She frowned, her brow furrowing as she tried to dismiss the sensation. Her imagination was playing tricks on her. She'd been amongst the dead for too long.

She continued on her path, farther, deeper, and she broke into a run again. Turning a corner, she collided with someone. They grabbed her arms to steady them both.

She pulled away, ready to run again, but a single word stopped her.

"Mira?"

December 14, 1888: Afternoon

PROFESSOR EDWARD BURKE STOOD IN FRONT OF her, in the flesh. Breathing. He wasn't even pale. He stood there as if he hadn't been shot forty-eight hours before. Gone was the zebra costume and mask. Instead, he wore a new suit, with just a bit of limestone dust on the cuffs of his trousers.

"You're alive," Mira breathed, stepping back.

He schooled his surprise and confusion into something unreadable. "Are you alright? What are you doing here? Did they take you, too?"

Her thoughts were whirling. "Take me? You mean Circe took you?"

If that were true, he would have been locked up for two days, at least. But his face was clean shaven. Circe wouldn't have given him access to a razor, would they?

He nodded. "I've only just escaped. Were you looking for me?"

"We thought you had died!" She turned away, putting a hand to her head. "You'd fallen into the river and," she took a shaky breath. "He shot you."

And yet he seemed to be in perfect health with no evidence of a bandage or sling whatsoever—as if he had never been injured in the first place.

"A graze, if that. Enough to throw me off balance. I swam to the shore, but they knocked me out and brought me down here."

She hugged him tight. He didn't flinch at all the way he would if he were injured. And his cologne was strong. Strong enough she had smelled it further down the tunnel.

She hid her face in his shoulder, maintaining the hug so he wouldn't see the conflicting emotion spreading across her face.

Relief. Horror. Resignation. Disgust.

She wished she could believe him. That she could pretend that she didn't know who he was.

But how could she ignore the evidence? The facts? She mentally reviewed her notes.

1. *They have reason to keep me alive.*

Professor Burke had been her godfather since before she was born. And even if he was part of Circe, their entire relationship wasn't built on a lie, was it? He wouldn't want her dead.

2. *They have access to commerce, shipping, routes of travel, politics, etc.*

His relationship with her uncle would give him access to all sorts of things that other people wouldn't be aware of. He could know about shipping routes in advance and be put in contact with valuable connections. It was the perfect cover.

3. *They travel frequently to France or have contacts there.*

Burke would go on lecture tours at least three times a year. Most often to France, but all over Europe. That gave him plenty of opportunity to make sure the smuggling routes were running as they should.

She could be kept in the dark no longer, because from the moment she saw him in the flickering lamplight, she knew. Professor Burke was the Charger. And he was behind everything that Mira and Byron had fought so hard against.

He pulled away from the hug and searched her face, expecting her to say something. Anything. Did she tell him to drop the act? Yell at him for deceiving her for so long, for making her believe him to be dead? Or did she play along? If she could convince him that she didn't know, there would be a much higher likelihood that she would be able to escape alive. They could arrest him and return to the catacombs to apprehend the rest of the smugglers.

She pushed down the anger and the hurt and the burning questions that lined her tongue.

"I'm so happy you're alive!" The sad thing was, that statement wasn't even a lie. She was happy he was alive, and she felt like a traitor for it.

"How did they get you?" Burke asked, a sharpness to his eye. She'd seen this expression dozens of times before, but she had never realized the danger behind his gaze. He slotted himself into the role of the doting and protective godfather with such ease. But now she could see through the mask. He was always the Charger. Even now as he seemed concerned, he fished for information. Not to protect her, but to determine who had acted without his orders. And she could tell him that without any guilt.

"Selene came to me and told me that Byron was in trouble," Mira said. "But Alexander sent her to lure me here. He intends to use me to stage a coup within Circe."

That was all true enough. And hopefully Burke would

realize the danger of staying, and would agree to get to the surface as soon as possible.

"Use you? How?"

Mira shook her head. "It doesn't matter. I have a map. We can get out of here."

He nodded. "Which way?"

She pulled out the map again. "I think the closest exit is going to be here." She pointed on the map. "Which I think is down that tunnel there."

"Let's go, then." Burke led the way down the tunnel, and she hurried after.

He seemed to know where he was going, which made sense. Somehow, she felt safe in his presence, as if she could trust him, even if she knew that she couldn't. He was the Charger, and that made him dangerous. How long would it take for that realization to fully sink in?

As they approached the next turn, they heard muffled voices. Burke stopped, pressing into the wall, and Mira followed suit. After a few moments of listening, it was clear that it was a search party. There must have been another way into this section of the tunnels. Burke motioned for her to go back the other way.

Once they were in an area of relative safety, she pulled out the map again and consulted it under lamplight.

"Can you see another exit?" Mira asked. The professor likely didn't even need the map to know which way to go, especially in the part occupied by Circe. And he'd know the fastest way to get out.

Burke took the map from her, examining it. He opened his mouth, but another voice sounded.

"It seems that I underestimated you, love," Alexander said, moving around the corner. He had two men with him. All three were armed. "I promise you it won't happen again."

Mira took a step back, ready to run.

A shuffling came from behind her, and Mira glanced over her shoulder. More guards blocked them in. They were trapped. Her breath caught in her chest. Burke's gaze flicked to each of the men in turn, and he straightened.

"You thought that it would be that easy to leave?" Alexander said. His eyes exuded danger, his voice cold, dark, and mirthless.

"I had hoped so," Mira said, standing her ground and stalling for time. There had to be a way out! "I have a previous engagement that I'd hate to be late for."

"I'm afraid that too much is at stake for me to let you go." Alexander snapped and his guards stepped forward. "This way, if you would."

Mira glanced at the professor. His fists were clenched at his sides, his shoulders tense, and rigid. He couldn't say anything, lest his identity as the Charger, or at least a member of Circe would be revealed. If she told him that she knew, would it make it easier for him to get them out of there?

Before she could make a decision, the guards ushered them forward, back into the center of Section A. They went past the tunnels that Mira had come through, and up into the largest chamber in the catacombs that Mira had seen up to that point. Once they were in the center of the room, Alexander stopped and turned towards them, a haughty smile fixed to his lips.

"I see that you already had your reunion. Which really is a shame, seeing as I had such a marvelous plan." He sighed. "But I suppose this will have to do."

He stepped away towards a desk. He opened the drawer and pulled out a gun. It wasn't the revolver he used before. No, this was a flintlock pistol with a single shot.

"And what do you intend to do with that?" Burke asked.

"I'm not going to do anything with it. What happens next is entirely dependent on you."

"Me?" Burke raised an eyebrow. "You'd hand a pistol to one of your hostages?"

Alexander chuckled. "You of all people are not held hostage here, Burke. Or should I say, Charger?"

Mira felt Alexander's gaze on her, gauging her reaction. After all, this was the reveal he had been waiting for. She glanced at the professor. His eyes were set on the ground.

She held her chin high and looked back at Durant. "If you're waiting for me to fall into hysterics, don't bother," she said. "I already know."

"You told her?" Alexander said to Burke, face turning red.

Burke lifted his gaze to her. "No. But she's always been clever." A softness came to his eyes that Mira couldn't stand.

Alexander scoffed and turned to the other men in the room. "Do you see now? This is our beloved leader, weak-willed and disloyal because of what?" He grabbed Mira by the arm and pulled her a distance away, throwing her to the ground. "A little girl that he's grown fond of."

She pushed herself up, palms bleeding from the impact and stinging from the limestone dust. Two of the guards moved towards her as she stood again.

"I'd be very careful what you do next, Durant," Burke said, voice low.

Alexander tapped the flintlock in his hand as he approached the professor. "No, I believe you are the one who needs to be careful. This gun is loaded. It has a single shot. A single choice."

Alexander continued as he pressed the pistol into Professor Burke's hands and stepped away.

"It comes down to this: Do you care more for Miss Blayse or for Circe?"

Mira swallowed, her breathing becoming more erratic. Once she would have known that the professor would have protected her. But that was when she was blind. Now that she knew the truth, she realized that she didn't know him at all.

Grief constricted around her heart, and tears pooled at the corners of her eyes.

Yes, she was terrified that she was about to die. But as she watched her godfather stare at the gun in his hand and cock the hammer back, the grief she felt was not for herself.

Before she had mourned because Circe had taken the professor from them. Today she mourned because he had been lost to Circe long before that night on the bridge.

Burke held the gun up parallel to his chest, pointing it at the ceiling. He took a deep breath and released it, even as Mira fought to breathe. His eyes locked with hers, and he lifted the gun towards her.

Mira closed her eyes.

But the shot never came.

"A clever plan, Durant," Professor Burke said. "Forcing me to show my hand. But it seems that you have overlooked something."

She opened her eyes. The professor uncocked the pistol. Alexander stood a bit away from him. The guards were watching with interest.

"And what is that?" Alexander asked.

"I know you far better than you know *me*." He moved over to the desk and set the pistol on top of it. "You thought that I would attempt to shoot you or one of your men, so you took the precaution of handing me a gun that wasn't loaded."

Alexander protested, but Burke put up a hand.

"It's no use trying to deny it. It was easy enough to tell by sending a breath over the top of the barrel. If a bullet were in place, it would block it, but I could feel the air on my fingers."

He turned back towards the group.

"From this, I know two things. That you are a liar and a coward. But I already knew that. I knew that when Number One assigned you to work under me."

Alexander reached for his inside pocket where his revolver

was. Burke snapped and two of the guards moved to restrain Durant.

"The second thing you assumed about me, was that I was not aware of this little plan of yours. On the contrary. Despite my not being privy to everything happening here in the catacombs, I do have men, men that I trust, who have kept me apprised of every little thing you were doing. And that's another tally in the negative for you. The moment you moved on your plan, they informed me. Which means I had to leave a crucial meeting with the Trio early because of you."

Mira's eyes widened. He had been scheduled to speak at the University in Provence. Was that all a cover for his dealings with Circe? He took so many trips over the years. How many of them were for Circe? How many were lies?

Durant struggled against his captors as they tied his hands behind his back and searched him for weapons. "But the Hound said—"

Professor Burke chuckled. "Oh yes. The Hound told you to infiltrate the Crossroads and figure out why I had suddenly gone soft. I realized that almost immediately. And so, whilst you were busy threatening my goddaughter, I went to speak with Number One. We managed to come to an amicable agreement about the situation."

He turned to the two remaining men of Durant's. "I would suggest that you leave and consider why you chose to go against the Trio. Don't bother leaving the catacombs. We'll find you if you run."

The two men didn't make a sound as they fled from the room. Burke stepped closer to Durant, towering above him. "You thought that by seizing control from me that you would gain the respect of the other members of the Trio." He lowered his chin, considering the man in front of him. "Perhaps that would have been true, if you hadn't already proved that you are incurably incompetent, reckless, and hot-headed."

"But I—"

Burke cut him off. "Shall we go over your more recent examples of ineptitude?" He smiled, all teeth as he turned away from Alexander and walked towards the center of the room. "First. We assigned you to kill Vincent Sutherland and frame Ambassador White. You managed the first part of the task well enough, but chose to overcomplicate the affair. In doing so, you failed to frame the ambassador. And not only that, you involved Mira in your alibi, despite knowing full well her connection to Detective Constantine."

He threw a hand up. "Why, you didn't even dispose of the evidence properly until weeks after the murder! By that point it was too late. Circe had two goals for that murder, and neither were accomplished. We lost two of our good men and had to send you to France to avoid your arrest as well. And even that you failed at, because you told Mira where you were going. Senseless. Absolutely senseless."

He leaned against the desk. "You always had more of a flair for the dramatic. Drama has its place, mind you, but often it is not worth the trouble. That letter you left behind, for instance, was entirely unnecessary. When I discovered that Constantine had tracked down your apartment here in Paris, I sent you a telegram and ensured you would have enough time to escape."

Mira's mouth fell open. "You stalled us so he could clean out his apartment!"

Burke turned to her. "Yes, being your chaperone was incredibly convenient." He chuckled. "You even sent me in first to see Selene. That was a stroke of luck, as it allowed me to show her this." He pulled a cord from under his collar and held it out towards her. A ring was attached to it. She let it fall into her hand and turned it up to see the face. A symbol of a horse's head was engraved on it.

He pulled it away and tucked it back beneath his shirt and readjusted his tie. "She didn't realize that I was the Charger. In fact, she thought I only worked for him, but that was enough to convince her to keep us there as long as possible. And she did a good enough job of talking in circles without telling you anything important."

He whirled back on Alexander. "And yet, with all that, you left two things behind. The tailor's receipt I could forgive as it had fallen between the floorboards. But you chose to write a letter taunting the very people who were after you. And in doing so, you set a target on my back. Very few people knew that Mira was in Paris, and I was one of them. And while the Trio had a plan in place to fake my death eventually, you forced me to expedite it."

He moved over to the desk again and opened the drawer, pulling out a small box and setting it on the top.

"I will say you followed my directions to a fault during the masquerade, but I believe that was only because Circe would have known if you had chosen not to miss. No, you needed witnesses to what you thought was my weakness."

"It is weakness, Burke!" Alexander said, gritting his teeth. "If she and that detective had been taken care of to begin with, we would still have Vaporidge. We would still have Emoria-Sutherland. But no, you insist on holding onto some twisted view of sentimentality."

Mira's breath caught in her throat as Burke pulled out a powder flask and funneled the powder down the barrel of the pistol. She needed to leave, regardless of how many questions she had. She stepped towards the shadows, hoping to go unnoticed as Burke continued.

"And this is why you could never be the Charger. Your view is much too narrow, and aside from that, you don't trust the Order to take care of itself. You think yourself the sole protector of it."

He shook his head with an aborted laugh. "We have existed for centuries, Durant, and we will exist for centuries more. One man cannot make that much of a difference one way or the other. Yes, Constantine may be irksome, but the cases he solves are sixpence compared to the greater magnitude of Circe. And he can be useful. After all, he was the one who inadvertently tipped us off to Ms. Vermielle's operation. What a treat to have someone with such skill operating parallel to us! Pity that someone had to silence her."

"She betrayed us!" Alexander spat.

Burke pulled out a small square of fabric and set a bullet in the center of it.

"Perhaps she did. But she was also in the perfect position to aid us. Because she betrayed us, she was paranoid. Always looking over her shoulder for us. Which meant that when she found us there, she would be much more likely to give us information. But you decided to kill her instead."

He pulled the ramrod out of the slot beneath the pistol's barrel and turned around. "The funny thing is if you had just let her go, your plan would have gone so much smoother. Her guilt about leading Mira here would have been too much, and she'd have gone straight to Byron. You wanted him down here, didn't you?"

Mira caught the briefest smile on the professor's face. The entire room was under his spell, and he seemed to enjoy every second of it. She was almost to the entrance of the tunnels and knew she should run. Everyone was so focused on Alexander she could slip out and into the catacombs without anyone noticing her departure. But seeing that smile made her freeze in place. That was her godfather, the man who introduced her to Dickens and Austen. Who first brought her to an art museum, and who kept her company after she broke her wrist falling from the swing. She shook herself out of her thoughts and crept closer to the exit. But she didn't have the map. The professor did.

Burke picked up the fabric and bullet with his free hand,

placing it over the top of the pistol's barrel and tapped it in with the ramrod.

The blood drained from Alexander's face as Burke stepped to the center of the room again.

"You want to know the truth, Durant?" Burke said. "I might have forgiven you for all of this. You could have had a chance. Even with all of your bumbling efforts, we managed a convincing death. One that wouldn't be questioned. You had already made yourself the villain. And I came out the hero, unscathed and able to work from the shadows."

He considered the pistol, testing the weight of it. "But you couldn't let things be, now, could you? You had to be right. And so, you brought Mira here. She knows everything now, and that makes things much more difficult." He let out a long slow breath.

Mira pressed up against the wall, unable to tear her eyes away. Durant tried once again to break free of the rope. The two remaining men, loyal to the Charger, pushed him to kneel on the ground and stepped aside.

"There's just one other thing that you don't know about me, Durant," Burke said, voice a low, dangerous growl. He brought the pistol down, pointing it at Alexander's chest and cocked the hammer back.

Mira shrieked and turned away as the shot rang out. A slow silence replaced the echo, her heartbeat pounding in her ears. Hesitating, she opened her eyes. The bullet had embedded in the ground behind Durant, leaving scorch marks on the surface. It must have gone straight past his face. He was still kneeling there, face bone white and lungs breathing heavily as he stared up at Professor Burke. But no. That wasn't Professor Burke anymore. Every line of his body spoke of danger. Every word from his mouth was sharp and precise.

The Charger lowered the flintlock, still smoking and stepped forward.

He leaned down, eye to eye with Durant. "I. Don't. Miss."

Straightening again, he blew on the end of the pistol to clear out the smoke and walked away. He gave a small shooing motion to the guards.

"Take him to the cells and guard him."

"What will be done with him?" one of the guards asked.

The Charger placed the flintlock and ammunition box back into the drawer.

"That will be up to the Council."

The guards nodded and dragged a shaking and eerily silent Alexander away.

Number Three turned to her. "Mira."

She lifted her head, swallowing.

He reached a hand towards her. "Come with me."

December 15, 1888: Morning

MIRA FOLLOWED, BRUISED AND NUMB AS THE Charger led the way through the catacombs once more. He didn't consult the map that he had tucked into his pocket. He didn't take pause at each crossroad. Soon, they came to a curtain affixed into the ceiling. He pulled it aside and allowed her to enter first. The room was dim, lit only from the lamps in the hall. He dropped the curtain behind them and moved over to the desk, lighting a decorative kerosene lamp. With the room illuminated, Mira found that the space had a strange familiarity to it. It looked almost exactly like the office that he kept in his rooms in London. The items on the shelves were different, but the size of the room and the orientation of the furniture were the same.

When she made no further movement, he gestured for her to take a seat in the armchair across from the desk. She perched on the edge of the chair, skin tingling. He grabbed a pitcher of water from the side table and filled a glass, setting it in front of her.

"You've been down here for a while. Drink up."

Mira hesitated only a moment before taking the water and sipping at it. If the professor wanted to kill her, he would have done so already. The water was cool running down her throat, and she set the glass aside.

"Thank you."

The professor took the seat behind the desk. "It's the least I could do."

It was strange sitting across from him. A sense of déjà vu tickled her brain. As if they had sat this way before. It felt almost mundane, but perhaps that was the shock wearing off.

"What day is it?"

"The fifteenth. Just before noon, if you were wondering."

So her chronology had been off. She'd lost an entire day. She sat back in her chair.

"I'm sorry that this happened to you," the professor said.

Her gaze narrowed. The liar! "You're only sorry that I know."

He pressed his lips together, a harsh sigh escaping him as he leaned back. "It's more than that. I do care for you, you know. Circe aside, you are my goddaughter."

Mira went silent. He was acting differently to how he was in the other room with Alexander. Not as cold. It was as if he had put on the mask again, but it continued to slip. As if he could convince her to pretend that everything was the same when everything had changed.

He turned back towards her. "I'm sure you have questions."

Her fingernails dug into her palms, making them sting even more. "I'm tired of being lied to."

"Yes, I would imagine you would be."

Once again, that gentle tone caught her off guard. A softness on the surface that made her want to believe that he really cared. But how could he? She looked up at him. "Why did you do it? Why work with Circe?"

He let out a slow breath. "Ah. Well. I didn't intend for my life to go this way. Circe sort of found me."

"But you still chose it. You could have walked away."

His gaze narrowed. "No. I don't think I could."

"Why?" Her voice cracked.

He paused a moment, as if to choose his words. "It didn't start with Circe. No. It started back at Cambridge." He rubbed the back of his neck. "I may have cheated on the Latin Previous Examination just before my final year."

She furrowed her brow. "Cheated?"

"A dreadful thing, I know, but my parents expected me to graduate, and I wasn't as good at Latin then as I am now. The college didn't realize until just before graduation. They brought me before the staff and expelled me from the college. I just begged them not to make it public. They agreed, but I didn't receive my diploma."

"Did my father know?"

"Heavens, no. He thought I graduated early. Instead of returning to my parents, I decided to try the Indian Civil Service. But my lack of a degree made it impossible to apply. So, I forged my documents. Did a fairly good job, too. At least well enough to get to India and start working. Met your uncle there. During that first year, however, the forgery was found, and I was brought in front of Sir Giles Elliot, one of the commissioners in Madras."

Elliot. She knew that name. Where had she heard it before? "Loretta's father? The previous Charger?"

"Why, yes." He chuckled, and a shiver ran down her spine. "However did you come to that?"

"Loretta has the Circe symbol on a necklace. She said that her father gave it to her when she was married. And told us about her and Cyrus. And Emilie."

He nodded. "At least something good has come out of this trip. I had hoped that they would make up. I always felt beastly that it was my fault they were separated."

"Your fault?" Mira frowned. "Wasn't it the ring that gave them away?"

"Is that what they thought?" He let out a breath of relief. "Thank goodness. No. Her father wanted me to marry Loretta. Keep the business in the family and everything. But I couldn't bring myself to do it. Not when she and Cyrus were so in love. So, I helped them elope. When Sir Giles brought up the topic of marriage again, I told him. I thought maybe he'd accept Cyrus and let them move to England."

He grimaced. "I was wrong. After it was all said and done, Giles took me aside and told me that such attachments would be my downfall. I suppose, in some ways, he was right."

"And yet you still saved me." That was what she didn't understand. Was his connection to her purely based on his friendship with Cyrus? It didn't make sense.

"I wish I could say that I have." He turned away, pulling the map from his pocket. Her blood froze. He tucked it into a drawer and brought his gaze to meet hers again. "Unfortunately, you still know too much. And I doubt that if I extolled the virtues of Circe that it would change your mind about the organization."

"You mean you actually believe that what you are doing is right?" she said, the numbness in her stomach dispersing. A dark anger coursed in its place.

"I believe it, because I can see the good on the horizon. Yes, what we are doing at the present time is terrible, but in the end it will all be worth it. We have to tear the existing structures down in order to rebuild it anew. There will be no more countries or boundaries. The world will be able to live in peace and prosperity because of us."

"How can you expect to build a world of peace when your

tactics are murder and destruction?" She kept her voice level. "I saw your plans. You intend to cause a global conflict."

"One that will end all wars, my dear. It is an unfortunate necessity."

"People will die!" she yelled.

"New ones will be born." He matched her volume.

She fell silent looking away. This was the man who had taught her to ride a horse when they went on holiday in the country. The man who had built sand castles with them on the beach. Her godfather, who had comforted her after her parents had died. And he didn't seem to care for the sanctity of human life at all. In fact—

A coldness settled in her heart. Her parents. She met his gaze, horror flooding through her.

"Is that what you thought about my parents?"

He flinched. "What?"

"You were part of Circe when they died. You knew, didn't you?"

He grew still. Slowly, voice barely above a whisper, he said. "That is the one thing I regret most in this life. I must assure you of that."

"What happened?" she asked, but with no question in her tone. Her words formed an order, a compulsion to know the truth after eighteen years of lies.

Burke fell silent for a moment, a sorrow in his eyes. "Do you really want me to tell you?"

"I have to know."

"Very well. But I need to explain it from the beginning."

Mira sat back in her seat, trembling. "I'm listening."

"Circe had lost valuable shipping routes when the East India Trading Company dissolved into the government. The Crossroads had been searching for a new way to smuggle goods. While Cyrus and I were down in India, I received a letter from your father. He'd been working under Henri Giffard on those new man-powered balloons. He mentioned that he was coming to India to source rubber for them. He'd arranged to come to Madras, because he knew I would be there and wanted to catch up on old times. I introduced him to Cyrus while we were there. And when we were all back in London, we got together, along with your mother. They fell in love and were married, as you know.

"Meanwhile, Tavian continued to work on the dirigibles after his apprenticeship with Giffard. He made an agreement with Vaporidge and started a project to make a dirigible that could cross the English Channel with passengers and cargo. He succeeded, and I had an idea. If I could find a way to get a secret hatch into one of his balloons, the Crossroads would have a new way of smuggling. An ingenious one. A method that would put me in line to become the Charger. And so, I set to work changing his plans and arranging for workers from Circe to build the balloon."

Mira felt herself slumping in her seat, her vision blurring. She knew what happened next. Her thoughts drifted back to what the Shadow had told her all those months ago. *Pennington's story is your father's.* "He found out," she said, voice hollow.

"Exactly. He came to me one night. Showed me the changed plans. He was distraught. He didn't know who had tampered with them, but he was concerned that someone would try to use his dirigible to smuggle goods across the channel. He asked me what he should do. I told him to wait while I looked into things and warned him not to go to the authorities. The dirigible was almost finished, at any rate. But he kept poking where he shouldn't. I thought maybe I could convince him to work for us. So, I arranged for him to be taken. Unfortunately, your mother was taken, too."

A small flame of hope blossomed in her chest. "You mean they weren't killed outright?" Could they still be alive? Working for Circe? She cursed herself for hoping for such an outcome. But if they were alive . . .

Burke let out a heavy sigh. "After I realized that the scum from Cypress had kidnapped your mother as well, I tried to play it off as if I'd come to rescue them. But your father saw right through me. And so I was forced to tell them about Circe. I offered for him to work for us. He refused. But I decided he just needed some time. I left them there to think about it. But regardless of their choice, it was impossible to let them go. Circe arranged for the explosion. We had a few," he paused a grimace coming to his face. "Bodies on hand that we could use to make people believe that your parents had died. And as I identified the bodies, no one questioned their validity. It was easy."

"Easy?" Tears were flowing down Mira's cheeks, and she didn't know when they started. "You took our parents from us. Let Cyrus grieve his sister and," Her breath stuttered. "Are they still alive?"

He paused and gave a small shake of his head. "Rose grew ill within the first month or so. Her greatest concern was for you and Walker. I'd bring her updates each time I visited, and I promised that I wouldn't let anything happen to you. She died just about three months after the accident. And your father would have been such a valuable asset, but he refused to work for us. Particularly after the death of your mother. After a year or so, Number One decided that keeping him alive came at too much of a cost. Especially with all of his attempts at escape. But I assure you, his death was quite painless. And I ensured that they were buried together."

Her mouth dried up as she sobbed. "How could you?"

His expression hardened. "If your father had heeded my warnings, your parents would still be alive today. If he had chosen to work for us to better the world, he would be standing here with us. I had no choice but to act as I did. And until you started working with Constantine, I'd managed to fulfill the promise I made to your mother to look after you and Walker."

Mira's muscles quivered, tears fading away. "If he heeded your warnings? You make it sound as if it wasn't your fault at all."

"It was an unfortunate set of circumstances."

"That didn't need to happen!" She stood, pacing away. "None of it was necessary!" She whirled back on him. "You murdered my parents and turned right around to comfort us as if you hadn't. We trusted you, and all the while, you were the reason that our family was broken!" She choked on a sob. "I don't even know where they are buried."

"They had their chance and chose their fate. You can't blame me for the outcome!" He stood and moved around the desk.

She threw a hand out and stepped towards him. "You sound just like Alexander Durant. What was it that you called him? Reckless? Hot-headed? You had no reason to kill my parents. To even kidnap them. It was a last-ditch effort to save your own skin! And you aren't even man enough to accept the blame."

The slap came before she could blink, her cheek stinging from the impact.

"Don't you dare lecture me on guilt, Mira." His eyes were cold and sharp. "That's the only thing that's kept you alive these past few months."

She squared her shoulders, her pulse racing. "Is it? Or is it the fact that being my godfather was convenient? You said it yourself. Your proximity to me allowed you to spy on your enemy. I was useful. Your friendship with Cyrus allowed you access to the shipping routes. He was useful. My father, even, was useful until he wasn't. And then you betrayed him. If you felt actual guilt from your actions, you would have left Circe from the weight of it. Instead, you rose to the top and you justify every evil action that you do."

"I would tread carefully, girl. You forget just who you are dealing with."

"No, I think for the first time I know exactly who is in front of me. A manipulative, self-serving, ba—"

"That's enough!" The Charger growled. He grabbed her by the arm and yanked her through the curtain. Stumbling along after him, she tried to pull out of his grip. He kept a steady gait as he forced her through the tunnels. They came to a row of alcoves set with heavy iron bars. A guard stood to the side, eyes widening when he saw them.

"Open that cell." Burke pointed, and the guard hurried over, pulling his keyring from his coat pocket. He unlocked the door and opened it.

Burke threw her inside, and the door closed behind her with a clang.

"It seems history repeats itself," he seethed, turning away. "First your father, and now you."

"So, you'll kill me too? And here I thought you were a man of your word."

He kept walking. "You may soon wish that I wasn't."

As soon as he turned around the corner, Mira sank to the floor, pulled her knees up to her chest and let herself mourn. Her parents were dead. Her godfather was their murderer. And she was left with the luxury of counting down the minutes until he would kill her, too.

December 15, 1888:
Afternoon

LAUGHTER SOUNDED FROM THE CELL NEXT TO her. Mira couldn't see who was in it—she hadn't seen into the cell when she was brought in—but her stomach dropped as she realized who it was. She slowly raised her head to rest on the stone wall between them.

"So, he's gotten rid of his lap dog at last, has he?" Alexander said. "At least that part of my plan worked."

"Stop talking," the guard said, pulling a flask from his pocket and taking a long gulp.

"Oh, come on, Duncan," Alexander said. "You have to admit there is humor in it. And there's nothing wrong with talking. Weren't you getting tired of the silence?"

Duncan grunted, but went quiet.

"Did you see how red Burke was?" Alexander said. "I don't think I've ever seen the man lose himself like that. What did you say to him?"

"It's none of your business," Mira ground out.

"Yes, but there isn't much else to keep one occupied down here." A loud yawn sounded from where he was at. "Do you think your detective is on his way yet?"

"Why? Would you prefer to be executed by the government?"

Alexander went silent. He was right, though. Byron might be on his way. But he probably wasn't. Even if he did figure out that she was down in the catacombs, how would he possibly find her with so many tunnels? Although Alexander's plan had been built on Byron's arrival, hadn't it?

Hesitating, she said, "Did you end up sending someone to leave clues for him?"

"No. While we were discussing it, I found out that Burke was back early. And then you escaped." A pause. "How did you do that, anyway?"

"Wouldn't you like to know?"

"Don't be making any plans for escape now," Duncan said, voice gruff.

"Heaven forbid it!" Alexander said.

Mira stood and examined the cell. Unlike her previous cell, the hinges sat on the outside of the door. The ceiling stopped a few feet above her head, with no access tunnel or ladder that she could try to climb to. And, of course, this time a man stood guard outside, which meant that though she could reach the lock, she wouldn't be able to pick it without notice. Instead of being thrown together as an afterthought, this cell had been designed to hold people from the beginning.

She couldn't plan on Byron. But there didn't seem to be any way out. She placed her hands in her pockets. She found the matches, the handkerchief, her letter, and the lock of her hair. Her eyes widened as her fingers found the knife handle. She had forgotten that she even had it.

But what use was it to her when she was stuck behind bars?

"Excuse me, Duncan, but do you have a light?" Alexander asked.

Mira groaned. "You can't be serious." The tunnels were already teeming with smoke from the kerosene, and he wanted to add to it?

The guard shuffled over, disappearing from Mira's line of sight. "I suppose there ain't a rule against it."

"Much obliged."

A match struck the edge of something, fizzling into the air. Then the scraping of boots on stone. A cry that cut out with a gurgle before the body fell limp in front of Mira's cell.

She gasped. "You killed him."

"Still holding onto those morals, are you? He's just unconscious."

Sure enough, the guard's chest rose and fell in time with his subtle breaths. Alexander's arm came into view as he snaked it through the bars on his side. When he couldn't reach the coat pocket, he attempted to pull the man closer to him but couldn't move him more than a few inches.

He cursed and went silent. A moment later he said, "Can you reach those keys, darling?"

"I'll try if you stop calling me by those ridiculous pet names." Mira crouched down and slipped her hand through the bars. With a bit of twisting, she could squeeze her arm through the gap up to her elbow. Duncan's pocket was within reach, and with a stretch of her fingers, the keyring fell into her hand. She brought it up to the lock and tried each key until she found the right one for the cell. Unfortunately, Duncan was in the way of the door. With a silent apology she pushed the door into him enough for her to get through, and stepped over his body.

"Good. Now unlock mine," Alexander said.

She turned towards him and took a proper look at him. His entire demeanor was disheveled and wild as he gripped the bars. He seemed more like a wild animal than a gentleman, especially in the flickering light.

"And why should I?" Mira asked, crossing her arms.

"We don't have time to argue," he said. "Duncan will come to any time now."

"Good for him. Then you can explain to him why I've gone."

"Please don't leave me here," he said, voice desperate. "I know I've lost any respect you had for me, but you can't leave me here."

She clenched her fists. "Perhaps you should have considered the consequences before you kidnapped me."

His demeanor shifted. "If you had told someone where you were going, instead of wandering off like a fool, then this wouldn't be a problem. Your detective would have saved us both."

She scoffed. "You're trying to blame me for this? If that plan had worked, Byron would be dead." She stepped closer, staring him down. "No, Alexander. I think you deserve everything that Circe will do to you."

She turned away. Now faced with freedom, she wasn't quite sure where to go. The map was in the Charger's office, and she couldn't escape without it. But which way was it? Forward? Left? Right? Dash it all, why did these catacombs have to be a labyrinth?

"Something wrong?" Alexander asked, a smarmy lilt to his voice.

"No," she said, short and clipped. The lamplight flickered, and the shadows danced.

"You don't know the way out. Do you?"

She knew he was smirking, even with her back to him. A headache pulsed at her eyes.

"They must have taken that map you stole from me," he continued. "Clever thing you did there, by the way. Didn't even realize it was missing. Of course, at that point I didn't need it, as I know my way around these parts of the tunnels."

He was trying to convince her to get him out. And she hated that it was working. Alexander couldn't be trusted, but she knew that, for once, he wasn't lying. With a grimace she turned towards him.

"You know the closest way out?"

He laughed. "You think I strangled a man without an escape route in mind?"

Her gaze narrowed, and she pulled the knife from her pocket, moving over to the bars, but keeping enough distance that he couldn't reach her.

"You listen now, and you listen well, Durant. Against my better judgment, I'm going to let you out, and you are going to lead me to that exit. If you try anything, I will use this."

His eyes widened, and he nodded.

She pulled the keys out with her free hand and tried each of them on the lock. *Click.* Alexander pushed the door open and a feral grin spread across his features.

"You are so *trusting*, Mira. It's going to get you killed one day."

He lunged for her, grabbing the wrist that held the knife in one hand, and her opposite shoulder with the other. As she tried to pull away, his grip tightened. So, she switched tactics. She pushed with all her strength, and the knife cut a jagged line across his cheek. His grip lessened from the unexpected pain, and she pulled away, bringing her knee up hard into his groin. He pushed her to the floor with a groan as he keeled over in pain.

The knife skittered off as Mira found her bearings. She had fallen next to Duncan, who had yet to stir. Now on the other side of him, she caught sight of a revolver in a holster at his waist. She grabbed it and managed to stand, pointing it at a still recovering Alexander. Her heart raced as she caught her breath.

It took another minute or so before Alexander uncurled himself and looked up at her.

"Get up," she said.

He did so, slow and steady as he used the bars for support. "You know how to use that?"

She cocked the hammer back. "Do you really want to test me right now?"

He touched a hand to the cut on his face and pulled it away with a hiss. After examining the blood on his fingers, his gaze flicked to her. "Not particularly."

"Good. Now, which way to the exit?"

He glared up at her with a heavy silence, but after a moment he deflated and let out a sigh. "The only exit I'm aware of is at the center of Circe's base. The rest, I would need a map for."

"You said you had a plan." Her grip tightened on the gun, but she kept her finger off the trigger.

"That plan was made when I thought you still had a map."

"You were going to let me out?"

He smirked. "I wouldn't have left you here, love."

She was about to retort, but Duncan moaned and both of them jolted. Mira caught Alexander's eyes. They didn't have time for banter.

"The Charger took the map," she said. "It's in his desk."

Alexander said, "I know the way to his office. Let's take care of our friend here first."

He picked up Duncan and dragged him into the cell. Before leaving him, Alexander rooted through the guard's jacket pocket.

"What are you doing?" Mira tightened her hold on the revolver.

"Looking for this." Alexander pulled the flask from Duncan's pocket and held it up for her to see. He stepped out of the cell and took a swig from it.

He coughed. "Whisky. Strong stuff, too."

"You disgust me," she said, lip curling.

He shrugged and closed the door behind him, stowing the flask in his own jacket pocket. "It's been a long day for both of us."

Mira gestured for him to move away from the door, and he obliged while she locked it and put the keys in her pocket. With the guard safely tucked away, she turned back to Alexander.

"Which way?"

He turned down the hallway to the right. "This way, if I'm not mistaken."

With one last glance at the unfortunate Duncan, Mira hurried after.

They kept close to the wall as Alexander led them back towards the center of Section A. After a few minutes, they heard footsteps and ducked into an alcove. Mira kept the gun trained on Alexander. She wouldn't let her guard drop. Not again.

When the footsteps were gone, they continued down the path. Soon enough, Mira recognized the area. Burke's office was just around the corner, and raised voices came from inside. There was an alcove closer to it, and Mira followed Alexander into it, hiding away.

"No, Moreau! We need something that can't be traced." That was Professor Burke. "Arsenic isn't going to cut it this time."

Mira's gut churned. They were planning a murder.

"Ah, you need one of my more special brews, oui?" the man, Moreau, sounded more than pleased. A clicking noise, like the opening of a briefcase, accompanied the clinking of glass bottles.

"This is one of my more favorite concoctions. Just a little on the skin, in the tea, or even breathed will kill a person. And it has no odor or taste if you let it dissolve in liquid."

"And what if our man happens to touch it?" the professor asked.

Moreau made a non-committal noise. "Can he not wear gloves?"

"Isn't there anything else?"

"Well, there is one method. Although, I haven't tested it thoroughly."

"What is it?"

"When I was in Japan, I witnessed a death. Complete paralysis occurred within minutes. My guide said it was because of the fish the victim had eaten. A common occurrence when not prepared correctly. I brought some dried specimens back with me to attempt to isolate the toxin. But there is no guarantee."

Silence for a moment. "And if you had test subjects?"

Mira locked eyes with Alexander. He wasn't referring to them, was he? She swallowed back her fear. Echoing shouts and footsteps came from further down the tunnels. They must have discovered that they had escaped. She strained to listen for the response.

"That would change things," Moreau said.

"I'll need to discuss this with the Trio, but I believe that could be arranged."

The yelling grew louder, closer. A rush of air swept past Mira and Alexander as a man ran down the tunnel and ripped down the curtain as he entered the office.

"*Police! Police!*" he shouted in French. "*We've been discovered!*"

Mira's heart leapt. Byron. It had to be Byron.

"*Which section?*" Burke asked as the men left the office and hurried down the hall.

"*Section B!*"

Once the men had moved past their hiding place, Alexander entered the office.

"Sounds like your cavalry has arrived. Which drawer is the map in?"

Mira pointed. "That one, there."

Alexander opened the drawer and took out the map. He spread it across the desk.

"Our closest exit would be in Section B if we want to brave the fighting. The alternative would be in the darkened tunnels here."

"Byron will be in Section B." And it sounded as if he brought help. If she could just keep Durant in her sights, they could arrest him and finally go home.

Alexander looked up at her with surprise. "You're certain about that?"

"I know it." She gestured to the door with the revolver. "After you."

He paused a moment. "You know, we could always part ways here. I helped you get out. Doesn't that mean anything to you?"

Her jaw tightened. "Move."

He raised his hands above his head and moved towards the door. "I just thought I'd ask."

She knew that Alexander was leading them in the right direction because the sounds of fighting got louder. Soon, they were back at the entrance of Section A, standing by the well. The corridor beyond wasn't lit. Mira didn't like the idea of walking behind him in the dark. Anything could happen. But before she could voice her concern, Alexander pulled the torch from the old bracket above the well.

"It won't light," Mira said. "I've already tried."

"Humor me, won't you? Do you still have my handkerchief?"

Serena's jaw tightened. "I believe it's still dripping with Selene's blood somewhere in the catacombs."

"Ah, never mind." He stooped and picked up a bit of old canvas, wrapping it around the end of the torch. "This should do it."

He tucked the torch under his arm and pulled the flask from

his inside pocket. Opening it, he poured some of the contents onto the canvas, soaking it.

"I'll have to light it further back." Alexander took one step closer to her, pausing as if he were afraid she would shoot him. What he didn't realize was that she had uncocked the hammer long before with no intention of using it. Unless absolutely necessary, of course.

"I have matches." She slipped her free hand into her pocket and passed the box over.

"Resourceful as ever, I see."

"Just light the torch."

He did so, and led the way down the corridor towards Section B. It was a much shorter walk with a torch, and soon they were turning the corner into the lighted area again.

"Put it out," she ordered.

"I retract what I said about you being too trusting." He dragged the torch against the dirt as they continued forward.

As they approached the storage area, the sounds of fighting grew louder, and footsteps echoed down the tunnel. Smoke from gunfire clung to the humid air.

Mira ducked into an alcove as a man emerged from the smoke. Alexander was not as lucky. She winced as a fist collided with Durant's face, sending him sprawling to the ground. Her heart leapt as she recognized the man as Byron. A slow smile spread over her face, and she wobbled on her feet.

"What have you done with her?" Byron said, voice harsh as he stood over the murderer, pointing his own revolver at him.

Alexander moaned in pain as he pushed himself up, nose bleeding. "Ask her yourself."

But Byron didn't have time to ask her anything, as she threw her arms around him and kissed his cheek.

"You came." She relaxed for the first time in what seemed like days.

"I was afraid I was too late." His hand pressed into the small of her back, holding her closer.

"Never." She pulled her head back so she could see his wonderful blue eyes. A cut bled just below his hairline. "Are you alright?"

"Better knowing you're alive. What happened? When I called at the boarding house, they said—"

"Just a moment," Mira interrupted. She twisted to raise her hand, pointing her revolver at a retreating Durant. "Don't take another step, unless it's back towards us."

Alexander raised his hands again, his own blood on them for once, and moved back towards them. "I was only giving the two of you some privacy."

"Come on." Byron moved his free hand to take hers and guided her so they were both behind Durant. "Let's see if the police have any more handcuffs."

UNFORTUNATELY, HANDCUFFS WERE IN SHORT SUPPLY, AS the police had managed to apprehend almost a dozen men. They were all positioned on the floor in various states of duress. Mira noted that the Charger was not amongst them.

Fred ran up to them, wincing as his grin tugged on his split lip. "You found her!"

"She found me. Didn't need rescuing after all." Byron smiled down at her. "But we do need to do something about him."

"Oh, don't worry about me," Alexander drawled. "I'd be happy most anywhere."

"I'll take care of him." Fred grabbed him by the arms and dragged him away towards the others. "I'm sure there's some rope around here somewhere."

Byron turned to Mira. "Ready to see the sun again?"

Relief flooded through her. She wanted nothing more than

to see the sun. But a part of her paused. "There's something I need to show you first."

She led the way down the corridor just off of the storage room and brought him to the little sitting area. The fire continued to rage in the hearth, and the teacups still sat on the side table, the tea long forgotten and cold. Mira pulled Byron into the next chamber where the long conference table was.

"I know that you already know about their plans for war, but perhaps these can help us stop it."

Byron let go of her to look at the documents. Mira stepped to the side, running a hand over her face. Had it always been so hot down there? Byron's eyes widened as he picked each piece of evidence up. "This could certainly help. I'm sure they have more documentation somewhere."

Mira nodded. The professor probably had more papers in his office. She froze.

"Were those the only men that were arrested?"

Byron frowned. "Yes. Why?"

"The professor. If he's not there, then . . ."

Byron's expression darkened. "He was here then? You know who he is?"

Mira's eyes widened. "You know?"

"I've had my suspicions for a while now."

She let out a shaky breath that ended with a cough. The smoke from the kerosene was getting to her. "We can talk about that later. But if he wasn't caught, that means he's in the tunnels somewhere. We need to get back to his office before he does!"

A harsh light came from the sitting room as Mira turned towards it, heat on her face. Her steps faltered as she realized that the room was on fire, spreading across the curtains that lined the walls.

Alexander Durant stood amidst the flames, Selene's knife in one hand and a lit torch in the other. His eyes were manic, with a too-wide smile on his face. Was that blood staining the blade, or just the flickering of the light? Her stomach dropped. No! How had he escaped? He must have grabbed the knife before they left the cells. Was anyone hurt? How could she have been so stupid?

Alexander gave a crazed laugh. "It seems my plan has worked after all! The detective and secretary are together in death, Circe will come to its knees before me, and—"

His monologue was cut short as Byron raised his pistol and shot. The bullet hit Alexander in the shoulder, and he wrenched back with a moan of pain. The motion had the torch flying from his hand, landing on the table. Mira jumped back from the flames as Byron readied the gun for another shot. Durant placed a hand over the wound and stumbled back into the smoke, disappearing without another word.

Byron tried to run after him, and she followed. They caught sight of Durant running across the sitting room towards the exit tunnel. But he was unable to go further as the men from Scotland Yard came down, flanked him, and disarmed him.

"Thank goodness," Byron mumbled as he uncocked his pistol.

"Are you alright?" Constable Simons called over the roaring blaze.

"We're fine!" Byron called. "Don't let Durant out of your sight."

Mira wasn't sure if Alexander could go far, in any case. His shoulder was dark with blood, his face pale and gaunt. He finally accepted defeat as the room burned. Her breath of relief at his capture turned into a cough from the smoke.

"We won't. Wensley had him but we didn't know he was armed," Hayworth called. Mira's chest tightened before Hayworth amended, "Don't worry. Fred's had worse!"

"Do you think you can get across?" Simons asked, gesturing to the fire.

"We'll try." Byron placed his arm around her to lead her

across. But as they moved to join the others, a curtain rod snapped and fell into the center of the room, and soon they couldn't see anything through the thick smoke as the heavy flames consumed everything in their path. It would be impossible for them to cross safely.

Byron pulled her back the way they came, coughing from the smoke. The flames had engulfed the entire table by that point, the documents shriveling away to nothing. Mira watched in shock. They had been so close. They could have brought down Circe, escaped this prison, made it to the surface, but now everything was going up in smoke.

"I'm so sorry," she looked up at Byron, eyes stinging.

"Don't apologize." He crouched, pulling her with him so that they were below the smoke. "We'll make it out. You'll see."

She shook her head. "There isn't another way out down here. I tried before and," She stopped. That was strange. The flames were licking closer, but the smoke was being pulled away as if by an updraft. Hope stuttered in Mira's chest, and she took Byron's hand, leading him back towards her original cell. The door was still off its hinges. She stopped beneath the access tunnel and let go of Byron's hand. The smoke was thick above them, but little beams of light clung to it as it made its way through the tiny cracks in the blockage above.

"If we can reach the rungs of that ladder, we can get out," she pointed.

Byron nodded. "I can boost you up."

"But what about you?"

He cupped her face. "I can boost you up."

Her eyes welled with tears again. "No. I won't leave without you."

"And I'm not letting you die!" His voice cracked. "I've thought that I'd lost you the last few days, don't let me mourn you again."

The flames were getting closer behind them. Mira looked around the cell. The last time she was there she had given up on using the access tunnel to escape. Of course, last time, she didn't have the door to help her.

"Will you hold the door so it won't topple over?" she asked Byron. He nodded and held on tight.

She pulled the keyring from her pocket and prayed that one of the keys would work on the padlock. The skeleton key worked, and the door came off from the other side. Together, they moved the door underneath the rungs of the ladder. They pushed the cot into it to hold it in place.

"You need to go up first," Mira said.

"But—"

Mira interrupted. "I won't have the strength to break through the barrier. You're our best chance."

With reluctance, he nodded, but pulled a handkerchief out of his pocket. "As long as you wear this to help with the smoke."

She pulled her own handkerchief from her pocket. "Only if you'll wear mine."

He gave half a laugh and took it from her hand.

A few moments later, they both had makeshift masks around their mouths and noses. Byron gave her hand a squeeze and climbed up the horizontal bars on the door, easily taking hold of the first rung of the ladder. Once he was up halfway, Mira placed her foot onto the bottom bar of the door. It held for her, too, although it was shakier than Byron made it seem. Once she reached the top of the door, she found that her arms were just inches too short to reach the ladder. Byron had already made it to the top of the ladder and was working on dislodging the wood that blocked off the tunnel.

Summoning all the courage that she had, she jumped and caught the first rung. She took a few steadying breaths and let go with one hand to grab onto the next bar, arms screaming from the tension. The cuts on her hands stung, but she pushed on.

Sunlight flooded over her, but the air was cold and wonderful. If she had any tears left to cry, they would be flowing down her cheeks. Instead, she pulled herself up to the next rung, and then the next, using the holes in the wall as footholds until she could get her feet onto the ladder. Soon, Byron was reaching for her, pulling her into his arms above the surface.

She pulled the handkerchief away from her mouth, shaking all over. Byron hushed her, running a hand through her tangled hair.

"We're alright," he said. "We're safe."

She burrowed further into his shoulder. They were alright, and safe, and together. She was free of that wretched place beneath the ground, the hellish landscape of the dead. They were alive and swathed in the sublime light of day. She brought her face up, a slow smile forming on her lips.

He caught those lips with his, and she sunk deeper into his arms, her legs failing her. But he held her close, and that was all that mattered as she kissed him back and the world faded away.

December 20, 1888

"*Y*OU NEVER DID TELL ME HOW YOU found me," Mira said. She and Byron were once again in the sitting room at the Lavigne boarding house. Ever since she had returned, her uncle had refused to let her leave. It suited Mira just fine. Her entire body was stiff and sore. She only wished that everyone would stop hovering so much. Klasha had forced several gallons of soup into her. Loretta kept flitting in and out, asking if she needed anything. Her uncle had given up the pretense of excuses and just stayed with her everywhere she went. Even Emilie, who had only come for dinner on Sunday, wouldn't leave her alone for her entire visit.

Mira didn't want to be alone. But she didn't want them. She wanted Byron.

And he couldn't be there all the time, even as he wished to be. He was back and forth between the police station, Rue Geoffroy, and the boarding house. The first, to debrief and ensure that everything worked out well with the law enforcement. The second, to make sure that Fred was recovering from the minor stab wound that Alexander had left him. And the third, to check on her. Durant and the rest of the smugglers that hadn't died from the smoke inhalation were being held at Le Santé prison before their trials. The smugglers would be dealt with together, but Durant's would be a special case. Murder and arson.

His trial wouldn't be held until after Christmas, and because he was arrested for crimes committed in Paris, they couldn't move him to London. But that was for the best. Less chance for escape that way.

Loretta graciously offered to let Mira's family and the men from Scotland Yard spend the holidays at the boarding house.

With all the excitement and hovering, it had been days since Mira and Byron had been alone together. This particular visit was only possible because Klasha had volunteered to chaperone while Cyrus and Loretta had gone Christmas shopping. Once they were out the door, the Russian woman had promptly disappeared to some other place in the house.

Byron looked up from where he was stoking the fire. "I didn't?"

"No. I told you my side of things, but you never told me yours."

He dusted his hands off and came to sit next to her on the sofa.

"You remember that night before you went to the cemetery?"

"Of course." She doubted she would ever forget it.

"You said something that tickled a memory of mine. That we were shooting in the dark, or something like that. The night on the bridge, Durant had pulled out his revolver, and I had turned to you to make sure you were behind me. But I could have sworn that he was aiming towards the ground. At the time, it didn't register because I was more worried about you. But it would have been impossible for him to hit the professor."

She stiffened at the mention of her godfather. They still hadn't told Cyrus. She wasn't sure she wanted to.

Byron turned towards her, placing a hand on top of hers. "I had already suspected the professor before that night."

She nodded. "That's why they faked his death. He said it was already in the works, but that Alexander's note forced him to do it sooner."

"His note?" Byron frowned. "Interesting. I actually suspected him before that, when we went to visit Selene. She was trying too hard to appear calm when we first came in, and he was fiddling with his tie. Potentially a sign of nervousness, however . . ."

Mira sat up straighter. "He keeps his ring on a cord around his neck and had just shown it to her, ordering her to stall us."

"That would explain it. He also sent a telegram before we went to Selene's. Only I noticed that it wasn't to the university in Provence. The address was for somewhere in Paris. But I didn't dare tell you about my suspicions. And then he died, so any thought of him being the Charger left my mind. You were mourning, and," he took a breath. "Well, I was beastly, wasn't I? Accusing your uncle like that."

"You were trying to find a solution, like you always do."

"I'm still sorry for it. It seemed like the only solution at the time. But you were mourning, and I just made it worse."

"I forgive you," she took his hand and gave it a squeeze. "And I'm alright."

"Thank heavens for that," he smiled. "Now where was I?"

"I had just said, 'Shooting in the dark?'"

"Ah. Right. You said that, and everything started to fall into place. But how could I tell you that your godfather, the one you just watched be murdered in cold blood, was the Charger? No, I needed to find evidence. That afternoon I went back to the bridge and found the bullet embedded in the concrete. He hadn't been shot!

"But that left the question of how Burke got away. I knew he had fallen in the water because I heard the splash. And surely, one of us would have heard him getting into a boat if a rowboat was waiting beneath the bridge."

Mira's brow furrowed. "You're right. Before he found out that I knew about the Charger, he told me that he had floated downstream and swam to shore before being taken by Circe. But if he had done that, surely we would have seen him."

"There's that walkway on either side, just at the level of the water. I found a way down there and came under the bridge. It took a bit of poking and prodding, but I found a secret door hidden in the brick that led to one of those tunnels. But it was getting close to midnight by that point. I decided to wait until the morning."

"And by that time, I was already in the catacombs."

He nodded. "When I went to the boarding house, Mrs. Lavigne told me that you had sent her for tea and by the time she returned both you and Selene were gone."

He cocked his head, his brow furrowing in confusion. "Why did you listen to her? You never said."

"Well, I didn't trust her entirely. Not at first. She said that you had come to her, asking about the quarries, and that she had directed you to the cemetery. She made it sound as if you were in danger, so I came."

"Did they ambush you at the cemetery?"

Mira shook her head. "No. It wasn't until we were in the catacombs. And by then, I couldn't run."

"How did she get you in the catacombs?"

Mira blushed. "In one of my letters to you, I sent a lock of my hair. So that even though I wasn't with you, you could always remember me. But Durant was intercepting our correspondence. He wrapped the lock in a handkerchief with the letter and left it at the entrance to the catacombs. I thought that you had dropped it there by mistake. It never occurred to me that you had never set foot there."

"He read our correspondence?" His countenance darkened for a moment before he recognized what she had said before. "You sent me a lock of your hair?"

"It seemed proper, seeing as we are courting now."

He grinned. "I keep forgetting that."

"I'll have to keep reminding you. But once you realized I was missing, how did you find me? I didn't tell anyone where I was going."

"You said Selene's name and Loretta remembered it. There are only so many Selenes that I know of in Paris, and so I immediately headed to the Gallerie. Her right-hand man, Theo, was there. He was worried sick. Apparently, Durant had come there and had a private meeting with Selene the day before. Theo had heard something about the tunnels. After Durant left, Selene was quite pale and said, 'I could be free.' And then she disappeared. Theo agreed to use his own map from his time in Circe to lead me down there."

"Poor Selene," Mira said, wishing the image of the thief's death would leave her.

Byron paused. "Yes. We found her before we found you. I was so worried."

"They wanted to use me as bait," Mira said. "They were going to kill you."

"I was more concerned about you, my love." He kissed her forehead. "But you always seem to rescue yourself, and me."

"I'm quite tired of needing to be rescued. I've been kidnapped enough for a lifetime, don't you think?"

"One would hope so. And we've thoroughly maimed the Crossroads. I don't think Circe will be bothering us for a while."

They settled into silence for a moment. Mira fidgeted with her hands, thoughts racing through all the possibilities.

"Something's bothering you," Byron said.

"When Alexander started that fire, it didn't just trap us in. It destroyed all those documents. All those papers. Just because the Crossroads is licking its wounds, doesn't mean that the rest of Circe is going to stop planning for that war. And we're left with nothing."

Byron sighed. "It does put a damper on things, doesn't it? I doubt that Durant will want to tell us anything before his," he cleared his throat. "The trial."

Mira closed her eyes. She hated to think of the trial. And she'd have to be a witness. Byron put an arm around her shoulders.

"Why don't we forget about Circe for a little bit?"

She leaned into him. "I've been told that you're rather good at forgetting. Can you teach me?"

"Of course. The best way to forget is to set what you're thinking aside and distract yourself with something else. That's why I like keeping you around."

Mira laughed. "Is that it?"

"Among other reasons, yes. Now, since I'm obviously not distracting enough for you, we need something else."

"Did you have something in mind?" She turned to him.

He leaned closer. "I may have thought of something."

Author's Invitation

Welcome to the end of the book! Since you've made it this far, I have a favor to ask. Whether you enjoyed the book or not, please leave an honest review on Amazon or Goodreads. It only takes a few minutes and makes a significant difference for the future of this book. Reviews are essential for its success and longevity, and you'll be helping other readers decide if it's worth their time. If you loved the book, don't hesitate to recommend it to your friends!

To make it even easier, scan the QR code below to go directly this book's page on Goodreads:

AND IF YOU WANT TO KEEP UP with my news and inklings, you can join my newsletter by scanning the QR code below.

Acknowledgements

I would first like to acknowledge, that when I first started writing I didn't have any idea that I would be writing so many acknowledgement sections. If I were to give advice to my younger self, it would be to leave some people out the first go around so that you still have people to reference later down the road. That being said, I do think that I'll acknowledge a few people, even if I've called them out for being fantastic before.

Lenore, your covers are absolutely incredible and I am so grateful to have you as a designer.

John, I am so glad that Holli keeps assigning you to me! Quite literally, your suggestion to remove the torches from the catacombs for accuracy made the ending of my book five times better. Everyone needs an editor, and I'm so grateful that I get to work with you.

Musicians: There are too many to list all of the musicians I listen to by name, but I do want to shout out Joe Hisaishi and Abel Korzeniowski for writing some incredible music. I have almost exclusively listened to music they composed throughout the entire process of writing this book, down to writing these acknowledgements. Music is such a fundamental part of my creative process, I don't know if I'd be able to write nearly as well without it.

Merlin, Luke, and Becca: Thanks for being the best alpha readers I could ask for and giving such good feedback for every twist, turn, and bit of character development.

Mum: Thanks for sticking with me through all of this. I know it can get a bit crazy with my manic writing sprints and obsession over catacomb maps. You continue to be one of my best rubber ducks, and I'm so sparked that you came up with the idea for the corset bone. It is one of my favorite parts of the book, and it wouldn't be there without you.

Byron and Mira: I had no idea how far this journey would take me. I know that we still have several books left, but I would be remiss if I didn't acknowledge you here. You've pushed and prodded, nudged and needled, and wormed your way right into my heart. And if you can keep pushing your story into my head, at any time regardless of convenience, I'd appreciate it. We have to get the two of you married at least whether that happens in the next book or the fifteenth.

About the Author

NATALIE BRIANNE'S love of writing might be traced back to an old Rainbow Macintosh Laptop she received for her 8th birthday. Perhaps it came from years of improv storytelling and the discipline of wonder. Or maybe, she was born to write and didn't realize it until her first book sprung out of her fingertips somewhere between a house in Pleasant Grove, Utah and a bus on its way to Edinburgh, Scotland.

She received her degree in Interdisciplinary Humanities from BYU. While she could have studied English or Creative Writing, she opted to learn more about culture, distant lands, and people in hopes of writing better stories. Much of her first book, Constantine Capers: The Pennington Perplexity was written when she lived at 27 Palace Court, London, walking the streets as if she were her characters.

When Natalie isn't writing, voice acting, playing the guitar very badly, traveling, and forgetting that she has vegetables in her fridge.

CONSTANTINE CAPERS SERIES:

The Pennington Perplexity
Flashes of Memory
There Comes a Midnight Hour

THE 13TH ZODIAC SAGA:

Keepers of the Zodiac
Heart of the Meridian

SHORT STORIES AND NOVELLAS:

FROM CONSTANTINE'S CASEBOOK

Byron's Oblivion
The Great Sheep Panic
In the Silence of the Catacombs

FROM SAMIRA'S SKETCHBOOK

A Constantine Christmas

GENERAL FICTION

The Glade of Sionn O' Shea

www.ingramcontent.com/pod-product-compliance
Lightning Source LLC
Chambersburg PA
CBHW022026240626
47154CB00007B/2281